A Selection of Stories & Poems
from the Magazine

Visionary Tongue

A Selection of Stories & Poems from the Magazine

Edited by Storm Constantine

With assistance from Louise Coquio, Jamie Spracklen and Donna Bond

NewCon Press
England

First edition, published in the UK 2017
by NewCon Press

ISBN
hardback: 978-1-910935-59-0
Paperback:978-1-910935-60-6

10 9 8 7 6 5 4 3 2 1

Cover art and design, and interior illustrations by Ruby, except for page 84 by Billie Walker-John
Text layout by Storm Constantine

Contents

Introduction: Giving Voice to the Visionary Tongue – Storm Constantine   7
A Photocopier and a Giant Stapler – Louise Coquio   13
The Sin Taker – Katherine Roberts   17
Pumpkin Man – David Rain   25
Tides – Tanya Brown   27
The Gift of Flight – Eden Crain   31
In That Unquiet Earth – Chris Amies   33
Mad Love – Ray Girvan   43
A Traveller Meets One of the Minotaur's Younger Brothers – Justina Robson   52
The Bull Leapers – Justina Robson   53
A Tale from the End of the World – Fiona McGavin   65
See You Later – Suzanne Gyseman   79
Ptolemy's Recording – Jamie Spracklen   85
Finding Mary – Tim Lebbon   91
The Arena – Lachesis January   97
The King of Hearts & the Jack of Frowns – Jason Gould   103
Succubus – Chris Green   114
Dancing Day – Liz Williams   115
Storm – Sian Kingstone   124
Deities – Austin McCarron   126
The House by the Lake – Lisa Pallin   127
Awakening – Isabel Taylor   135
The Satanic Sex Machines of Dr Zhinn – William Eve   145
An Angel's Effigy – Dylan Kinnett   153
Sympathy for the Devil – Paul Whyte   160
Forgotten Sounds – Simon Williams   161
Luncheon with the Last of a Kind – Colin James   168
Féa – Janine Jones   169
The Magus of Inner London – Austin McCarron   178
Collector of Broken Things – Lauren Halkon   179
Toe in Water, Hand in Flame – Brian Maycock   189
What You Came For – Jaine Fenn   195
The Heroic Acts of Strangers – Ian Whates   201
Chess – David Graham   207
Casamundi – Douglas Thompson   213
The Lady of the Fog – J. H. Fleming   219
Mother Mary – A. N. Calaway   227
Appendix 1: Lex Visionaria – Jamie Spracklen   239
Appendix 2: The Female Fool – Donna Scott   242
About the Contributors   249

Acknowledgements

Thanks to Louise Coquio, Jamie Spracklen and Donna Bond for helping me to compile this anthology. To Ian Whates for suggesting the idea for the collection and then offering to publish it. To the gang of helpers Louise and I had back in the day – Yvan Cartwright, Paul Kesterton, Mark Hewkin, Jim Hibbert, Paula Wakefield and Simon Beal among them. To Ruby for her illustrations for the original magazine and the beautiful cover for this collection. To all the writers who sent us their work, and the volunteer professional writers who acted as editors for them – Cleo Cordell, Joe Donnelly, Christopher Fowler, Steve Harris, Graham Joyce, Kim Newman, Brian Stableford and Freda Warrington.

Giving Voice to the Visionary Tongue

Storm Constantine

Last year, I was chatting on the phone with Ian Whates, (as we often do), and the subject of the magazine *Visionary Tongue* came up, which I created and edited with Louise Coquio, and a band of volunteers, back in the 1990s. Ian asked if I'd ever issued an anthology of some of the stories. I confessed I hadn't, and Ian promptly offered to do so through NewCon Press, if I'd be happy to edit it. I was, and here is the result. I asked artist Ruby to revamp the cover she created for issue 20 of the magazine to adorn the book.

Before talking of how *Visionary Tongue* magazine came to be, and what aims its editors had for it, I must say that revisiting these stories after twenty years or so has been wonderful. I'd forgotten how good they were, how fresh, sometimes funny, sometimes poignant, often dark, always entertaining. Some of the authors you'll find within these pages have gone on to have very successful writing careers, and their names will be familiar to fans of the genres of science fiction, fantasy and horror. *Visionary Tongue* was lucky to publish some of their earliest stories. (This includes our publisher, Ian Whates.)

Some authors branched off into other genres and found success there. Others, who didn't attain the success of their more fortunate contemporaries, deserve to have their work read *now*. Perhaps this book might encourage them to take up the pen once more, or give them some leverage to get their work published again.

Sadly, in at least three cases, the authors are no longer with us. Ray Girvan wrote the delightful and mischievous 'Mad Love'. I was able to track down his widow, Clare, who kindly allowed us to reprint Ray's brilliant story. Chris Green was a student of mine for a while at Stafford College when I taught creative writing there in the 1990s. I was told of his death years ago, but can find no further details about him. David Rain was an acclaimed Australian writer, who died in 2015; his partner Antony Heaven gave us permission to reprint David's horror poem, 'The Pumpkin Man'.

Several writers, some of whom were regular contributors to the magazine, have disappeared without trace, leaving no 'foot print' on the internet, vanishing into the murk of uncatalogued history. It's doubtful that would happen today. Just about every writer posts their work on the internet or talks about it there. It's become rather difficult simply to disappear – even if you might want to!

We've made considerable effort to track down the 'missing' authors to no avail, but have decided to include the stories and poems anyway, because I didn't want the anthology to be published without them. Should these writers come across this book, I ask them to be tolerant of the liberty I have taken and to contact the publisher to receive their free copy. We have no idea whether any other of these apparently 'disappeared' have – like the three authors I mentioned – gone on to the great library in the sky.

As to how *Visionary Tongue* came into being, the idea evolved from music fanzines. When I was working with Goth bands in the 80s and 90s, sporadically managing and helping with fanzines, fan clubs and mailing lists, the part I enjoyed most about the work was creating the magazines. Once the band Empyrean disbanded, (with whom I was working at the time), the urge to make mags did not diminish. I had the idea to create a dark fantasy magazine, but with stories edited to a professional standard, which would help fledgling writers get their work noticed. Too often, independent publications lacked this professionalism. My good friend and colleague, Louise Coquio, was also interested in working with me on this. It was Louise who came up with the title for our proposed new venture – *Visionary Tongue*. We sub-titled it 'Dark Fantasy for the Millennium'.

We decided that if we were to produce a fiction magazine, it would be innovative to have a team of 'guest editors' – established authors who'd work with newcomers, passing on their tips and advice, helping people to learn their craft and refine it. In addition to the bonus of new writers working with seasoned professionals, it would mean that Louise and I wouldn't have to do all the editing ourselves, which would enable us to spend more time on designing and distributing the magazine. We spoke to writer friends, asking if they'd be interested in editing for us. Initially, we recruited Graham Joyce, Cleo Cordell, Freda Warrington and Brian Stableford, who were later joined by Kim Newman, Christopher Fowler, Joe Donnelly and Steve Harris. This was an impressive stable of editors indeed! We were grateful so many successful authors were keen to be involved.

We also thought it would enhance the magazine if established authors contributed articles to pass on their experiences and advice to new writers. Most of the consultant editors donated pieces in this vein, and also Neil Gaiman, who generously supported our independent venture with the article 'Where Do You Get Your Ideas?' for Issue 4.

When Louise and I first thought of publishing a magazine, we didn't have the convenience of the internet, with its Facebook, Twitter, blogs and such like, and not everyone had email. We didn't even have a web site for quite a few years. Making contact with authors to trawl for submissions required effort. We had to distribute flyers at conventions and band gigs, gain the co-operation of other magazines and advertise in fanzines. The editing process often involved sending printouts back and forth by conventional mail. To be completely honest, I can't even remember now how we managed it – finding quality submissions to fill a magazine four times a year. It brings home to me just how much we rely upon the internet now, which has trivialised a lot of the hard work that was necessary back then. The magazine itself was photocopied, collated, folded and stapled together by hand. Subscriptions had to be parcelled and mailed out. Luckily, we had a team of volunteers who helped us with all the manual work.

Eventually, as our volunteers diminished – due to university courses, moving away, or taking demanding jobs – Louise and I found it increasingly difficult to keep the magazine going. We too were becoming busier. Yvan Cartwright, who'd helped us throughout, but had now gone on to study at university, was still able to assist us by moving VT onto the web in 1999. The last printed issue was number 13. We continued for a while by publishing electronic issues, (14-18), although sadly all of those are now lost. Time continued to present a problem to all three of us, so that eventually we came to the sad decision we'd have to fold the magazine. Then writer/poet Jamie Spracklen, who had contributed stories and poems over the years, came to VT's rescue and offered to take it over. He – along with a team of co-editors – kept VT alive. It has never officially folded, although it's been a while since its last issue, number 27. Jamie and another of his editors, Donna Bond, have helped me enormously in compiling this anthology.

The earlier stories in this collection, those from issues 1-13, are touched by (if not soaked in) the Gothic, reflecting a decade when the Goth scene was still a prevailing sub-culture. The 90s were perhaps the tail end of its hey-day and, although it still survives in darkened corners of our cities, if perhaps upon smaller stages, it has diminished, rather like a vampire deprived of sustenance – an appropriate metaphor, I feel. Yet even if starved, it is still potent. Back when we were first publishing VT, so many people in the Goth scene were creative. If they weren't in bands, they were writers, and if they weren't into fiction they produced fanzines to support the bands, film-makers and writers they loved. Nowadays, I feel it's rare to come across the ardour and promise we once found in so many aspiring young authors of those earlier decades.

Not all our contributors derived from the Goth scene, but in selecting stories for our magazine we were drawn to those with dark, compelling atmospheres and narratives. Jamie extended VT's scope, taking stories of a wider range of genres and including more non-fiction articles.

It was difficult for me to choose the tales for this collection, because there were too many for all to be included, but ultimately, with an editor's privilege, I chose those I liked the most. Not that I disliked *any* of them.

In this anthology, you'll glimpse ghastly and gorgeous locations – sometimes both at once. You'll wander through rooms redolent of passionate melancholy. Scenes ooze opulence and decadence, or else romantic skeins of dust and decay. Characters live in or create fever dreams, luring others with treacherous spells of glances, scents and sighs. Water conceals tragedy or propels victims to their inevitable fates. Murderers hide behind smiles or beauty or clever words. Demons dance. The visionary tongue speaks. Now listen to its voice.

Storm Constantine
February 2017

Yvan, Louise and Storm caught unawares by the camera

(Some of the Editorial Team, circa 1996)

A Photocopier and a Giant Stapler: Working on Visionary Tongue

Louise Coquio

The seeds of what would become *Visionary Tongue* were planted in the fertile soil of the caffeine-fuelled, late night discussions, following the weekly creative writing classes taught by Storm in the early 90s. These classes ran at Stafford College – back in the days before teachers were buried under avalanches of paperwork – and when it was not yet frowned upon to adjourn to the pub.

Each week a group of misfits and sometime writers met and, after classes in which we frequently surprised ourselves by producing actual words on paper as directed, talked books, writing and all things related. Those with proper jobs invariably sloped off as the last orders bell rang. The rest of us would gather around Storm's kitchen table and drink tea and coffee, until we were wild-eyed with caffeine and delirious with 'good ideas' that made less sense in the cold light of day.

The conversation that led to VT went something like this:

"Let's start a magazine that isn't crap."

As goals go, it seemed achievable. Even the next day.

"Let's print the sort of stories that we like to read."

These, by turn were: weird, spooky, odd, Gothic, frightening, magical-realist, fairy-tale inspired confections.

"OK."

"We can get established writers to work with new writers and edit their stuff. It'll be like a workshop but without the uncomfortable chairs and vending machine coffee."

"Let's call it *Visionary Tongue* because, well, it'll be visionary and words come out of mouths…"

"Well, we have a photocopier and a giant stapler; I'd say we're ready to go."

So, we did.

Storm press-ganged some of her fellow writers into taking on the roles of guest editors. Lots of people said yes. Lots more offered support by way of articles, stories and other contributions. At the time, many of these writers, like Storm herself, were part of the newly created Penguin imprint, Creed, which specialised in Dark Fantasy. That helped us to define *Visionary Tongue* as 'Dark Fantasy for the Millennium' – we figured that it would attract the sort of writing that the team of editors themselves enjoyed. We began with a team comprised of: Storm, Freda Warrington, Graham Joyce, Christopher Fowler, Brian Stableford and Cleo Cordell. After a couple of issues, Joe Donnelly joined them.

Submissions came in fast – the stories went out for editing – all by snail mail – and came back polished and ready to go. We fired up the photocopier and then, well, then we realised that we would need a bigger boat! It took us HOURS (and by hours, I mean DAYS) to make the masters and assemble the zines themselves. The process was not made any easier by what turned out to be my complete and total inability to photocopy pages:

a) In the right order.
b) In the appropriate size.
c) The right way up.

How Storm didn't throttle me I'll never know. I nearly throttled myself. In the end, we cajoled, bribed and black-mailed our friends to help us. We began to look forward to 'making' days, as they quickly turned into wine-fuelled socials, masquerading as work. The pages would be spread out over the floor of Storm's workroom and a band of willing volunteers, armed with staplers and high on toner fumes from the overheated photocopier, would miraculously produce piles of zines from the chaos. It was fun.

Issue 1 came out in the Autumn of 1995, and had its official launch at the *Welcome to my Nightmare* convention in Swansea, over the Halloween weekend. The issue included stories by Tanya Brown, Paula Wakefield and Yvan Cartwright, as well as poetry from Eden Crane and Chris Green (Chris and Yvan were alumni of the Stafford college class). Issue 1 received some good reviews and was followed, in winter 1995, by the second issue. This saw the inclusion of a 'How to…' article about an aspect of writing. Covering topics as diverse as self-editing, horror writing, or the mystery of where ideas spring from, these were donated by one of the regular editors, or by guests like Neil Gaiman.

In 1996 *Visionary Tongue* was nominated for the Best Small Press award at the British Fantasy Awards. This was repeated the following year and, this time, there were also nominations for Best Short Story for Justina Robson's 'The Bull Leapers' and Best Artist for Ruby. The magazine went from strength to strength, eventually under the editorial eye of one of the earliest contributors, Jamie Spracklen, whose work had first appeared way back in issue 6.

Re-visiting old issues when writing this article, it strikes me how lucky we were to attract such talented people. Many of the contributors have gone on to achieve success with their writing. It was a great pleasure to meet them first in the pages of *Visionary Tongue*.

The Sin Taker

Katherine Roberts

I am the Sin Taker, and this is my final duty.

As I clothe myself in the traditional black silk, my flesh shivers. Then, as it often does, a corresponding shiver touches the darkest place in my mind.

I finger the chain that will serve as both belt and symbol of my sacrifice. I should be using this time to prepare myself. Yet, as so many times before, the whisper that floats from the shadows distracts me.

"No, Ahanh... You can't possibly consider this thing! A girl from a family such as yours will never be without suitors." Even the bitterness comes through. "You'll get over him, Ahanh, I promise you..."

Smoke scented with flowers of forgetfulness silences his words. Memory only. No one is there.

My mind clears. I apply the chain, feed stray hairs into the neck of my robe and lift the mask. I feel calm.

Mask in place, I close my eyes a moment before turning to examine myself in the mirrors that line my chamber. No part of my body remains visible. Only the suggestion of a gleam shows through the eye slits. The chain drags at my hips, dull and thick. Darkness shrouds me, cancelling the light of a hundred candles. All is as it should be.

I have no past. I have no name.

I am the Sin Taker.

The sins given into my care are three.

There is a man in the prison who beat his wife, though he loved her more than he could say. He confessed he struck her every night for a year until she would not venture out in daylight without a veil. She was too ashamed to tell anyone. But one day the wind blew under her veil, people saw, and there was no more hiding the truth.

I accepted his sin, and he will walk free.

"Ahanh! Listen to me!"

That is not my name. I am the Sin Taker.

"Ahanh!"

It is harder here to ignore the whispers. My chamber lies behind me. The smoke of forgetfulness grows thin. Yet reason tells me he cannot be real. This is a sealed tunnel. It leads only to my chamber, which is underground and has no other exit, to the cells where I work, and to the fire where I go now. For many months, there has been no other way for me. I wish for no other.

'Ahanh, stop!"

A hand jerks my waist, cutting my breath like a knife. "Don't you understand, you crazy girl? They've twisted your mind. If you go in there, they'll kill you. This way. Quickly."

I turn, puzzled. Through the eye slits, I see two halves of the same face. It is dirty and fuzzed with a day's growth of beard. We are in shadow between two torches. I am the Sin Taker, and he is... I frown. I think I have seen him before, so he must be one of the prisoners trying to escape. Apart from the old woman who feeds me dreamflowers, the Sin Taker sees no one else.

"Let me go, Sinner," I say softly. "Soon you'll be free."

He stares at me. He does not let go. Instead, his other hand comes up and rips off my mask. I have time to feel exposed before his palm crashes into my cheek. Echoes whirl along the tunnels. My head goes with them.

"What have they done to you, Ahanh?" he cries with an anguish.

I do not understand. "Who's Ahanh? I'm the Sin Taker. How did you get out of your cell, Sinner?"

"How do you think? I swallowed the key before I let them arrest me. I'll explain later. There's no time now."

I am being led by my chain, but we are going the wrong way, back to the cells. I am filled with sin now. I can take no more. I resist him. "Ahanh... I'm sorry..." His fist slams me into the dark.

The sins given into my care are two.

There is a woman in the prison who murdered her husband. She said she did it because he was violent with her, demanding love when she had none to give. One night she hid a knife under her pillow, waited until he was deep in passion, then stabbed him in the neck. His blood covered her, soaked the sheets, stained the very flags on the floor. There was no hiding what she had done.

I accepted her sin, and she will walk free.

I wake to lozenges of sunlight that drip heat onto my cheek from a high window. The sun brings strange memories after so long in the dark. I might believe them to be yet more dreams, if it were not for the whispered conversation taking place at the far side of the room. I cannot see who is speaking, for there is a fretwork screen about my bed. Through the holes in the pattern, it is possible to tell only that I am no longer in the prison. This place has the airy tranquillity of an upper room; maybe a tower, for the walls are curved. The man who hit me is talking to someone whose face is veiled by shadows. A woman.

Her dry, crackly tones seem familiar. "So what do you intend to do now, Jhakahr?"

That name. Jhakahr. It makes me think of a garden where I am clothed in colourful gowns, racing in my diamond slippers round the corners of a maze while a scruffy boy chases me. "Can't catch me, Jhakahr! Can't catch me!" I always let him, though. He used to grab my hair and tug it out of its coils, and then I was in trouble because Mother wanted me to stay clean and neat for my suitors.

But the woman is still speaking, and something about her makes me uncomfortable. I hold my breath and do my best to concentrate through the echoes of long forgotten dreams.

"They'll be looking for her all over. It's unheard of for the Sin Taker to run away, and when they see your cell's empty, they'll know you helped her escape. Remember that as far as they're concerned, you're a sinner now. I'm the only one who knows you set the whole thing up, and it's too dangerous for me to show my face in the prison now. I can't help you again, Jhakahr. If they catch you, they'll put you to the torture to discover where she is."

"Do you think I care?" It is the same whisper that haunted me back in my chamber. The same man who hit me. It makes no sense. "Just look after her while I make the arrangements to get her of the city, old woman. Then it won't matter what they do to me, because I'll know she's safe."

"Ah, you must love her terribly."

A dry chuckle, like dead leaves falling through my dreams, distracts me from the man's answer. When I drag myself back, the woman is speaking again.

"...but you were only in that prison two days, and that with the knowledge you could open the door to your cell just as soon as you shit. You don't appreciate what it can do to a man in the months you'll have to wait for your own Sin Taker. This time they'll make certain you've no key, inside or out. They have their methods, and believe me, they're not pleasant. You'll be in the dark, silenced and alone."

"I'll be thinking of Ahanh, who was in the dark and is now free."

Why does he keep saying that name? It makes my head hurt so.

I close my eyes as he slips round the screen. He touches the bruise he put on my jaw, but I control my pain as I have been taught. In the fire, there will be much pain, and a Sin Taker cannot scream, or the sins given into her care will escape, and then the prisoners will not walk free.

I can smell his sweat as he leans over me. His lips touch mine: a brief comfort. "I have to go now, Ahanh. I'll try to come back tonight. You get some rest and let old Sarha pamper you. Don't worry. No one'll think of looking for you here." He laughs, as if he finds this funny.

But Sarha... now I know why that dry voice has such power over me. I open my mouth to call the man named Jhakahr back, but he has already gone.

I struggle up from the bed. The cover falls from my body, and I realise for the first time that I am naked. It is too long since I drank my last cup of dreamflowers. My head screams with memory.

Mother betrothed me to the richest of my suitors, who begged an hour alone with me in a secluded grove so we might come to know each other as man and wife should. I was cold toward him, for as yet I felt no love in my heart, though he was handsome enough, and Mother said I would learn. He began by gripping my hand so hard I lost all feeling in my fingers.

Then he tried to kiss me. When I struggled, he grew furious, as suddenly as a cloud does rushing across the sun. He tore my gown. We rolled in the spilt pearls, me screaming and hitting him with anything I could, he grunting like a camel. He thought to beat me into submission, but I was no weakling. My play with Jhakahr had toned my muscles and given me a grip to match a man's. I managed to squirm out from under him and seize a rock. His skull smashed like a pomegranate. When they found me, I was clothed in his blood.

I start to scream aloud. The old woman pours something into a goblet and comes around the screen. Crystal dazzles my eye. Her voice, as always, is dry and monotonous and clouds my head. I struggle to rise once more, my fingers hooked in the screen. But I am weakened by my time in the dark and helpless to resist when Sarha sets the goblet to my lips. Sweetness coats my tongue, bringing with it a final dream.

The sins given into my care are one.

There is a serving girl in the prison who disobeyed her mistress. The lady used to admit men to her bower without her husband's knowledge, and commanded the girl to silence. But the girl saw with wise eyes. She saw how much her mistress' husband loved her, and she saw what her mistress' lovers were doing to the marriage. So one night while her mistress was deep in passion, she crept into the husband's room and told all. Her mistress sent her to prison for her disobedience, but the marriage was saved.

I accepted her sin, and she will walk free.

I wake to a feeling of confusion. It is dark, yet this is not the Sin

Taker's chamber. There are candles, yet only five. I am alone, yet I do not think I have always been. Before, when Sarha has given me dreamflowers, I have woken as the Sin Taker with shadows in my head. Now my head is full of tiny lights, like stars being born. They terrify me.

The door opens. A man comes round the screen and smiles at me. I remember him quite clearly now. He is Jhakahr, and from too poor a family to ask for my hand.

"Are you feeling better, Ahanh?" he asks, sitting on the end of my bed. He takes my hand.

"You... you... what have you done to me?"

He considers this a moment, then says with a grin, "Only rescued you from the most horrible fate, you crazy girl! Why did you do it, Ahanh? Whatever made you agree? I know you were upset by your fiancé's death, but take it from me, no man is worth burning yourself alive over."

"You don't understand." A moth fizzes in the flame of the candle nearest my bed. I stare at the ashes of its wings and wish I could escape so easily. But whatever dreams Sarha gave me in that final cup, they were not laced with the same flowers of forgetfulness she used to give me in the prison. The truth comes out with a sigh. "I killed him, Jhakahr. Me! With my own hand."

"You killed him...?" His confusion matches mine, but the lights in my head are flaring fast. I am remembering more and more; each memory a new pain.

"But I thought you loved him, and that was why you..."

"I disgraced my whole family. You have no idea, Jhakahr! If I had gone to prison and confessed my sin in the normal way, neither I nor any of my family would have been able to show our faces in public again. The family of a Sin Taker, however, has great honour. I didn't mean to kill him – I hit him too hard – but I did it, and there was no hiding the fact. When they offered me the chance of becoming Sin Taker, what choice did I have but to agree? It wasn't so bad. Sarha gave me flowers of forgetfulness every night. But now..."

I am no longer the Sin Taker. I am no longer Ahanh. I do not know who I am.

"No one had the right to demand that of you," Jhakahr says

22

quietly. Then he realises what I just said and his eyes widen. "Did you say Sarha?"

Before I can reply, his head jerks round. A look of horror crosses his face, and now I hear it too. Heavy feet on the stair. The scrape of swords leaving scabbards. My heart begins to pound. I am no longer calm.

"Sarha... I wondered how she got hold of that key so easily, the old witch!" Jhakahr leaps to his feet and looks round for a weapon. It is pointless. We are trapped up here. I should have made more effort to tell him before, but I was so confused. How was I to know who to trust? Sarha was my friend in the prison, with her gifts of beautiful dreams.

Now it is too late. The door crashes open. The candle flames flatten and all but one smokes out.

Darkness closes its hands upon me.

The sins given into my care are none.

I can no longer be trusted with them, for now I am a sinner myself. My cell is dark, and I have to wear a gag, which the guards remove only to feed me or when the Sin Taker comes, but such discipline does not worry me. Somewhere close is Jhakahr. I can hear him confessing in a whisper that makes me smile: "I escaped from prison before I could confess. I'm deeply sorry. I repent."

Outside my cell is a three-legged stool. On the stool sits a masked figure draped in black silk. As yet I cannot tell if the Sin Taker is a man or a woman. The whisper of the silk and the chink of the chain put shadows in my head, but I shake them out and concentrate, for I have promised. Nothing will be said concerning my time as Sin Taker; it is one of the conditions they have laid upon me and Jhakahr in return for us being allowed to confess. The other condition is that as soon as we are released, we will take a ship across the sea and never return. Sarha's betrayal has made it possible for us to start a new life. She is wise.

"I ran away from my home and family and all my responsibilities," I say, confessing the sin I have yet to commit. "I am deeply sorry. I repent."

The Sin Taker nods. "I accept your sin," she says in a monotonous, dry voice that clouds my head. She signals for the guards to replace my gag. She seems calm. Soon she will go to the fire, and Jhakahr and I will walk free. All is as it should be.

I have no past. I have no name, but I shall find one.

This will be my first duty.

Pumpkin Man

David Rain

Late night,
The Pumpkin Man comes down;
eyes and nose in diamonds, carved,
zig-zag mouth,
coal-splintered teeth,
candlelight in every pore.

On ragged straw-stuffed feet he comes,
unboned, in immolation dress,
woodlice nesting in the seams,
spiders webbing all that tatters.

To alleyways -
where waters drip,
where papers blow,
where rats dine out -
to black spots where the night is oiled
with methylated imprecations
belched by low-life,
cardboard scum -
here, the Pumpkin Man comes down.

What does it take to gouge an eye,
to fill these diamond hollows, new,
make good all that the kitchen knife
sliced up and punctured, cast away?

Such nightmares should be on the label: dread,
dissolved in hydro-carbons.
Body parts exchanged for peel.
Trousers taken.
Shoes removed.
Beware.

In alleyways where waters drip,
the sensitive are never found.
Late night, the Pumpkin Man comes down,
taking souls.
No pennies thrown.

Frontispiece by Ruby for Issue 2

Tides

Tanya Brown

Outside the old sash window, the sky was darkening over the saltings, and the long flat fields stretched away into the dusk towards the village. It was December, the day before the old winter solstice, but Jeanne did not feel cold in the high, unheated room.

Below her, the house was empty and they were dead. The smell of old clothes and lives filled the other rooms. As a child, she had slept here, at the top of the house. Now she kept the window open all the time, letting in the cold. She did not care if something else came in.

In the summer, the room would be full of flies. In the winter sunset, little glittering molecules of air were drawn in by her breath.

Across the salt marsh, the lights of the village flickered on. She could see the moon rise behind the church steeple. Once it had been in front of the steeple, but her mother had said she was making up stories. Outside the window, something fluttered in the branches of the oak tree.

Jeanne lit another cigarette and blew the smoke spirals towards the night. The room was very quiet, and in the silence, the door creaked, hesitantly, as if someone was standing outside.

The house was old. Once it had been flooded by the sea. Now there was a wall at the edge of the marsh to keep the water out; but the tides were getting higher and nobody came to raise the wall.

They were dead, but the house did not remember that.

Last night at this time, she had stood at the gate for nearly an hour, staring towards the town. Her mother's presence had been strong in the kitchen; the cat howled at her chair. When the last light had faded from the sky, Jeanne had gone back into the kitchen and fed the cat in the dark.

She was here to sift through their lives and take what she could find. The house suffocated her. She talked to her lover, an angel from a Botticelli picture. Of course he was long dead as well. Dead enough not to hurt.

"Is it full moon tonight, my love?"

"The air hangs heavy in the firmament." He was always so vague, now. The house stifled him as much as it did her. Somewhere, in one of the rooms, was the picture where she had first seen him. She could not leave without that. But first she must go and meet him.

Jeanne lined up the little white tablets along the edge of the inlaid dressing table. She spaced them precisely along the bramble pattern, one for each cluster of blossom. She swallowed the first. In the mirror, a glimmer of light came and faded.

"Listen, my heart," he said to her, "that's the basilisk climbing up the ivy on the wall. Don't be afraid. I will not let it in."

"I love you," she said gently, looking out at the oak tree. The shadows gathered in its branches where she had lost the gold ring on her seventh birthday. Maybe a magpie had taken it. Magpies are of the crow family. They will eat young pheasants. One for sorrow, two for tears, three for hopes and four for fears. She picked up another white fleck between her bitten fingernails. There was a glass of wine on the table; he must have brought it for her. "Thank you," she said, and raised the glass to toast him. The tablet was bitter but the wine was sweet.

Somewhere, out on the marshes, the tide was coming in, folding gently over the samphire and sea lavender. The thick black mud would look like water in the dusk. She knew people who had drowned there; her lover had drowned there. She wondered how it had been. She could hear the waves, although there was no wind.

"It was a gentle death. Nine days and nine nights, lying there in the soft mud, feeling the tide come in and go out over my face and under my eyelids. There were small creatures in the mud and I felt happy I could feed them. The moon rose when the evening tide came in. The water tasted like tears." He stroked the cat. It purred at him.

She swallowed the third pill and went to the window, slowly, as if she might stumble into him. An early star was tangled in the branches of the oak. One of the diamonds from her mother's eternity ring was gone.

Today, she had found her mother's diary. Her mother had written of a lost lover who had drowned. Jeanne smiled, and wondered if she was living in her mother's death-dreams. She wondered if her mother had thought of her as she died. She sat herself on the narrow window sill and stared through the air.

"She loved you, never think not." His voice was soft, and although he was very close, she could not feel his breath on her neck. "Darling, I do not breathe," he whispered, and she laughed.

"Did you know my mother, then?" she asked him.

He said, "She had a lovely face."

She turned back to the room, hunting for his reflection, but the mirror was cracked and showed nothing but fragments of the room.

It was time to walk and Jeanne was out in the lane in front of the house, the cat twining astonished about her ankles, purring. Through the gap in the hedge and over the bridge made from a railway sleeper her father had pulled back from the river shore. Bats fluttered subliminally around the chimneys of the house behind her.

"I mislike the marsh," he said to her, "but I will walk with you to the wall and see you safe."

Jeanne smiled, knowing that he could not see her in the dusk. "You are kind. Did my mother ask you to look after me?"

"Of course," he replied, as if he had just remembered that himself. "I am your guide."

Together, they walked down the pebbled track to the gravel pit, a pale heron lifting from the water into the night at their approach. She heard the rustle of its feathers as it flew above them. He walked three paces behind her, soundlessly. The rusty sign at the field gate glistened with dewy spiders' webs. Jeanne opened the gate and went through into the sharp stubble, the cat leaping at moths in front of her.

"See how full the moon is, my love," he said to her. "The tide will be high tonight. The fish will be caught in the branches like stars."

"That's pretty. The cat can catch them," Jeanne answered, laughing. Almost, she turned to kiss him, but the cat came bounding back to rub against her ankles again, and she stroked its head.

The sea wall rose above the flat field, like a grave. Jeanne ran forward, dizzy from the wine and the dusk. The dead grass on the slope of the wall was very pale. It crackled beneath her feet. Behind her, the cat howled.

As she reached the crest of the wall, the first wave broke coldly over her feet.

The Gift of Flight

Eden Crain

I can feel my wings growing again –
Just there, knobs beneath the skin, below the bone.
I thought they'd gone for ever,
Would never grow back.

It was terrible:
First they were clipped
And I just flapped around a while.
Then they turned black and fell right off.
But now they're growing again;
I can feel it.

Whatever passes between us, or not,
Whatever the future holds in its shadows,
Whether we pass beyond these ruins into light
Or remain here, hiding,
Know only this:
You have given me the greatest gift;
The hope of remembering how to fly.

Cover by Ruby for Issue 13

In That Unquiet Earth

Chris Amies

I. Carcosa, Nest of Ghouls

Carcosa was a darkened labyrinth of crumbling colonnades, cracked wet tiles underfoot, and cascades of slime down ancient walls. In the abandoned godowns by the river, strange shapes slithered and gibbered in half-dark. The dead crowded howling in the graveyards by the river, cold white faces turned to the darkness of the slow water. The living sat in the dark towers, using drugs and slow loving, anything to keep out the all-pervasive death-in-life of Carcosa.

That summer, Carcosa was a hot sweaty maze under an aching blue sky, the meat-and-metal stink of the dead town climbing up the staircases. People crowded the shadows and sat on vine-wreathed balconies. The days were hot, and heavy with the buzz of flying creatures. Down by the river, funeral pyres burnt day and night, consuming the city's ever-increasing dead.

Danny Salom and Marceline Legree had been living on the twelfth floor of an ancient apartment block for a month now. Danny was tall, dangerously thin, and wiry. He tried to make a living as a painter. He had ridden with the Bad Boys once, but then the Incident had happened, and he no longer liked even to go out at night.

Marceline was small, brown-haired, and dark-eyed, a taut young woman whose poetry rang like angels and demons together. She had tried suicide seventeen times and now seemed to attempt it desultorily, when she wanted to amuse herself. Carcosa attracted suicides like Paris called lovers, and New Orleans lured magicians. Marceline's suicide attempts were now no more than high-spirited pranks: jumping off the city walls or into the river, or turning on the gas and lighting a match. In a city where a third of the population suicided every year, Marceline and Danny surfed on the death ambience.

At twenty-four years old, both Danny and Marceline were growing old for the death games of the young. Most of their friends had killed themselves off; and some of them, whose bodies were not found and burnt in time, became ghouls, living on the lush pickings of the vast ornamental graveyards that surrounded the city of Carcosa. A handful became the more fearsome night-gaunts, which impatient of waiting for the dead, would swoop from the shadows on the unsuspecting living and tear out a throat. It was said that any of the dhole-riding Bad Boys, who sometimes made raids on the city, would become night-gaunts if they died in action. Danny hadn't died, but his friends had; and what he had seen was in some ways worse than mere death.

One morning at sunrise, Danny set up his easel at the end of Mahon Street and looked down the steep, tiled street at the river. His view covered the corner of the Sant Pau cemetery; and as he looked, he caught sight of a white figure perched on one of the tombstones, caught in the act of chewing on something nameless. The ghoul looked up and for a long, chill moment, it stared right into Danny's eyes. Danny swallowed hard; was that recognition in its dead eyes? Did it know who he was, what savage thing he had done, and what sicker vengeance he had witnessed?

Then both painter and dead thing looked away, and Danny picked up his brush and began feverishly to paint. He painted the ornamental tomb, its cross tilted at an angle, the grey stone sepulchre tilted into the soil; and he painted the thing that crouched atop it, chewing. As Danny painted, a second creature clambered onto the tomb and began grabbing at the lump of flesh the first ghoul held. Eventually, it took a bite from the lump, and turned round to present its rear. The two ghouls crouched quivering, pressed against one another, for several seconds before Danny realised they were fucking. He stopped painting and watched, fascinated. What feeling would a ghoul have while it fucked? That cold flesh would not be welcoming as a living person, and there could be no biological function; but the sex reflex must still be there. The ghouls went at it feverishly, slavering from long teeth. Danny started to paint again.

Danny went home in the late morning, canvas under his arm, paints and brushes in his satchel. The people in the streets were subdued, and Danny kept his gaze fixed on the roadway. At home, he showed Marceline what he had drawn: the white creature perched on the tomb, and the two copulating mindlessly.

"Like dogs," Marceline said. "Just like a pair of dogs screwing in the sun." She was wearing a white shift this day, her arms bare, her hair loose. "Do you think they remember? What it was to love?"

"They aren't human anymore," Danny said. Marceline tightened her grip. For someone so focused on death she was fiercely jealous of life.

"But do they remember?" Marceline insisted, her Levantine accent becoming stronger as her emotions took more of a hold on her.

"You'd have to ask them," Danny said. "And I doubt if they would be able to tell you. As you said, Marceline; they are like dogs. Screwing in the sun."

Day after day, and night after night, the dead became more pervasive. Ghouls hung around in doorways; white shapes glimpsed at the edge of vision down by the river crowded into a single vast shade. A sickly smell of burning flesh from the pyres wafted over the city.

In the old *Jardins de Sant Ferran*, Danny and Marceline shared a bottle of rough red wine with Azrael Shah, a shapeless figure of dubious sexuality who lived in the gardens. Azrael could empty half a litre bottle in a single gulp, taking it all down into some improbable part of his body, so his friends kept a close watch on how much they passed his way. The gardens had once been formal and correct, carved arches draped with climbing vines, ornamental urns and tiled pathways; but now the *Jardins de Sant Ferran* had fallen into a lush degeneracy, swarming with birds and animals and wayward plant growth that cascaded down to the river's edge.

"I'd keep in well with the dead," Azrael said when Danny told him about the ghouls fucking, and the way the first one had stared at him. "They know a lot, dear. Never turn my back on 'em, I don't. Not just 'cos I don't trust 'em, but 'cos they can be useful." Azrael patted his hand. "Remember that, sweet thing."

II. The God Who Has No Name

The four arcane symbols painted on the doorway of the Temple of Askileth, whence the Sacred Scarab came at the dawn of time, may be interpreted as meaning 'The Way of Beneficent Peace'; or 'The Queen Has Left the Tomb'; or 'The Farmer's Cow is Sick', though those mooting the last meaning are clubbed with stones before they can spread their treason. At the height of Carcosa's forgotten civilisation, the townsfolk sacrificed animals to the God Who Has No Name (and whose invocation is answered with, "May he be praised, whoever he is"); few could forget the screams of crucified goats as the butcher's axe swung down and lopped the goat's head off. The God Who Has No Name is not interested in meat, but in blood, and in death. He is depicted with a bloated belly and an open maw rimmed with sharp teeth. He sits on a mound of skulls. Skulls adorn him as a necklace, and his body is slimed with blood.

Nowadays ghouls meep around the doorway of the Temple of Askileth; though even the bolder ones dare not enter, Luther Maximilianus is Pope to the creatures of the night. He lives in a secluded room at the back of the Temple of Askileth. He is a lean, cadaverous man, whom some mistake for one of the ghouls to whom he ministers; years of living among the living dead have turned him into the replica of one of them.

Out of the setting sun, from beneath the crumbling arches that mark the edge of the city, come the Bad Boys. Astride strange beasts, whose pallid necks twist and turn, and whose blind questing snouts prod the air for scents, they ride, four of them, up the street to the Temple of Askileth. A white creature gibbers to them from beside the Temple's doorway, and one of the Bad Boys aims at it with his crossbow. He fires, and the ghoul is pinned to the wall, kicking and meeping feebly, leaking thin pink blood. Other ghouls flee up the street like sheep before a sheepdog.

The Bad Boys are back in town.

They climb off their beasts and lope into the Temple. They pass by the hideous statue of the God Who Has No Name, sneering as they go. The stink of blood cheers them rather than sickening; thus they are immune to the effects of the God's excesses.

They are also immune to the aura surrounding Luther Maximilianus. The Pope comes bustling out of his sacristy, hands sticky with goats' blood, face white with the pallor of long years spent indoors. He raises his hands and prepares to greet the travellers; but their leader, Yukio Narvaez, raises his crossbow and shoots the old man in the chest.

Luther smiles benevolently. "So kind," he says, falling to his knees, blood bubbling from around the metre-long shaft. He falls sideways and dies, glubbering horribly, his hand outreached and spasming towards the statue of the God Who Has No Name.

The Bad Boys grin and turn to go.

Behind them, where there had been the open chancel of the Temple, stands something bloated and blood-streaked, taller than any of them, grinning down at them with a mouthful of sharp teeth. It is so close the boys can hear the skulls of its necklace chinking together, and droplets of blood splashing onto the chill stone of the chancel. And it stinks, of blood and shit and ancient flesh.

Yukio Narvaez's bladder spasms and he wets himself. The God Who Has No Name grins wider and extends a limb, half-arm and half-tentacle, to seize the boy. It wrenches his head off like a peasant killing a chicken. Then it turns its attention to the others, scooping them up and tearing them apart. Bones crack and splinter; flesh tears like wet paper. When it has eaten all three victims, it burps massively, farts and slithers back to its pedestal, where it becomes, once more, a statue.

The only survivor watches in chill horror from behind a pillar. Walking in the shadow at the edge of the Temple, Danny Salom slips out of the building, leaps onto his blind beast, and gallops into town. Behind him, the other, abandoned dholes whine, and the ghouls crowd round, pointing and cackling. Somewhere in what remains of their minds, the ghouls understand what has happened, and remember what they have seen. As he rides, Danny is aware of their rotting eyes watching him.

III. The Memories of the Dead

"The dead have long memories," Danny Salom said to Marceline, in the silence of the night. He could not sleep, remembering that day so long ago and the stink of the creature that somehow, despite all logic, came alive in that temple. Although she was sleeping, he told her the story, leaving out nothing, not even the delighted look on the old man's face when he was dying.

"Why did he look so pleased?" Danny asked. "Because he knew what our punishment would be? That must be it."

"Must be," Marceline murmured.

Danny lay down and put his arms around her, whether to protect her or so that she could protect him, he couldn't have said.

When he woke up she was gone. He pushed himself up from the bed, and called her name twice. When there was no answer he walked through into the bathroom, but she was not in there; nor was she in the tiny kitchen, and there was no sign of her having brewed her habitual first-thing-in-the-morning pot of coffee. There was no note on the table, nothing saying where she'd gone. Danny shoved the streetside window open and looked down into the narrow street. He couldn't see her there. She was gone.

"Oh gods," he murmured. "She's making another attempt. Why, dear heart?"

He went back into the bedroom, pulled on his clothes and street shoes, and went out.

In the street he passed a café owner setting out his tables. He took the man's elbow in his hand and asked, "Have you seen a woman passing by?"

The café owner looked pityingly at him. "Many women," he said, shrugging, and turned away.

Danny walked on, wondering where she might have gone. To the river, he guessed; she would have gone down to the river. Maybe Azrael would know. So he headed for the *Jardins de Sant Ferran*, looking for the old fellow there.

Azrael was sitting on his customary bench, arms outstretched along the seatback, face uptilted to the dawn sun.

Danny came and sat beside him like a predatory bird. "Have you seen her?" he asked. "Marceline?"

"No," Azrael said, languidly, then registering the urgency in Danny's voice, turned to face him. "I will help you look. We will search along the river. Sometimes they go there."

Danny didn't ask who went there, but it was clear: they went there to die, among the drifting stink of the pyres.

When they reached the Terrace, an area of cracked flagstones above the river, Danny had a sudden hot flush of foreboding. He ran across the Terrace like a man possessed; though he did not want to see what he knew he would see, he could not keep away from it. At the far side, where the balustrade overhung the river, he looked over. A pale figure lay in the water several metres below, face down, but her floating hair and the shape of her body told Danny what he needed to know. She was wearing the primrose-coloured dress that she liked to wear when she was writing poetry; she claimed it helped her imagination.

"Help me carry her up," he said, his voice thick and heavy.

He and Azrael descended the narrow weed-choked stone steps, almost slipping off several times. At the bottom he crouched, and reached out for her. His warm hands touched her cold arms and he was suddenly revolted, bile rising in his throat. But he got a hold on her arms and pulled her towards him, all the time saying, "Why, dear heart?" under his breath like a mantra.

In the end Marceline's body lay against the steps. He turned her over. Her face was not calm in death; her mouth was open, one eye was closed, and there was a small fish clinging to her cheek. Danny pulled the fish off and squeezed it until it popped and fish guts spewed over his hand.

Together, he and Azrael Shah pulled the dead woman out of the water and onto the bottom step. Danny pushed at Marceline's chest, forcing water out of her mouth, but all efforts to bring her back to life failed.

Azrael put a hand on his shoulder. "She's dead, Danny," he said.

Danny looked up at his friend's face and saw a kindness he would never have expected. Together they carried Marceline up the stairs.

"I want to bury her," Danny said, "where none of those creatures will get at her."

"The body," Azrael said impassively, "must be burnt."

They were sitting in the gardens again. Marceline's body lay a hundred metres away, in a dark room in the Temple of the Winds, an ill-named place of weird smells and unholy pictures. Azrael and Danny were drinking wine, and this time Danny was drinking faster.

"Never," Danny said. "I shall not burn her. Neither, my friend, shall you."

"Very well," Azrael said. "But she may turn. Had you thought of that?"

"Gods, no." It wasn't true: he had thought of it, but tried to send the thought back whence it came. There could be no similarity between his warm, loving Marceline and those pallid horrors that lived in the graveyard. "We have to bury her, Azrael. Bury her deep and say prayers over her. Bury her and keep her buried. I want to remember what she was, not live with the fear she might ... turn."

"Why do you think she did it?" Azrael asked, gently.

"I don't know. Suicide is infectious around here. If you live in this city you have to expect it, like flies and religion. But Marceline ... I know she'd tried, many times, but I thought it was over. And it was just after I told her ..."

"Told her what?"

Danny sighed. "A few years ago," he said, "I ran with the Bad Boys. We killed the priest of the God Who Has No Name."

"May he be praised," Azrael said in a shaky voice, "whoever he is."

"And then," Danny went on, "the God ... you won't believe this, but the God came to life and killed my friends. Killed and ate them, Azrael, and I alone survived to tell the tale. I think this is the punishment I missed that time."

Azrael said, "no, no," but it was plain from the look on his face that he thought that it might be true. Danny felt as though that dark day had come to life yet again. He hadn't even suspected that Azrael might be a follower of the God. He certainly didn't seem the type to cut animals' throats, or to slash his arms and legs to feed the God on his own blood; but you could never tell, not in Carcosa where suicides hung at street corners some mornings like the sides of ripening meat in the butchers' market.

"Where can I bury her, Azrael?" he asked. "Where will the ghouls not get to her?"

"There is only one place," Azrael Shah said. "Where even they do not dare enter unbidden."

Cover by Ruby for Issue 5

Mad Love

Ray Girvan

When I was a child, other boys hoped merely to drive steam trains when they grew up. I aspired to be a mad scientist.

Blame it on cinema. One of my formative memories: Colin Clive in the 1931 *Frankenstein*, looking up wild-eyed and exclaiming "It's alive!" Another: Ernest Thesiger as the creepy Dr Praetorius in the sequel, setting out his supper in a crypt, and looking up unfazed to offer some to Karloff's Monster. A third: Rudolf Klein-Rogge as Rotwang, creating the robot doppelganger of Maria in Fritz Lang's *Metropolis*.

That last was my favourite. Surly and long-haired, Rotwang wore a single black glove eighty years before it became fashionable, and owned a laboratory rivalling Frankenstein's for electrical hardware. Oh, how my budding sexuality was roused by Brigitte Helm lying bare-shouldered in a hooped cabinet, the apparatus copying her likeness to the robot. Roused even more because Rotwang's duplicate of Maria had a different and exciting personality: not a nice girl who did Good Works, but one who danced in decadent night-clubs and stood by while German aristocrats duelled to the death.

I scarcely followed the rest of the plot (why, I was only ten when I first saw the film). But I was left with that image of transformation, of the wimpy Maria turned into a sexual being by a dark technological magic known only to mad scientists.

Unfortunately, mad scientists need as long and tedious apprenticeships as sane ones. I had my grounding at Cambridge.

"Science is sexy" went a slogan of the time, but I found it more so than that catch-word implied. Others may have been bored by the endless chore of lectures and practicals, but for me there was a frisson of perverse sexuality. In physics, I read of master and slave circuits; in chemistry, of bonds and chains; in mathematics, of dominant variables, the constraints of an equation, and degenerate cases.

Though hard-working and above reproach by day, I confess that my evenings were often filled with solitary drinking. Hardly scientific, but it led me to what a mad scientist needs: a laboratory. At closing time, (I thought of Michael Ripper as a Hammer landlord saying "Drink up, lad. Don't you think you've had enough?"), I would stagger back to college to sober up on black coffee or read *Films and Filming*, sipping port, until I fell asleep.

One night I came back, port-thirsty, half-fell up the three storeys to my room, and – damn! – my bottle was empty. I had heard a rumour that down in the B staircase cellar was a stock for the dons to drink at high table. Grabbing a pocket torch, I set out to raid it.

A ridiculous scheme to a sober mind, but with caution anaesthetised by a skinful of alcohol and the prospect of more, I somehow managed to stagger down to that cellar and break in by unscrewing the door lock with my pen-knife. Disappointment. No stacks of port bottles there, but a low room cluttered merely with cabin trunks and tea-chests. Still, a minor mystery consoled me: at the rear, baulks of two-by-four half-hid another door, this of iron.

Secret places in familiar buildings always intrigued me. I had ridden the paternosters and explored the crannies of the University Library in search of the fabled cache of pornography in its tower. There too I had been unsatisfied; my quest had ended in a room revealing only heaps of yellowed *National Geographic*. But what could be here?

Rapidly sobering, I moved the timber and hauled the door ajar, (it creaked alarmingly), to reveal the foot of a narrow spiral staircase. I climbed, losing count of my steps, until I lifted the final obstacle of a trapdoor and came out into an open space.

I swept the torch-beam about me, and was awed. I was under the roof of the college. Beams loomed, arched and fanned over me, a cathedral in miniature. Stepping through years of untouched dust, cobwebs billowing about me, I reached the single window and looked out. I saw moonlit rooftops, spires dreaming in the small hours, the River Cam far below. This was the place of my imagination, where I would make my laboratory.

Over a period of weeks, I equipped it. Usefully, a hall of residence opposite the college was being renovated, and the sound of pneumatic drills disguised my own work. I toiled there a few hours a day, then crept downstairs to carefully replace the timber over the staircase door before leaving.

My raw materials were harvested from all over the city in dozens of furtive and mostly illegal expeditions. The Sedgwick Geological Museum was a gloomy labyrinth of high wooden shelves. There I took spiralling ammonites, trilobites, spears of quartz and kidney-shaped masses of red hematite. There was the Whipple Museum, an unwatched treasure trove of animal specimens, stuffed or preserved in jars; and in the Old Cavendish, (where Rutherford split the atom), antique physics apparatus and modern circuit boards lay side-by-side wrapped in newspaper.

My own college's library supplied armfuls of books. At night, I took leather buckles from bicycle saddlebags, a pair of swimming goggles from the sports changing room, and the iron frame of a single bed, spanned by a diamond grid of springs.

All these I dragged up the spiral stair and arranged by the light of many candles; no power points here. The place was as ready as I could make it.

Now I needed someone to share my obsession, and Jessica fitted my requirements. I found her by a cynical exploitation of my earliest love, of cinema. My college's Film Society was all but defunct, and it was easy for me to join and inject new life into it. Within weeks, I was in a position of responsibility that allowed me to arrange a season of vintage screenings, and to observe who came.

I wanted to draw those who liked the scientific, the perverse, so I plied my audience with James Whale's *Frankenstein* films, with *Metropolis*, with the Fredric March version of *Jekyll and Hyde*. When the supply house could provide no more classics, I moved to 50s science fiction B-movies, then Corman's Poe adaptations with their prisons and dark machinery.

And, as inevitably as a fractal orbit circling toward an attractor point, I homed in on Jessica. Every week she was there, visible even in the semi-dark by her shock of red-dyed hair. After, I watched as she drank coffee; hardly Gothic heroine material in Doc Martens, efficient culottes and pullover, but I was attracted by her retroussé nose and up-tilted eyebrows. She had a punky charm reminiscent of Elsa Lanchester in *Bride of Frankenstein*.

I introduced myself, and soon we were dating. We walked the Backs, went on punt trips, talking camera angles, chiaroscuro, subtexts, literary analogues. After three weeks, we shared a meal at Waffles and returned to my room and to my bed.

As I had suspected, I was impotent. I could respond to the covers of my collection of 1930s pulp magazines: *The Mysterious Wu Fang*, (a Fu Manchu clone), gloating over a captive heroine, or Doctor Death leaning over a bare-breasted woman with hypodermic poised. But with Jessica, I was flaccid, as dead and unresponsive as one of my formalin-pickled specimens.

She asked me why. "Are you just nervous?" she asked. "Or gay?"

"No, nothing like that," I said. "There's something special I want you to do for me. Come with me."

Puzzled, she put on her bathrobe, (I donned a lab coat), and followed me to the cellar. Then nervously, up the winding stair, through the trapdoor into the dark space beyond. I lit the candles, and she inhaled in what I hoped was wonder.

Now the attic was an alchemist's dream: ranks of shelves, some stacked with minerals and fossils, others groaning under dark tomes with marbled covers. Yet more held jars: biological specimens swimming in formalin, vials royal blue with copper, purple with permanganate. A stuffed alligator and tortoise hung from a slanting roof beam. There was a bank of modern circuits with red and green diodes flickering, and another of antique apparatus, all brass, ebonite and gutta-percha, with shellacked copper windings.

"It's weird, but all perfect," said Jessica. "Why go to such trouble?"

"An ambition," I said.

She laughed. "You're crazy. It's games that turn you on, is it? Just like playing doctors and nurses as kids."

I smiled. "How conventional. No. My dream is of scientist and..." I searched for the word, "... and subject."

With a flourish, I whipped the drapes away from the centrepiece of my laboratory: the bed-frame, now converted with rubber padding and a bed-sheet to a white-draped table, suspended like the one in *Frankenstein*, leather buckles open and waiting.

I had reached that moment we all fear, when we have revealed our darkest side to someone we care about and wait to see if they will run or stay.

"Will you be my subject?" I asked.

Her eyebrows rose, but she didn't flinch. Why should she? I knew her mind already; we are what we watch. "Sure," she said.

Realities don't match fantasies. Film heroines are solemn, frightened. Or they faint, and the scientist's assistant carries them effortlessly to the table. A brief dissolve to some other scene, ("But Sir Henry," exclaims the hero. "I thought Lucy was with you!"), and then the camera returns to the heroine, lying tastefully draped in a white sheet.

In contrast, Jessica giggled a little as she undressed. The table wobbled like a hammock, and I had to lower one end to the floor for her to stand against it, arms at her sides and legs slightly parted. Several of the straps were at the wrong level, (I hadn't particularly thought about the subject's height), and I had to bodge fresh holes through the sheet and rubber.

But finally, it was done; naked, she stood strapped at wrists and ankles, elbows and knees, waist and forehead. I hauled the table up horizontally again, and everything was right. I put on my goggles, and in my mind Igor was flying kites on the roof, millions of volts were massing in the skies above, and all the electrical tat I'd collected was no mere window-dressing but truly working, wheels spinning, arcs sparking blue and reeking of ozone.

I gazed at Jessica with the intimacy of knowing the name of each corded muscle, each bone in her slight frame. Did Rotwang take advantage of Maria, I wondered? Was Frankenstein turned on by the Bride? I put a tentative hand on her breast, leaned to kiss her deeply. As if a spark of lightning had animated her, she gasped and convulsed in the straps and I felt the thrill of that illicit scientific magic flowing in me.

Finally, I truly was a mad scientist. My groin stirred. "It's alive!" I yelled.

Maybe that shout gave away our presence. Maybe it was the candlelight showing through the attic window. Whatever the reason, I was not to know a convention was about to work itself out: mad scientists are never allowed to consummate their plans.

Even as I began shedding my own clothes, there was a scraping from the stair. "I knew someone must be up 'ere," someone said in a rich Cambridgeshire burr. Then, more sternly: "Hoy, what's going on? Christ, George, look!"

Like the poor Herr Doktor Frankenstein, I realised that men with torches were at my door, and hammering to get in. I turned, covering myself, and squinted into a dazzling beam; the trapdoor was open, faces peering in. A shudder crossed me as I thought of the scene in *Mad Love*, when Peter Lorre is disturbed while manhandling the heroine. Lorre's character dies when the hero Orlac, (Colin Clive again), finds that his transplanted knife-thrower's hands can be put to practical use.

But the figures clambering into view resolved merely into the college night-porters. The two could have rushed me then, but they paused, seemingly amazed, at the sight of the room and its contents.

"Oh, shit, let me loose," Jessica hissed. "If my tutor hears about this, I'll never live it down!"

But I was still absorbed in my new persona. I dashed to the shelves and began to throw at the intruders everything I could lay my hands on.

"Out, you fools! Must you always destroy what you don't understand?" I raged, hailing them with sharp crystals, stuffed animals, jars. Rubbery, fleshy things splattered around them, spraying the stink of formaldehyde. They retreated down the stairwell.

Then, my mistake: I threw one more jar. Glass burst around a cat foetus, the liquid flooded a candle, and I realised this specimen had been preserved in alcohol. A sheet of blue flame zipped across the floor, catching ancient wood and spreading.

Trapped, Jessica screamed and writhed. More flashbacks: at the end of *Metropolis*, the robot Maria lashed to a pillar, raving and burning. The heroine of *House of Wax*, nude in the mould with molten wax pouring inexorably toward her. Spencer Tracy's dream of Hell in *Dante's Inferno*, with chained figures wailing in the fire.

This wasn't what I intended. I came to my senses. Ignoring the flames at my heels, I scrambled to undo the buckles. As I fumbled at the last few, a corner of the tablecloth ignited. Desperately, I dug fingers under the straps, and tugged; my nails broke, my fingertips bled, but the tough leather snapped. I pulled Jessica from the table, shielding her with my body, and carried her to the square hole in the floor where the porters cowered.

They took her from me. One seized me by the arm, but I tore free and dashed back through the flames.

A moment's freedom. I stood, back to the window. Through a wall of flame I could vaguely see Jessica beckoning to me, draped in a borrowed jacket. One porter started forward, arm shielding his face, but then another of the alcohol-filled jars burst, splattering me with fresh blue fire. Burning, I spun and dived through the window.

Like a film freeze-frame, there was an instant when I seemed suspended, surrounded by flames, shards and ruptured window leading. Then, blazing and torn, I plunged like a meteorite, and the waters of the Cam rose to meet me. Cold burst about me, currents and weed tendrils tugged me this way and that, and then I surfaced in an echoing dark. I felt a ledge, crawled on to it, and lost consciousness.

I wake, chilled and damp. It's morning, I think. My fingers don't work properly; the right of my face is charred, roughened. I hear organ music, and crawl mechanically toward it. I am in a tunnel beneath a college chapel, (I don't know which), and through a ventilation grille I can see a young woman practising. The organist plays a chord; she sings a scale, up an octave, then back again. The chord repeats, a semitone higher. "Again!" says the organist in a testy German accent, and the woman sings the scale, shifted up likewise. In the dark, I manage a smile.

Cover by Ruby for Issue 6

A Traveller Meets One of the Minotaur's Younger Brothers

Justina Robson

I, Voyager,
wandering the transparent world
looking for the ancient earth beneath;
populating the empty landscape
with mythical beasts,
was surprised to say the least
upon finding you -
lost son of Pasiphae,
with your black bull's poll
grown to such a length.

You and I,
eye to eye.
One of us is out of place;
you with your athlete's disdain for clothes,
I with my maps, my guidebooks, my cyclopean camera.
You put your head down,
ready for a struggle.
I keep mine aloft,
ready to leap

To follow you
back to your hidden home
and your life which I have built
in my fevered imagination
to be as heated and wild as any rodeo.
We have watched each other for less than a second,
But I am already lost in the labyrinth of your possibilities.

So, it was me after all.

The Bull Leapers

Justina Robson

The journey from England to Crete was lengthy and exhausting. We arrived in the outskirts of Knossos later than expected. On the final voyage, by fishing packet, the glare of the sun had brought on a headache even more severe than the one started that morning by yet another abortive attempt at conversation with my husband, George. I sat in the cool shade of the courtyard at our rented house and fanned myself with my hat.

George's voice, always so cultured and quiet in response to me, was animated as he blurted gouts of unfamiliar Greek to our guide. If I had not known it was him I would have thought another man was there; Ashton perhaps, my first husband, who had been most alive when he was with me. I did not need to speak the language to know that George was already immersed in plans for a rendezvous with Sir Arthur Evans; that was his real reason for coming to Crete.

My real reason seemed as idealistic and stupid as his dreams of Classical perfection. I had hoped that this voyage out of Europe would be a chance to save the marriage. I put it down to the war, of course. So much can be put down to the Great War, but the only reason I was still there was that any sign that I might leave threw him into such a depth of despair I couldn't bring myself to be that cruel. But this silence...

My sister in particular had high hopes that allowing George to pursue his mania for the ancient world would kindle a similar reaction in him towards me. She was fond of saying, "But Elizabeth, you are such a passionate woman," meaning I was wasting my time on someone as cool as George. "If only Ashton had come back instead," she sometimes added, for which I could occasionally hate her a little.

If Ashton had come back, I would not have been married to his friend. My sister was not the only one in our society to think I had done it out of pity. It was not pity. It was despair to grab back anything of Ashton's that I could.

George turned to me, his face lit with happiness. I smiled automatically. It was after all, not happiness because he was here with me. "Darling," he announced, "He has already sent me a letter," he waved the note, "inviting me to the dig tomorrow morning and for a visit to the site this evening. I'm to go there now with this chap here. He whirled quickly across the tiles and bent down to give me a peck on the cheek. "See you tonight." And that was that. He strode out without even pausing to change from the stiff tweeds he had travelled in.

The housekeeper, a woman of my own age, with long dark hair curled in a bun and dressed in a clean apron, brought me a large glass and a jug of lemonade without being asked. She lingered for a moment beside my table. When I looked up, eyes and mouth watering from the tartness, she smiled at me. Her dark eyes looked straight through my face. She nodded, then turned and walked away, brushing the leaves of a laurel tree with her shoulder and releasing some of their distinctive scent. I was about to call after her and ask her what she meant by it, but the lack of words stopped me. I could not shake the conviction that she had recognised something in me that needed no translation. I was ashamed for a moment that my displeasure with George must show so openly that I needed sympathy from her.

The next day, George was gone before breakfast. When I could loiter no more, I took my sturdy shoes and a stick, put on a large-brimmed straw hat and went out for a walk. It was fortunate the fashion had changed to loose, long-waisted dresses. They were just the thing for Crete's dry summer heat. I was thinking about abandoning my silk shawl to my bag, where my cologne and book rested, when I realised I was lost in the twists and turns of the town's narrow streets. On either side of me whitewashed walls rose to form a narrow alley, which ran uphill. Looking back, I saw the bright colours of the market below, which gave me confidence. I was thinking about retracing my steps but was startled by the appearance of two men in the alley before me.

There was no obvious opening from which they could have come. They were simply there. After a split second of surprise, I saw how different they looked to the men of the town, who wore spare, peasant clothes and whose dark eyes followed me with a kind of covert insolence. These two had a similar regard, but one which went unchecked. They were also nearly naked. Half tunics of folded linen were wrapped around their waists in a manner that seemed almost Egyptian. The material, far from being dingy and stained, was pure. Jewelled belts held these skirts in place and also secured to their sides long knives in elaborate sheaths. One had a handsome gold band around his forehead, holding back his hair which, like his companion's, was unbound and flowed in thick black tresses to halfway down his back. Any of my London friends would have scalped them for such heads of hair and robbed the owner of his fillet with its enormous fine peacock's feather or somesuch – I didn't recognise the plume except in that it denoted nobility. In London, we wore feathers aplenty, in Crete, on a man, the finery could only signify some kind of station.

Taking this all in at once I was stuck to the spot, not knowing whether to scream, run or stand aside. I did none of them, but my hands of their own accord clutched the sagging shawl up around my shoulders and tight across my chest. One glance back into their gazes – fixed on mine like hunting lions' – was sufficient to confirm my instinct. Their golden skins were glistening with sweat or oil and their lips were parted in anticipation. They moved forwards as one, the black centres of their huge eyes growing darker, larger, as I watched them come. As they closed in on me, the thing I was most impressed by was their youth and beauty, and it was this which held me fast there on the path, until it was too late to escape. They halted before me, close enough that we almost touched without needing to move. I smelt their breath. It was sweet and grassy.

"It has taken a long time for you to come here," one said. He had an easier smile than the one with the feather, who seemed older and more sombre. I thought he said that. I wasn't sure his lips moved. From the town, small noises of normal life went on It was so bright in the alley. My heart was hammering.

"Please let me pass," I said, trying to be bold, and made a determined movement with my foot, looking to go back into the comfort of the market. Neither of them twitched a muscle. The air was full of their scent – a sleek smell, redolent of healthy animals; powerful and musky. The one to my left closed the gap between them with his shoulder.

"I must get back to the hotel. I am late," I lied quickly. They seemed to have edged me in further in the last few seconds. I could feel the touch of one leg against mine.

"But you are lost, Mrs Stowe," the elder said in heavily-accented English. This time his lips moved carefully. His teeth were snow-white and even. How had he known my name? I backed off in fear, until I was pressed against the hard stone wall.

They stared at me, almost without blinking. My hands clutched harder in the knot of my shawl as I strove to cover myself from their gaze. It did no good. My mouth was dry, then, as I looked from one to another. Their lips lifted into small smiles of predatory hunger, and my tongue was suddenly wet with a rush of saliva. Perspiration shocked out all over me. The younger one leaned in. I saw his mouth become gentle. His breath rushed over my face. Without thinking, I was leaning also, stretching forward to him like a girl eager for her first kiss.

The knife hilt of the straight-faced one brushed against my elbow with a cool metal touch and brought me to my senses. I jumped back and bashed my arm on the wall.

The elder one let his forehead down and nodded, his feather bobbing. I watched a bead of sweat curl past one of his nipples and could not help noticing that although his dark native skin must have been hairy he was waxed as smooth as an egg. Despite having me well cornered they made no further advance. I rubbed my elbow, but did not respond so that they were forced to do something first.

"Entertainment, Mrs Stowe," the younger one said, apropos of nothing. He stepped aside and gestured for me to move back into the alley proper. "We will show you an old Cretan entertainment. You will enjoy it. Come with us." They both kept their hands at their sides. The politeness with which they conducted themselves now was so at odds with the weight of their physical presence not two minutes earlier that I hesitated. But the order was also so very odd that after a moment of wavering, I went. A will bigger than my own was in possession of me.

As we climbed further, crossing the city through narrow back ways, the older murmured, "The labyrinth. You see it. All around us. The presence of mystery. You will see." He spoke so quietly I was not certain he meant me to hear. I wondered abruptly if they were both mad, but it was too late for such a judgement. On either side, their oiled bodies moved like heavy engines. In the still swelter of afternoon, the smell of them wound around me in a net. It was dark, earth. It reminded me of the moon. I floated between them.

Just outside the town they led me away to a little hillside grove of olives where there was a small sandy arena laid out among the sparse grass. In the arena, there was a girl, smaller than they were, darker skinned and naked, except for a string of coloured beads around her waist. She was holding a thin gold chain which was attached to the heavy ring in the nose of a giant skewbald bull. The animal swung his massive head around as we started to descend the little slope. I saw his wet nostrils flare like bellows as he checked our scent. The fine skin of his muzzle was the same as that of the brothers and the girl. If someone had been with me, I would have been shocked. As it was, I was the one who felt awkward and overdressed.

The brothers disbanded. I found a nearby rock and sat down. The sun was falling out of the sky. On the distant hillsides, I could see animals and people on the farms as normal, so I was not bothered I was the only spectator. The girl took out a switch from her belt and together, she and the brothers, even the haughty one, began to tease the bull out of his complacency with touches and taps and small flicks of the switch. Soon it was making little rushes towards them, snorting and shaking its head, more with annoyance than real intent, I thought. It seemed used to the proceedings and wishing they were over, but was too slow to remember this fact and eventually gave in and played the game.

The brothers danced around the animal, twin streaks of gold darting around the great white cloudy shape of the bull. They sharpened the animal's attention so that the girl, light as a little cat, could jump and spring off the broad back with her hands. The first time she leapt, I could not help but take a sharp breath and smile in delight. She saw I was pleased and swaggered a little with pride, her narrow, strong limbs easy and shining in the heat. As I watched her move, I was ashamed of myself for the sharp jealousy that came out of the blue and tried to wither my heart. It is always a shock to be jolted into remembering you are not what you once were. It also becomes easier to let the brief pain go, and I let it go; it was, after all, only the dying spasm of a young and silly vanity.

The girl sauntered up to the bull and tickled his whiskers as he tried to cross his eyes, watching the antics of the brothers who took the opportunity to jump over his back, rapping him smartly on each flank. He shook himself all over, very cross, and charged the girl, who simply took off like a kite, planted her hands on the lumpy fat behind his neck and sprang to the ground behind him to swing on his tail. Then the girl took the bull by his nose ring and led him off. After a long look at me, the reserved brother followed. His sibling leant against the barrier, puffing gently, and looked at me. "Good entertainment for you. I see you like it," he said.

"Very much," I agreed, wondering if he were expecting money or was building up to something else. He simply watched me as he caught his breath and wiped a sheen of sweat from his forehead and neck, flicking it away from him and drying his hands on his short white tunic. "It's where the story of the minotaur came from, isn't it?" I asked him, remembering from one of George's pamphlets. "The jumping of the bull. A long long time ago."

"You know the labyrinth," he said, again in that same tone that might have been question or answer.

"Pardon?"

"The labyrinth," he repeated. "It is here."

I looked around in confusion, "I thought it was at Minos' palace."

"No," he said, shaking his head in the twilight. "The mystery. The labyrinth. It is everywhere."

I was listening to him as hard as I have ever listened, as hard as I used to listen for the knock at the door telling me Ashton had been found alive after all. In the soft gloom of the coining night, he seemed to speak from another world, in which there were more possibilities than this one, and more time. He sketched out an invisible view with his hands, "The labyrinth," he repeated, "I can see it." I knew he was talking about something esoteric. His voice and figure were charged with a subtle force, its harshness deflected by his manner, which was gentle. He put his hand out and took hold of mine in a soft, reassuring touch, "You are in it, Mrs Stowe."

I snatched my hand back and felt myself grip my stick, but not out of fear, out of surprise and embarrassment, as if he had seen me undressed. I suddenly knew that he was talking about my relationship with George.

He was nodding as he watched me, approving of me and my wallowing realisation.

"Who are you?" I demanded, glancing towards the home track. I thought I could see a light coming down the path.

"We are the sons of Pasiphae," he said, "brothers of the minotaur. We can show you the heart of the bull and the heart of man. Will you come?"

His eyes were blue and black. Night was pouring down through the small branches of the olive trees, colouring the fruit black. The air was warm, cooling, smelt of grass and animal and man. When I looked down from the sky, both the Cretan youths were there. I stood up and walked between them without thinking.

"Where are we going?" I asked, since they seemed ready to talk.

"To the Bull of Minos," said the younger and reached back to take my hand.

I lost track of time. There was only the walking, the heady air, the bright moonlight and the sliding planes of the city. When they stopped walking, their hands tugged me to a halt.

I saw that we were at the palace, recognising its thick pillars and heavy, smashed lintels from pictures that George obsessed over. The markings and posts of the dig were clearly visible to the right, but they were deserted. Only a lone donkey wandered around on a short tether and messed with a small pile of hay. Behind us, Knossos was sparkling with tiny lights and I could hear music. At our feet, the tiny pink bells of a flower that grows like a weed on Crete's rocky ground were nodding in the evening breeze.

"Will you go?" one of them said, which one I couldn't tell now. This time he was asking a question. Between the pillars of the doorway, the dark seemed to pulse like the skin of a drum. I could feel its vibrations in my bones and skin, but heard nothing I didn't want them to let go of my hands. I didn't know what waited there, only that it was a place of revelation.

"I will," I said.

"We will guide you," they both said, and one continued, "and we will stay with you through the night. You will not leave until dawn, and you will not be able to touch this earth or speak under this sky until then."

Easy to be calm when your fate is in another's hands.

We passed under the broken mass of the lintel and into the impenetrable darkness within the palace ruin. It was peaceful, walking those unseen corridors, feeling without understanding how the walls were narrowing, closing in, as we took turn and turn again, walking down passages unlit from the beginning of time, the air fading, changing, becoming heavier and more stale with the smell of the brothers and an even more powerful and clinging musk.

I thought many things on that inward journey. I remembered my girlhood and my mother, my father with his dogs and guns. I remembered Ashton, my first husband and what a riot we had had before the war. I remembered my friends at home with a love felt honestly, now it was not circumnavigated by propriety, and I remembered George with warmth and well-wishing. I hoped that when I returned I could bring something of this to him, whatever it was.

We came into a large space very suddenly. The change of the sounds must have signalled it to me but, as one, the three of us stopped walking. Underfoot, a soft earthy texture deepened, like dry ground pulverised by the passage of thousands of head of cattle. It killed all noise of our feet. The smell here was palpable and the air warm and moist. It wrapped me in a thick velvet of distilled masculinity. It seemed as if my nose could read smell; every taint a distinct aspect of male character and makeup. The dark was also inhabited.

On either side of me, the muted presence of the brothers faded. Their hands slipped from mine and they vanished. At some distance I could hear breathing. It was not a human sound, but a ponderous snorting breath with a lot of liquid in it, very slow, the breath of a heavy beast. Footfalls thumped through the damped earth, and the air shifted against me, as something butted through it and forced it to move on.

I could see nothing. I heard the bull-man approach and felt his smoky, misty breath as he sniffed me over, his head moving around me generally, accompanied by the thuds of his two feet. Once or twice his whiskers brushed me, but that was all. He snorted a few times and paced off to one side, making a low noise in his throat. I recalled with alarming suddenness the detail of the story George had recited in our drawing room – the Minotaur was fed on young women and men from Athens, sent in placation when the Minoan Empire was at its height. There was a powerful reek of dung that did not smell entirely of cattle.

Then the bull returned and breathed a different kind of breath over my face. It was dense and full of strange floral scents, as well as the reek of musk and something vaguely fetid. It was heavy and within two of my own breaths, unable to avoid it, I was feeling sleepy. I thought I felt the cautious hands of the brothers lowering me gently to the earth, and then I was falling down into the soft ground in a new darkness, held in silent, still warm darkness. My body seemed to be all one surface and through my skin I could feel the shimmer, as if I was contained inside a larger body, whose powerful heartbeat made the blood vibrate around me. I wondered if I dreamed of my mother, but this dark had a male smell. I rested in the body of the bull. Through the slow visions that followed, I was always aware of his presence, picking out the dream for me, showing me something of the men I had loved.

My father. I saw myself a little girl, through his eyes as he looked down at me. I had a pipe jammed firmly between my teeth and the taste of the tobacco was bitter and awful, its scent sweeter. The little girl was smiling – had I ever been that young? She was holding out a card she had made, and it was an awful card, I could see that, covered with glue that was still wet. I was repulsed by it as an object, confused that she thought it was a worthy present for me, but also terribly, painfully, touched with an intensity that made me almost pathologically afraid. She terrified me, because of the power of the emotions that even this pathetic gesture of hers could make rise in me. Fifty times more powerful than the effect her mother had. I could not stand the contrast – my life of evenness pierced like this, without mercy, and with no defences to stand against it. It hurt in my chest so much, I thought I might be having a heart attack. I had to go back into my study and shut the door, just to make it stop.

The vision faded. I expected to be consumed by sadness, but within the bull-man all emotion was gentled, rollered, measured. I understood my father without grief and marvelled that there was no pain. I could see without suffering...

I saw Ashton and myself getting married. I felt how he adored me, the depth of his passion like the ocean, lust and admiration, wonder and a ferocious need to possess, all tangled up together in a Gordian knot inside him. We had a spectacular few months before the war. I was grateful to find that this vision had little of newness in it. I knew him well, then and now.

In the third vision, I saw the brothers. They were with me in a dark place, cold and filled with wet and mud. I was George, trying to load some kind of gun, but my fingers were slippery, and I kept dropping the bullets and losing them. The sound of gunfire and cannon was incredibly loud and seemed to be coming from all directions.

In the night, we returned to the trench to sleep, in huts made of a few planks and cloths. I was glad when I saw Ashton there. He welcomed me, but the sight of his face nearly flung me out of the dream, because it held the same expression that had welcomed Elizabeth on her wedding night. I, George, secure in the cover of night and exhaustion and despair, flung myself into his strong arms. As we often had, we slept together, wound tightly limb against limb, me and my tender comrade. In the morning, we rubbed our faces clean with one another's spit. We kissed. The love was brighter for the closeness of death.

That day we received an order to go over. The shelling was intense. Bombs exploded to our left and right in the trench. I saw the brothers there fall. Some of them covered the mud with sprays of red and grey. Flayed skulls smiled forever. Hoarse from screaming, I loaded my gun. Men were scrambling over the top, some on the order, but some just to get away from the shells, mad. I saw Ashton ahead of me; breast the top of the trench, so brave. I got up and out behind him. I had no fear, because we were certain to die, and there was no need to think about that. I hoped that we went together. There was a scream in the air louder than the rest. Before I knew it, I was on the ground. The explosion threw me back to the lip of the trench. When I looked up again it was hours later. Twilight had come and it was quiet. I searched for Ashton. I found him, here and there. Night fell. I never fought again and neither did any man from our trench. The only difference was that I went home and they never did.

I was like an automaton. This remained until long after I returned home and married. I copied the expressions of those around me to show affection. The idea of having any kind of real feeling filled me with a nauseous dread, until that in itself became too much of an emotion and I switched it off. I pitied my wife. I should not have married her. She deserved a whole man, not a pasty-faced deceiver. Probably she would leave me. At least that would free me of the danger. I dare not think of him.

The last dream faded away very slowly. I listened to the blood in my ears and upon my skin. The bull breathed for both of us, until the morning, when he let me up out of the earth, and the brothers led me to the palace gate and home through the cool, fresh day.

It was quiet. I walked unimpeded through the door and up the stairs into our room. George was slumped on the bed, asleep in his clothes. He was almost as dusty and raddled as I was. I sat down beside him. He woke instantly.

"Lizzy!" he exclaimed, sitting up and clutching my arms fiercely. "Where have you been? My God I was out all night! I thought... that wretched woman downstairs kept trying to insinuate you'd gone for a walk all night, as if that were likely." He broke off as he saw the state of me. "Where did you sleep, in a stable?" But although his words were fierce with concern, his arms were gentle.

"Let's not talk about it now," I said, "I'm so tired. I've been a long way. We can discuss it tomorrow."

"Tomorrow is today," he said, but I was already curling around him and he was too tired to argue.

I copied the shapes I had felt in the dream. "Ashton and I used to sleep like this," I said. George stiffened all over. "You and he were such good friends, weren't you?"

"Yes," he said. His one hand plucked nervously at mine, as if he were toying with the idea of escape.

"I'm glad," I said.

The hand stopped moving.

"I'm glad he wasn't alone out there. And I'm glad we'll never be."

His hand pressed over mine where it lay tight, holding his shirt close to his chest. "Elizabeth."

I don't know if he knew that I knew his secrets. It would have been demeaning to bring them into the open. But in the morning, he did not go to the dig. He put on a Panama hat and a linen jacket and we walked through the groves, where the olives were ripe and unripe on the tree together.

A Tale from the End of the World

Fiona McGavin

For a long time, the sea had been crossed only by screaming gulls, but one evening, as the sun began to set, a small boat with a white sail drifted between the rows of needle sharp rocks and into the shadow of the towering cliffs. A man stood tall like a prophet in the prow of his vessel, his silvery blond hair billowing about him. He stared expectantly up at the crumbling settlement that perched above the sea. He smiled to himself as he drifted with the wind, but his smile was cold, and his eyes were as grim as the choppy waters. Then, once the village was passed, he spied the old crooked house and its spreading gardens and he laughed aloud. This must be the place.

It seemed as if Cliff House stood at the end of the world. This was the way of things now: cities, towns and villages had become isolated, as separate from one another as countries and continents. The village around Cliff House was ancient, but had long been forgotten by the outside world. The houses had crumbled away to nothing, while the sea slowly ate at the cliffs. One day, the rusting fairground had fallen away from the land and now it reared monstrously from the waves. In time, seaweed, salt crystals and barnacles had covered it, turning the sad, corroding merry-go-round horses into magnificent, magical sea creatures. Steeds for Neptune and the mermaids. All the villagers were dead or had fled. Only Cliff House remained; a paradise in the wasteland.

The Blood family had lived in Cliff House for centuries. They were a family who, at one time, had been notorious for their wealth, their history of insanity and the twins they produced in every generation – always a boy and a girl. Although the world was falling apart around them, Gabrielle and Raphael Blood continued to live in the manner to which their ancestors had become accustomed. To the twins, this meant taking hemp and opium, and being beautiful, inbred and vicious until the day they died.

Cliff House was surrounded by hedges of rose briars, nettles and barbed wire. The twins had two black hounds with red eyes and slavering tongues to protect them from outsiders. Their garden was wild and crooked, falling into the sea. It was filled with mutating topiaries, statues, wind-chimes and curious little summerhouses and gazebos. An uncanny place, filled with eyes. Raphael kept cats, and they prowled around the gardens claiming one-armed, decapitated statues for their own, filling the gardens with their scents and the sounds of their yowling.

Through the maze of statues and topiary, it was possible to come upon great banks of lupins and daffodils; hogweeds and briars; shimmering masses of pink willowherb; ponds choked with lilies and acid green algae; herb gardens neatly planted with sage, marjoram, valerian, and all the other herbs Gabrielle thought would give her sweet dreams. The garden was strange, all askew.

The house was the same; a perfect reflection of the twins' combined personalities: a place of dark, ugly furniture; strange empty rooms; cobwebs; twisted candelabras; burnt-down candles; antique lace and moth eaten, velvet draperies. There were wasps' nests in the back rooms, and the cellars were filled with vintage, dark red wines and rats. The twins let flowers die in cracked vases until the petals turned papery. They kept butterflies in glass jars and painted contorted, dark portraits of one another. They played peculiar old stringed instruments and left archaic books face down on the floor, with their spines bent and broken. The long corridors stretched away into perfect, inky darkness. Sometimes there were only two candles burning in the whole house.

The twins lived mainly in the attics. Here, they thrived with the darkness and dust. They breathed it in and then out onto everything they touched.

Gabrielle and Raphael Blood were named after angels and they looked almost like their namesakes; golden-haired, blue-eyed and perfectly turned out in dark silks, velvet and lace. They went everywhere together, as if bound by some invisible chain. Gabrielle was the leader and she led her quieter, perhaps more dangerous brother through numerous indiscretions.

The twins had no family. As far as they knew, they were the last of their line and now it seemed the Blood family was destined to be swept forever from the world. And yet, in the dusty old books of family history, they had read of ancestral relatives who had left Cliff House in order to marry into other families, to fight in the War or to make their fortune in some far-off city. Someone, somewhere, must have survived to generate a second great dynasty of Bloods. Often, the twins talked of finding these people, but they were afraid to leave Cliff House. Beyond it lay the savage moors where the roads were overgrown. Only peddlers travelled there now, and even they were becoming fewer and fewer. The forests and wild animals were creeping back. The land was wild, and the people who haunted it were wilder. The world was full of distorted folk; victims of the War. It was better to stay at Cliff House where it was safe. And besides, the twins were secretly proud of the tragedy of being last.

They lived alone, save for Hump, their hunch-backed servant. Sometimes peddlers rested overnight on their wanderings between settlements, but they never stayed for longer than one night. The twins made other people uncomfortable. Raphael watched them unblinkingly, while Gabrielle asked incessant questions. Sometimes, it seemed that the twins could talk to one another without opening their mouths.

The peddlers were always eager to tell stories of the twins. They felt that talking of it cleansed them of whatever poisons the occupants of Cliff House had breathed onto them. The twins were so beautiful and golden, while everyone else in the world was crippled or deformed in some way. It seemed unnatural. When Gabrielle wore Raphael's clothes, the peddlers could not tell which twin was which.

One man had stayed in Cliff House on the night the twins' parents had died. He had heard movements in the night and had barred his door. In the morning, he had found the twins standing dry-eyed over the bodies of their parents. They had smiled identical smiles and told him it was their birthday. They were sixteen now and had grown up. They would be quite all right on their own. Their manner of speaking had chilled the man's blood. His dreams were still haunted by the way they had stood in the doorway to watch him leave.

So, although the twins knew almost nothing of the world beyond, there were those who knew about them.

One morning, watching from their garden, the twins saw a boat drifting slowly across the sea towards them. A single figure stood tall in the prow. The twins observed in silence. They believed in sea gods and mermaids and in lost kingdoms beneath the waves. They believed there really was a better place.

Raphael chewed his bottom lip in suspicion, while Gabrielle leapt up and called to the black hounds. She leashed them and set off for the cliff path. Raphael followed her, cats twining round his legs.

The twins made their way down the treacherous, crumbling cliff path to the shore below. The hounds growled threateningly, hackles raised, while Gabrielle waved a hand at the little boat. The man at the prow began to guide the boat towards them.

Gabrielle turned to her brother. "What if..." she breathed, but did not finish her sentence, for the man was walking through the water towards them. He was tall and slender, his face cold in its eerie perfection. He was like a man made from stone, ice and metal. Different from them, different from the deformed, sick people who passed by Cliff House.

Gabrielle drew back, uncertain. No one spoke, but the twins were suddenly aware of the cobwebs in their hair and the worn patches on the elbows and knees of their clothes.

"Good morning," the man called.

The twins did not answer. They gazed at the man and smiled nervously as he advanced towards them. His feet did not seem to touch the ground, and the sea water had hardly wet his robes. He looked at the twins and then at their home on the cliff top. "I wonder if you might help me," he said.

The twins exchanged glances. They waited for the man to continue.

"I am looking for Cliff House and the Blood twins."

"Who wants to know?" Raphael asked.

"I know of their family," the man said.

"We have no family," Gabrielle replied.

The man smiled benevolently. "No, you are wrong. In a city in the south, there are other Bloods."

The twins' hearts leapt and then fell again. This made everything different and they were not sure how they felt about it. The stranger was as tall and straight as they were. His beauty was eerie and familiar; he looked almost like them. They were frightened, yet fascinated too, filled with a strange kind of yearning.

"Are you one of us?" Gabrielle asked.

The man smiled. He held out his hand to her and she shook it tentatively. "My name is Nathaniel," he said. "Nathaniel Blood."

"We are Gabrielle and Raphael Blood," Gabrielle said.

The man smiled broadly. He swept his arms wide as if to embrace them. "I have been searching for you everywhere and by coincidence the sea has cast me up here."

The twins did not believe in coincidences. Everything had a purpose, otherwise it meant that the chaos and anarchy in the world beyond the village was all for nothing. It meant that there was no reason for the demise of the human race, no reason for its ever having existed. The twins believed in magic and to them, Nathaniel seemed like a magician.

They took him up to Cliff House. As they walked, Gabrielle talked nervously, her voice high and excited, the hounds fighting on their leashes before her. Raphael walked a little behind, stooping now and then to pick up seashells or pieces of coloured glass worn to opacity by the sea. Throughout the day, they showed Nathaniel around the gardens and the house.

As the sun began to set, they had their servant, Hump, cook a huge meal, which they spread out on the scratched oak table in the dining room. Gabrielle lit candles all round the room, and Raphael opened the windows wide to blow the dust and cobwebs away.

The twins drank too much wine. They laughed at secret jokes they could not share with Nathaniel, for all that they tried. Cats jumped up on the table and spilled the wine. Giant ghost moths fluttered and crackled in the candle flames. The twins shone with a vibrant, frenetic beauty: Gabrielle flushed and eager to please and Raphael brooding and quiet, his eyes bright with unasked questions.

Nathaniel studied the twins intently and did not drink the wine. His eyes remained cold throughout the meal, and he flinched when the cats touched him.

As the candle stubs flickered in the late evening breeze, Gabrielle said, "What do you do in the city, Nathaniel? Are you an artist, a musician, an architect?"

Nathaniel shook his head. "I am a scholar," he said. "I study people like you."

"Like us?" Gabrielle asked, frowning.

"Yes. Those special people who are not twisted or deformed."

The twins looked at one another. They had sometimes wondered why they were tall, straight and healthy in comparison to other people they met, and had decided it must be because of their breeding; something in their blood.

"Where I come from," Nathaniel said, "babies are born deformed; two-headed, Siamese twins or hermaphrodites. Many have diseases we cannot cure, and die." He leaned towards them a little. "In my city, we need people like you. We have to find out what makes you different."

The twins smiled at the thought of two-headed hermaphrodites. Raphael reached across the table for the wine and refilled the glasses. The wine spilled over the rim of Nathaniel's glass and splashed on the table.

"But our family have always been mad," Raphael said.

Gabrielle looked dreamy. "Yes. Our mother believed..."

Nathaniel interrupted her quickly. "If my people could be beautiful once more, I assure you, they would risk insanity."

"You are beautiful," Gabrielle said. She bit into an apple. "Beautiful and clever. We like you."

Nathaniel laughed his strange, cold laugh. "Unfortunately, I wasn't always like this."

Gabrielle put her head on one side. "What do you mean?"

Nathaniel paused for a moment, then said, "My bones have been straightened and reinforced with metal. I have had surgery..."

The twins looked at one another. Raphael fiddled with the buttons on his shirt and Gabrielle opened her mouth to speak, then closed it swiftly as if to silence an importunate question. Both twins shifted in their seats, smiled nervously at one another and at Nathaniel. He seemed false now, a lie superimposed upon some deformed, hunched reality.

"You don't need us, then," Raphael said at last.

"The process isn't always successful," Nathaniel said in a measured voice. "Nine times out of ten it results in death. I was lucky to survive. Also, the operations are very expensive, as well as painful and time-consuming. Sometimes they go horribly wrong and produce only monstrosities. That is why we need people like you."

"But what would you do to us?" Gabrielle asked.

"Simply run some tests on you, isolate the things that make you different." Nathaniel's mouth smiled. "It wouldn't take long..."

"Are all our family like you?" Gabrielle enquired. "Metal and plastic, not flesh and blood?"

Nathaniel nodded. "They need you. You will be their salvation."

Gabrielle smiled. It appeared she liked the idea of that.

"Tell us about them," Raphael said.

Nathaniel began to talk. He could feel Raphael's eyes on him, considering everything he said, half smiling.

Gabrielle listened, entranced. "We must write all this down in the family history books," she said. "We mustn't drink much more tonight, or we'll forget what you've told us."

Nathaniel nodded. "Very wise." He paused. "You will come with me, won't you? You would be with your family. We could look after you and make sure that you want for nothing. After all, what is there here for you, at the end of the world?"

The twins were indecisive. The thought of the city and all its splendours frightened them and yet Nathaniel himself was fascinating. They wanted to be with him, hear his stories. He knew, and had experienced, so many things: a magician who might save them, just as they might save him. If only he would remain here, at Cliff House. If only he did not want them to go away with him.

"We must carry on the blood-line," Gabrielle said.

"Exactly," Nathaniel agreed smoothly. "And if you don't like the city, you can always come back here."

"Good," Gabrielle said. She rose from the table, took Nathaniel's hand and led him out onto the terrace, Raphael following. Both twins still carried glasses of sticky wine. Outside, the purple half-light was perfumed with jasmine, roses and the scent of the sea. Night birds called among the trees. The garden was full of dark corners and weird shadows; beautiful but dangerous.

The twins and Nathaniel sat down at a weathered table beneath a desiccated vine. Gabrielle lit candles there.

"Once I've shown you the city," Nathaniel said, "you'll realise you live like savages here."

The twins nodded vaguely, and became silent in the narcotic air. Moths danced around the candle flames and settled on the rims of the wine glasses. Their feet stuck in the sugary liquid, their wings flapping frantically until the cats swiped them into oblivion with delicate, clawed paws. Gabrielle set out a game of solitaire on the table and Raphael lay in the hammock nearby, swinging gently and reading the family history books. From time to time, he glanced sidelong at Nathaniel.

When the twins' wine glasses had been emptied, Nathaniel produced a package from inside his robes. He unwrapped it and showed the twins its contents. In a bed of crisp tissue paper lay a stick of something. It looked almost like cinnamon, but with a silvery-grey, crumbly appearance.

"This is silvertree," Nathaniel said. "It comes from the bark of a special tree. Let me share its secret with you. Bring me some clear water."

Raphael went inside and returned with a brimming jug, from which he poured out three measures into the empty glasses. Nathaniel broke the silvertree into three and dropped a piece into each glass. The substance began to dissolve, turning the water a silvery colour.

"What is it?" Gabrielle asked. "What does it do?"

"It is good," Nathaniel answered. "It shows you things."

"What things?" Raphael asked suspiciously.

"Things you wouldn't otherwise know," Nathaniel smiled. "Perhaps you'll see my city." He offered them two of the glasses. "Try it."

He watched the twins swill the liquid round the vessels, as if to dissolve the last pieces of silvertree. Colours drifted through the mixture and faded away. The twins sniffed it, exchanged glances and frowned.

Then Raphael put down his glass. "No," he said politely. "No, thank you."

But Gabrielle was less cautious. She hoped the silvertree would show her Nathaniel's city and her family. She wanted to know these things. Without further pause, she lifted the silvertree to her lips and drank deeply. "Go on," she said to her brother. "Do this with me."

Raphael waited until he saw Nathaniel drain his glass, then drank from his own. After a while, the twins climbed into the hammock together. With eyes half-closed, they began to float, to drift away. Nathaniel, who had taken silvertree so many times it barely affected him, watched them curiously. He thought of Adam and Eve in their magical garden, founding the human race. He stared at Gabrielle's slender, elegant body, the curve of her breasts against dusty velvet, the tiny waist encased in silk. Dreaming, the twins seemed to have become a single person; a graceful tangle of arms, legs and blond hair. Their eyes were heavy-lidded, their whispers slurred, as they shared identical visions. Nathaniel considered them objectively. In the house, he had watched them laugh at their hunch-backed servant and entice hapless insects into the candle-flames. He had recoiled from the strange paintings they had daubed. The crooked house itself, with its fecund, untended gardens and startling statues, chilled his blood. And yet, he was intrigued by the twins' twisted innocence and amoral purity. In their innocence, they would become his tools.

Tomorrow, he would begin his journey home. Now, he was sure the twins would come with him, that he had enchanted them.

Nathaniel leaned back in his chair and sighed in contentment. It was almost too good to be true. He had scarcely believed it when the peddlers had told him of the twins and their cruel perfection. He knew all about their desire to find others of their strange tribe, and if they believed he was of their blood, they would surely go with him. Nathaniel had already made plans.

The boy would be killed, his body frozen and studied to isolate the precious genes that made the twins unique. Eventually, his pure blood would be decanted to fill the twisted veins of an eager recipient. His clear eyes would look out from a new skull. His skin...

The girl they would breed with. And if his people were lucky, the twins might never discover that there were no other Bloods in the city. As far as Nathaniel knew, there were no other Bloods in the world.

The twins were dreaming. They saw wide city streets filled with dancing people, who applauded as they passed. Their feet did not seem to touch the ground and their bodies were caressed by the finest silk. Around them, the city was white and silver in the sunlight. There were palaces and mansions, shady parks, galleries and museums. The twins knew that, in this place, they could have anything they desired. The people clamoured to touch them, as if a brief contact could heal them. The twins felt loved, needed and – almost – happy.

But there was something dark behind them. They heard it slithering and creeping, the hiss of its darting forked tongue. It whispered their names, tried to entice them, and it reached out to crush them in its coils. Beware the serpent: it tells lies. Lies. It is not what it seems.

The next morning, Nathaniel awoke in his seat on the lawn. The twins were having breakfast: camomile tea in a cracked, willow-patterned tea-pot; sizzling hermaphroditic fish from the poisoned sea and thick slices of home-baked bread. There were cats on the table again; flies buzzed around the food. The twins were wearing thin, white, summery clothes that looked alien on them. Nathaniel thought they must be trying to emulate his appearance. Gabrielle fed the hounds and chattered amiably, while Raphael read an ancient, paper-backed book, its title obscured by coffee and wine stains. He cut an apple into neat slices with a long-bladed knife.

"It was nice in the city," Gabrielle said. "We liked it, but how do we know it's really like that?"

"Trust me," Nathaniel said.

"In the dream, everyone loved us," Gabrielle said.

Raphael did not look up from his book. "Not everyone."

"No." Gabrielle frowned. "Something was after us. Something dark. It wanted to hurt us." She smiled. "We should stay here, and you should stay with us. It would be better."

"I don't belong here, and neither do you," Nathaniel said. "You'll see that when you come to the city. What about meeting your family?"

"We're not sure we want to meet them now," Gabrielle said. "We don't need them really. We have each other."

"You are being silly. There's nothing to be frightened of."

Raphael glanced at Nathaniel. "We are not going to your city. The thing that followed us in the dream: it was you."

Nathaniel laughed. "Me?"

"You're not part of our family at all," Raphael said. "Are you?" He laid down his book and stood up. "You're a scientist." He spat out the words as if they poisoned him.

"I told you: I'm a scholar."

"Who studies people," Raphael murmured. "Yes... we know. We understand."

Nathaniel spoke calmly. "I think you're over-reacting. You're alone too much."

"Then stay here with us," Gabrielle said. "We want you to. We really do, but we can't go to the city with you. The visions showed us that."

Nathaniel looked around at the twisted house and the sprawl of the gardens, nothing beyond them but moors and sea and desolation. He realised how alone he was in this place. When he looked back at the twins, it seemed an unspoken communication passed between them. Raphael's hand closed around the knife on the table top.

"Please, don't go," Gabrielle said. "Say that you'll stay."

"We're not going to the city," Raphael said. "And neither are you."

"If we let you go, you'll tell others about us," Gabrielle said.

"They'll come for us..."

"Strap us to tables..."

"Stick needles in us..."

"Scientists..."

"Serpents..."

Gabrielle smiled. "So, you'll have to stay with us."

Nathaniel's laughter was uneasy now. "You're being ridiculous!

You can't stay here for ever, and I certainly can't!"

"Please, don't say that." Gabrielle's voice was almost a whisper, pleading, desperate. "Say that you'll stay."

Nathaniel shook his head. "I'm sorry. I have to go back."

Again, a silent message passed between the twins. Nathaniel began to feel uneasy. He did not like the way the twins stared at him, with their identical blue eyes; unreadable expressions on their flawless, heart-shaped faces. The hounds and the cats were looking at him, even the dead moths on the table. Only then did Nathaniel realise the twins did not mean to let him leave.

The knife glittered coldly in Raphael's hand; the hounds growled softly at Gabrielle's feet.

Nathaniel rose slowly from his seat. He had to tear himself away from the cage of eyes.

He ran down through the labyrinth of the gardens towards the cliff path, and his boat. He heard the hounds behind them, drawing closer. As the great animals brought him down in the unmown grass, he thought of the twins and their family living here for centuries, isolated and inbred, growing strange and different until they were not like anyone else, until they were barely human at all. Sharp teeth ripped his clothes, his flesh. Fetid breath filled his nostrils.

Then he heard the twins call off the hounds, and opened his eyes to see them standing over him. But before he could stand up, and attempt to escape, Raphael lunged forward. Nathaniel felt the long-bladed knife slide between his ribs, tearing through flesh. He felt the warm spill of blood that flowed out of him, down onto the grass. Raphael leaned forward to pull the knife out, and Nathaniel saw bright splashes of fresh blood spatter the boy's white summer clothes. The twins looked down at him fearfully, as if they thought he might rear up and bite them. There was blood in their hair, on their faces. As he floated, drifted in his last agony, Nathaniel was glad he would not live to see the twins and their descendants inherit this dying world.

The twins gazed down at Nathaniel's body, and then at the blood on their white, summer clothes. They put their fingers in the blood and licked them. Nathaniel tasted of chemicals and sterile air. They did not like his taste.

"But we did like him," Gabrielle said sadly.

Raphael wiped the knife clean on his shirt. "Yes," he said. "We did."

"Do you think his bones really are plastic?" Gabrielle asked.

"We could open him up and see," Raphael suggested, but neither twin was really that interested.

About a year after Nathaniel came to Cliff House, Gabrielle gave birth to twins; perfect babies, a boy and a girl. She and Raphael grew fond of walking along the beach with the children. In their white summer clothes, they looked like angels. They sometimes talked about Nathaniel.

"What if Adam and Eve hadn't eaten the apple?" Raphael mused. "What if they had killed the serpent instead?"

Gabrielle nodded, then smiled. "What if they never, ever left the garden?"

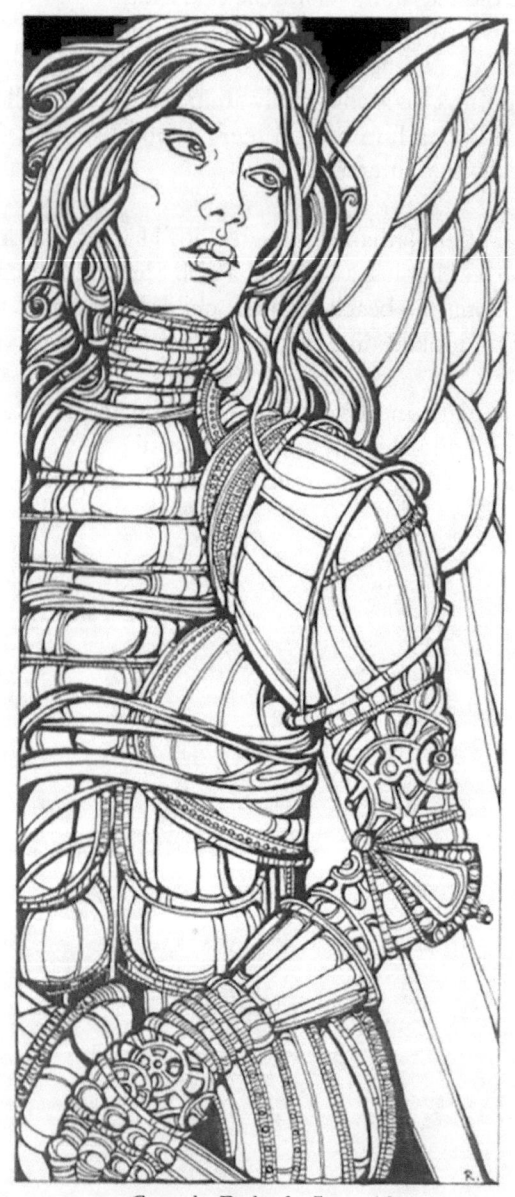

Cover by Ruby for Issue 12

See You Later

Suzanne Gyseman

I stand at the window. It is all snow outside, featureless except for the yellow stain of light that falls from my window. The sky too is bland; the nicotine colour of my grandmother's teeth. This is from the failing light of the sun.

Linda shares the room with me. We are kept prisoner here.

Our captors are reptilian-skinned, with lizard eyes. I am not afraid of them, because I have a gun in my pocket, hidden beneath a white handkerchief. I feel I ought to tell Linda about the gun. It will be our secret. I go over to her and touch her arm. She has her back to me and then she turns around.

I wake and sit straight up; staring, my heart racing. The beat shakes in my ears, and I breathe with my mouth open. It is still dark, and I reach to turn on the bedside lamp. At first, I fumble, because my hand is shaking. My clock falls from the cabinet and thuds onto the carpet.

When the light is on, I lean over and retrieve the clock. It appears to be unharmed and I am relieved. It would not do to be late for work.

I cannot go back to sleep now. I do not want to. I am afraid the dream will continue. I know, if I lie back down, that the atmosphere of the dream will flood over me. Probably, it will do so again tonight, even after a day's work.

I dress quickly and wrap my dressing gown over the top as well. The room is very cold. I do not have enough coins to put into the meter to use the heater as well as the cooking ring. I need coffee more than a heated room just now. I shuffle around in double socks that are wadded into my slippers, feeling cumbersome in all my layers.

As I drink my coffee at the tiny table between the cooker and sink,

I think about the dream. I wonder what it is that frightens me about it. Why I always wake up so suddenly and with such fear that I cannot remember what came next. I know that something happens because, until the end, the dream is not really frightening.

Outside the front door, Mark is waiting for me. Since Linda went missing along this route, he has taken to walking me to and from work. It is kind of him, but I do not feel I need an escort. I would not do anything silly. There are enough rumours about what has happened to Linda to prevent me straying from the main street. We pass ten side-streets on our way to work. I wonder which one Linda took.

When we reach the works, Mark lets us both in, then locks the black gate behind us.

"See you later," he says.

I am only on my sixth tray when the others start talking about Linda again. I wish they wouldn't. What's done is done. I suppose I can't blame them; it is still fresh in their minds. But if they are not careful, we will be split up. I don't want to be sent back to chopping; I prefer it here in sorting. The product is less recognisable by the time it reaches our section.

Maggie is the one who starts it. Leaning back in her seat, she lets her hands rest idly. Her gloves put slime on the edge of the conveyor, but she does not appear to notice. "Nothing new, then?"

"Is there ever?" Judy replies. She is the one who would know. She was the one called to the office, who was told what to tell us.

"I'll never understand why she did it. She never seemed unhappy."

"Always did her work. Faster than most."

"But never skimped." Maggie's eyes slide over me.

"Never left early, either," says Judy. She looks up from the tray she is covering, but drops her eyes when she meets mine.

"What's the use wondering?" says Mary. Coughing slightly, she peels off her gloves and searches in her apron pocket for a handkerchief. Mary hasn't been here long. She hasn't got used to the smell yet.

What none of us say is that Linda is not yet found. That is, Linda's body is not yet found. There are many rumours, but no evidence. We all know this, but it would be dangerous to say it.

While Maggie's hands have been idle, the machine has not. It has been extruding produce at its relentless rate, and trays have clogged together at her station.

"Watch that tray, Maggie!" Judy warns.

Maggie leans forward to separate the trays from one another. Her apron goes in the slime that her gloves have left on the conveyor.

While I am cleaning my hands before going home, Judy comes into the wash-room. "Another day done," she says as she closes herself into a toilet cubicle. I hear her peeing into the pan. "Mark walking you home again?"

"Yeah," I say.

She misinterprets my hesitation. "You could do a lot worse than Mark."

I turn on the dryer so I do not have to answer.

When I get to the gate, Mark is not yet there. I wait, obediently. Then four girls from downline come along and suddenly I decide to leave with them. My heart beats faster as the keeper unlocks the gate, but he does not even look at me as I go through behind the others.

As soon as we are beyond sight of the works, I slow my pace, and it is not long before the other girls are way ahead. I prefer to walk alone, despite the danger. My footsteps are incisive in the growing gloom. The laughter of the others ahead of me is faint, like a memory. I think of Linda and, as I pass each side-street, I wonder if it is the one she took.

I pause at the fifth opening, half-way home. I have to wait on the pavement while a car turns out onto the main street. The car has smoked-glass windows and I cannot see in. It is very clean, metallic grey, and even the hub-caps gleam, reflecting the orange glow from the street lamps. I do not look too long at the windows, because the occupants might be looking out at me. Part of me imagines Linda sitting inside.

It is not quite a conscious decision, and I have turned before realising. Instead of crossing, I walk down the side-street.

First, I pass large detached houses set behind gardens. These houses have bay windows. Many of the rooms are lighted. Within each house, I see a woman, sometimes with children. One woman lays a table ready for tea. Another is tending her fire.

I like this walking in the dark street, looking in at lighted rooms, where other people live. I walk slowly, taking time to watch the woman of each house, almost scrutinising. But none of them are Linda.

Then there are the terraces, and then the flats. The windows get smaller the further I go down the street, though the buildings get larger. Within each window that is lighted, a woman is working. As I go further, the curtains start being drawn, as if the women begin to feel eyes watching them from the dark.

I know I have gone too far when, up ahead of me, I see a group of men. They cross to my side of the street. A stubborn part of me still does not let me turn back, refuses to acknowledge the danger I am in. I carry on towards them, even though I know I should turn back, or it will be too late. But then, it is too late.

I do not meet their eyes as they come up to me.

"Looking for company, love?" There is the stink of his breath on the night air; he has been eating meat.

"I think she's shy!"

"Come on, darling, you're not shy of me, are you?"

I walk faster, which is ridiculous, for they simply lengthen their strides.

"What's the hurry?"

What a fool I have been. It is fully dark now; we have left the street lights behind. It is way beyond the time a single girl should be out of doors, and too far from any of the houses for help to come. My arm is grabbed and his claws pinch my skin through my jacket. Now, I know how Linda felt.

"Get off!" I pull back and hear my sleeve tear.

"Ooh, temper!" The one who grabbed me laughs. One of the others grunts. They do not say anything else as they close in around me.

My back is against a tall mesh fence. The wind blows cold through it, against my legs. On the wind is the smell of wasteland, empty night and, faintly, the smoke from distant chimneys.

There is a rasp as one of them strikes a match against his wrist to light a cigarette. The flame flicks light over his reptile skin and glints against his lizard eyes. The sheen in each eye is tiny and distant as moons. The wind whines through the fence behind my neck.

In my dream, Linda turns around. She smiles, and she has alligator teeth. In the same moment, I know that there is no gun in my pocket after all.

From some distance, I hear footsteps, running. Someone is coming from the lighted end of the street. There is shouting. The men look towards the sounds.

There is a scuffing of boots, no more. Their smell goes, the rankness of alcohol and cigarettes. But the carnivore breath stays in my nostrils. I look up at Mark. He is breathing fast. I know he is angry with me, and trying to remain calm. He expects me to be grateful; like he expects me to thank him when he walks me to work. But I find I have nothing to say. I am aware only of the discomfort of my body. My armpits are prickly; my skin chilled on the backs of my hands.

We walk back up the street together, towards the lights and houses. As we pass the blocks and the terraces, I do not look at the windows. In the houses with the bay windows, most of the warmth is curtained off. But in one room, a woman is standing, staring out at the night. She cannot see us. Possibly, all she can see is her reflection staring back at her. I turn my head to look as we pass.

Linda? A figure walks into the room behind her. It is her man. He lounges into an armchair near the fire, rubbing a hand along his jaw, scale against scale. The woman's face is expressionless as she reaches up and draws the curtains across.

My feet are aching. One toe is chafing inside my shoe. With each footfall, it sets up a regular rhythm of pain.

I suppose I shall have to breed with Mark some day soon. He has not asked me yet. But I know he will by the way he looks at me.

I hear the slither of his tongue as it slides out to taste the air.

Original Cover for Issue 2 by Billie Walker-John

Ptolemy's Recording

Jamie Spracklen

Ptolemy Webb was still a small boy inside, and was fed up with being walked over by everybody he met. He'd get even with the Devil this time, and all those who had hurt his mother, of that he was sure. No more silence for Ptolemy, or being talked down to. This is where it ended.

Before the Devil had come into his life, all his songs had been of secret things; the moonlight over the dark countryside, the vibrant screams of foxes catching rabbits, or the smell from deep, dark stagnant, pools. Before *her*, Ptolemy had known he had been happy, but now the Devil's insidious words and what *she* had done had ruined all of his songs.

Before *she* had come, he had travelled into town each day; full of his favourite breakfast of great slices of black pudding, crispy on the outside and dark red on the inside and peppered delightfully throughout with pale, glutinous fat. He liked to park his battered bike by the old station, marvelling every time at the old, forgotten chain locks that lay scattered and twisted like metallic snakes around the bike stands. He wondered why they had been left alone, uncared for, and where their owners had gone. He wished he had the keys and combinations to unlock and free each one and add their distinct songs to his own.

Reaching his favourite store, down the road, where battered wallflowers struggled to flower each spring, Ptolemy would look up at the music display, with a grin forming on his oval face, as he brushed his mousey brown hair away from his deep-set eyes, which roamed over the compact discs in front of him. They glittered in their uniform cases, so wonderfully different. He knew that the entire world would just melt away when he started to really listen to their songs, for these recordings eased the lonely fears that always plagued him; in their measured notes, he found order. Even in the wildest excesses of experimental jazz, or the chemically-induced twirls of trance, Ptolemy found beauty.

He remembered how he had used to sit for hours listening to his mother's old 78s, in that dusty old front room. It was the best their dark, dank old house had had to offer, and was therefore sometimes used when elderly relatives had come to visit. On those increasingly rare occasions, his mother would dress him in his best (and only) suit that smelled of ancient cologne and moth-balls. He would stand stiffly, drinking watery tea to the ticking of the often slow hall-clock, until the family would finally take their leave.

Apart from those troublesome visits, the room was usually his to use as he liked. His mother never interrupted him as, with the exception of those awkward tea parties, she just stared most of the hours away. Even his chubby hand in hers soon began to make little difference, and so the crackling, dust-filled sounds that issued from those huge, black records had lulled them both, as his mother had slipped away from Ptolemy more and more each day.

Yes, Ptolemy had loved that front room. He would scan the stern, picture-imprisoned faces that watched from the faded walls there, waiting for them to whisper to him their secret song. But they never did, they just stared back at the man who was the last of their progeny. It was there, in that room, that he first discovered that music could speak to him of his deepest desires.

Ptolemy loved his compact discs more than those scratchy records, though. Since he had first seen them in his favourite shop across town, he had bought as many as his allowance money would allow. It never mattered to Ptolemy what was on them, as long as he could sit back and listen to them, with a nice slab of toast that oozed margarine all over his thick fingers, and a sweet cup of tea. Their sounds and words held him close at night, when he'd lain awake listening to his mother moving around the house. The floor-boards would creak under her heavy, slow steps; steps that had in time began to rattle with the music that swam around in Ptolemy's head. And when he tried hard enough, he had found that it marched in time with the percussion of whatever music he happened to be listening to; it became its own, sweet melody.

As his mother deteriorated, it was only listening to his music that allowed him to fall into a blissful sleep, and often Ptolemy would dream of all the sounds he would one day fill *his* recording with.

This would be his special recording: a continuing soundtrack that played all his favourite tunes that only made sense to him. The dark at the end of the night was there; the mutterings his mother made in the day was replayed as his bedtime cacophony. Ptolemy's head was filled with drums muttering in the background, coupled with the wails from the rabbits as they were ripped apart in the shadowed fields. It would lull him asleep each night, and upon waking it would run through his day like some infernal tinnitus.

But the content of Ptolemy's recording was always changing, and the more he tried to keep in time with its tune, the more he had listen really hard to hear its joy. It demanded more of his attention each day, and cried aloud to be added to. Soon, he realised that the tune would need more songs.

Mother had loved Ptolemy and had been his friend. It was she who had taken him to the countryside once, when she still liked going outside. Ptolemy had often thought of that day when sitting alone in his new bedroom. It had been the best of his life.

But Ptolemy didn't see the countryside now. No more clean air for Ptolemy. No more love for Ptolemy, because his tune had changed, and he didn't like what it sounded like.

The recording had changed for Ptolemy one day when his mother had stopped muttering and lay silent in the day. The police had found him holding her hand and had taken him away screaming. Ptolemy hadn't wanted to leave Mother. When he'd held his nose, the smell hadn't been that bad anyway. Ptolemy and Mother would have been fine.

But instead, he was stuck on the other side of the large, grey town. And he was living where everybody thought he was strange, and looked down on him because he had trouble writing, and called him names when he rode his bike to the local music shop.

People could be so hurtful to him, but he knew inside that *he* would conduct the last melody.

And so, the music in his head played yet another tune for Ptolemy.

The killing teeth of the moon-silver foxes stopped savaging the rabbits. Instead they watched him from the dark, secret places with almond eyes and animal tears. The songs they howled now were all lonely without Mother, but also so full of rage.

And Ptolemy knew rage well. He hated the way he had been made to leave his home because the police had thought he was 'at risk', or the way that the other residents laughed when they caught him dancing to his music on his own. But he liked to dance and would spin round and round and round, until he felt all dizzy and funny in his stomach, with the blood pumping in his ears adding to the war drums in his soul.

Ptolemy's eyes narrowed as he thought about what it would be like to have somebody else who liked his recordings as he did, a friend he could whisper all his secret tunes to. Somebody who shared his fox-filled dreams.

But most of all Ptolemy hated the warden those police had appointed to him. She didn't know he saw the way she looked at him, when she thought he *wasn't* looking, or the way she washed her hands after she touched him. Everything was home-cooking, and cosy chats that 'worked through' problems. But all Ptolemy wanted to do was sit and listen to his recordings in his new, bright bedroom and try to block out the dull drone of *The Archers* that muttered away each afternoon from *her* front room.

Because Ptolemy knew that *she* was the Devil, you see. His mother had told him what to look for and what to guard against.

"The Devil always comes with soft words, Ptolemy," she would say, "and is a bad man or sometimes a person who says they love you, like your Papa, Ptolemy."

Yes, Ptolemy knew. Mother had told him, and that was that.

So, when one day the Devil bought him a football season ticket and told him not to spend so much time with his music, he tried not to let it show, but he knew *she* was the Devil. He recoiled at the very thought of spending any of his spare time standing with the bright and cheerful crowds watching the sportsmen as they postured and preened on the pitch. His mother had called football 'bloody silly, state-sanctioned tribal warfare' and Ptolemy agreed, even though he didn't know what all of those words had meant.

But he knew he had to be careful now, so he took the offered ticket but threw it away when *she* wasn't looking. He then went out to the grey town to look instead at some more compact discs.

But when he got back to his bedroom, all of his music was gone.

As he screamed, and screamed, the Devil just smiled sadly at Ptolemy and said it was for the best.

And Ptolemy hated the Devil more than anything then, and that night his recording played a new song for him, after he had fallen into a fitful sleep on a pillow wet with tears. The new song spun a tale of the dripping, bloody teeth of the foxes but instead of those angry foxes killing rabbits, they fought each other, until their pelts were slick with dark, shadowed blood.

When Ptolemy awoke, he left the house before the Devil could catch him. He rode all the way to the shop with the compact discs in, and looked up at the display that held the blank ones. There were so many types, thought Ptolemy, as he looked at the money he had in his pocket. Ptolemy had never bought a *blank* compact disc before. Until now, he had never had anything to fill it with, for he had kept all his special songs in his head, safe and sound, where the Devil couldn't get to them.

But he bought a very good one this time, so that those police who had taken his Mother away would be able to hear very, very well. Then he raced all the way back home, weaving through the traffic and feeling the happiest he had felt for a long time, with the wind gushing through his thinning hair.

When the Devil found him in his room, he had set everything up just the way he wanted it; the disc was paused and ready to record at a moment's notice with just a press of his fat finger.

And after the police had heard the screams of the woman as she was being stabbed to death by her lodger, they had read Mr Webb his rights.

But Ptolemy was so proud of his final recording. His rewriteable compact disc *was* a very good one, and that the laugh that could be heard throughout was clearly *his*.

Cover by Ruby for Issue 3

Finding Mary

Tim Lebbon

Every time I wake up, I bring another part of Mary back with me.

I sat at the kitchen table, my hair moulded into fantastic shapes by sleep, my eyes glassy, whether from tiredness or crying I was not sure. I held my hands tightly around the cup of steaming tea, enjoying the heat, a comforting sensation rather than one of pain. I could still remember the feel of Mary's hair wrapped around my fingers.

"What do you mean?" my mother asked. She took another bite from her toast, watching me guardedly.

I shook my head, smiled wryly, as if what I wanted to tell was foolish, as if the dreams I had been having were wet dreams instead of what they really were. I sipped at the tea. My lips burned, I took another sip.

"Come on, love, what do you mean?" My mother now sat to attention at the table, leaning towards me as if she would take me into her arms over breakfast.

"I dream about Mary," I said, playing down everything that had happened with such a bland statement.

"You're bound to. There's nothing harmful there, you're just keeping her memory alive." My mother was my guide, my guilt-sink.

I nodded, feeling the lump forming in my throat, but the strawberry jam reminded me of the inside of the windscreen. The smiling cuts on my palms ached now that they were open once more, their shape matching perfectly my uncut nails. I looked at them and saw a tear of blood seep from under one of the scabs. "I dream..." I said again, pausing, uneager to continue.

"Yes...?"

"I dream that Mary wants to be back with me. I have her in my arms, then something drags her away. Something black. Death, I suppose. Then, I grab at her, trying to stop her from going. She screams, lost. Then I wake up."

My mother sat quietly, considering what I had said. I could sense her weighing possible replies in her clever, wise mind. "You're remembering her. Trying to come to terms with the idea that you caused her death. In your mind, you're trying to make her live again." She took a sip of tea. "Is that bad?"

I was startled at first by her question. Then I remembered that she was always here to help. "Course it's not bad," I said. "But it's not all."

She did not say anything. She didn't have to. She could see that I was preparing to speak, struggling to form the words which would suitably convey what I had been experiencing over the last few weeks, since the accident.

Mother was great – she had soon dispensed with the banal, "You mustn't blame yourself" platitudes and now we talked, properly, about what had happened. She drank in my words of anger, blasphemy and guilt and nourished her love for me on the lie they contained. She knew the truth, and she knew also that to impart it to me, she first had to drain me of the lie.

"When I wake up," I struggled, "I have something in my hand. This morning... this morning it was hair. Mary's hair. In my hand, like ...a dead animal. Stiff."

Mother was silent for a long time. The tea went cold, the cooker clicked and groaned as the grill cooled down. "Oh, Jamie," she said.

I looked down at my dressing gown, remembered the tuft of auburn hair I had felt when I surfaced from the dream, the hair that had vanished when I woke fully and sat up in bed, my tears clearing. I remembered the itch on my palm as the memory of her hair spoke. My dressing gown had seen better days, my life had once been full. It was stringy and torn, now, fraying at the hems. I began to cry.

"I want her back, Mum." My face screwed up, the tears came, and I was a little boy once more.

My mother stood and walked around the table to me. Her slippers whispered soothingly in the chill morning air. She put her hand on my head, stroked my hair. I leaned into her, relishing her touch. I cried my heart out once more, staying that way for ten minutes, remembering

Mary as she had appeared to me in my dreams, struggling against the darkness that tried to tug her finally from my grasp. I had grabbed her hair, I knew.

I cried and cried, and my mother stood by me, crying as well.

That day, before going to college, I went back to my bedroom and there dressed in silence, combed my hair. The room was the mess that I was so used to, a Rorschach explosion of clothes, books, videos, comics, magazines and computer bits and pieces, in which only I could see a state of order. Scattered in among my belongings, like victims of a bloody battle, were parts of Mary; a perfume bottle here, half used, its contents destined to evaporate away to nothing; a hairbrush there, auburn strands curled and tangled into its plastic fingers; a book she had been reading with a bookmark half way through, the second half of a lost history fated never to be revealed. I stepped over a pile of my own books to fetch a jumper from the wardrobe, glancing down as I did so. I was trying to convince myself that I was not looking for a clump of hair amongst the mess. Yet still I kept the wardrobe open for a little longer than usual, kicked about in its base even after I had found the jumper, jerked back as a spider hurried away from its disturbed hiding place.

My eyes stung with the familiar morning feeling of having cried my way through the night. The guilt that burned in my chest had also brought the dreams to me, plaguing me with false hope, teasing me with things which could not be

Angry with myself I left, determined that the dreams would end soon. I caught the bus to college. I had not driven since the accident.

That night I dreamed of Mary once more. We were in the same endless place, with the same blackness, the corruption of my guilt, trying to rip her away from me. She held her hands out like an imploring child, and I reached forward to grasp her to me. But however hard I tried, however far I stretched, I could barely touch her. Her face became frantic as the blackness darkened even more, a shadow over a shadow, blindness in the night. I felt something huge moving at the periphery of my senses, a thing beyond size and shape.

Mary's face split into a scream, and I saw the marks on her skin from the crash, and I smelled the spilled petrol, felt the heat of the flames as I struggled back to the surface of consciousness. As the darkness brightened into an early morning haze, and the limits of my senses were once again defined within four walls, I grabbed one last time. My hand found Mary's, I held tight, then the darkness vanished in a blinding flash.

I squeezed my eyes shut against the sudden light. I felt Mary's hand in mine, her clasp cold now, skin clammy with the sweat of the grave. I wanted to open my eyes to see, but I was afraid of what would be there.

"Tea," my mother said.

I opened my eyes and saw her standing over my bed, the light cutting swathes through her hair.

My hand was fisted shut, beads of blood finding their way between my white fingers and running across the back of my knuckles, onto the sheets. I opened my fist, my fingers heavy and stiff with the tension I had been exerting. I had a sudden sense of Mary's perfume, *Obsession*, flood my nose, and I gladly opened my mind to the memories it invoked. I looked around the room, searching for Mary, the smell of the perfume so strong that I expected to lift the covers and find her snuggled in bed with me.

"Jamie, what have you done to your hand?" My mother sat on the edge of the bed and examined my bloody palm and fingers.

My tears began to flow, joining my blood on the sheets in a multi-coloured rain of guilt. "Can you smell her?" I asked. "Can't you tell she's been here, Mum? I nearly had her back. She nearly came back."

My mother frowned at me, shook her head, nearer to outright anger than I had seen her for months. "It's the bottle of hers you keep, you know that. The smell that reminds you. I'll get rid of it. It's time you started afresh." She looked away, embarrassed.

I went to college with red eyes again that day. My friends approached me carefully, and the lecturers avoided asking me any questions.

My mother was out when I arrived home that evening, a note pinned to the fridge, telling me that she would be home later on, and that my dinner was in the slow cooker, and that she loved me. I believed her.

She had tidied my room while I was out. I know where she had put things, what she had done, how she had confirmed my dreams and shown me the final way to Mary. I know all this, because now I know everything.

Mother had piled my books into a corner, picked up my scattered clothes and whisked them away into the washing cycle. She had dusted, deleting forever the mindless twirls of the distracted fingers from the few uncluttered surfaces. Air freshener had been sprayed, strafing the cupboards and corners with canned forest glade. She had thrown out Mary's bottle of *Obsession*, believing, in part, that the lingering odour was the cause of my strange dreams.

She had found a tangled, blood-matted clump of hair under my bed.

My shock at seeing the hair where my mother had left it – sitting innocently on my bed, a thoughtful sheet of paper beneath it to prevent any stains – was not as profound as I may have expected. I was scared, but calm, feeling a serenity derived more from relief than anything else. Relief that I had been right. Relief that Mary was still there for me, should I choose to look. My dreams of the last few days, my tears as I awoke, no longer seemed redundant. I now knew the way to beat the darkness, the way back to Mary.

What my mother had thought of the hair I cannot guess. Maybe she assumed I had unravelled it from one of Mary's old brushes, the blood seeping from my own tattered hands as I grabbed and twisted it in torment and guilt. Or perhaps she feared that I had taken the hair from the crash site as a grisly memento of our final, terrible seconds together. Nevertheless, she left it for me.

Perhaps because she finally believed that all I said was true.

I went to find Mary.

When my mother arrived home that evening, she came quietly up the stairs and opened my bedroom door. Her breathing was soft but fast, full of a barely-restrained tension. She could see that I was in bed, but still she ventured into the cool room. She saw the empty brown plastic bottle on my bedside table, a thoughtful note beneath it to discourage any blame on her part. But still she reached out and touched my cooler face.

She could see the shape in the bed next to me; she could see the greyness of my arm where I clung to the figure with whom I lay; she could see the auburn hair splayed on the pillow next to my head; she could see the smile of victory on my blue lips. She could see.

I sat by a river. Everything was light. The water reflected the summer sun, dazzling me with its brilliance. A kingfisher dipped suddenly from a branch and made two splashes in the water; one in, one out. A silver fish wriggled in its mouth, then disappeared. A soft breeze blew along the river, bringing the wonderful scents of woodland and life to my nose. I breathed in deeply, revelling in the solitude of the scene.

There was silence, except for the twittering of birds, the occasional splash of fish, the background whisper of the river on its never-ending journey from birth to an ultimate blending with the whole. I felt so relaxed, so at peace, that I did not notice the figure sitting on the bench beside me for several minutes.

It was Mary. She smiled at me. We did not speak, did not move to touch each other. We simply sat in peace, enjoying each other's company, swimming in the sense of love which surrounded us.

Nowhere was there any darkness, not even under the trees that hung over the river. Light found its way everywhere.

The Arena

Lachesis January

A dust circle surrounded by ascending rows of mask-like faces, eyelessly blind, earlessly deaf. Though they perceived nothing real, they were not devoid of spirit and passion. They had chosen to ascend to a higher level of existence, to listen to the heart's whispers, not the flagrant noise heard by everyone else. This was an assembly of wanderers and searchers who had come to rest, and with peace had found power; the recognition of something greater than the tangible. They did not feel the dry heat nor the stillness in the air. They could not hear the silence, nor smell the living scent of the Choreographer, who stood before them, down in the arena, shading his eyes against the bright sun's empty rays.

The Choreographer understood and translated the wordless wishes of the Audience into instructions. He picked up the fresh corpse of the suicide and carried it from the walled circle, returning for the paints the victim had used to help him transcribe his emotions. Finally, the Choreographer washed the spirals of colour and splashes of blood from the dirt. Without a word to those now burying the body, he slipped on his dusty coat and left the arena.

The desolate city with its mindless victims lay far across the sand on the edge of the horizon, but the walk never took him as long as it should.

The Choreographer found Lyn in an alleyway, drawn to him by the power of the Audience. There was no picture of Lyn in his mind, but he still recognised him, felt the Audience's mark upon him. Until that moment, the Choreographer had never doubted the Audience's decisions. Maybe he was becoming rebellious in his old age, maybe he was losing sight of the fact that appearances count for so little, but all those he had found before had looked more like chosen ones. This boy was mucky. His dirty blond hair hung in clumps and his clothes were in tatters. The Choreographer approached him from behind. The boy was eating something.

Closer.

There was a corpse on the ground. One of the boy's hands was deep in the torso, pulling at a piece of meat, trying to tear it away. The other was halfway into his mouth. Bloody flesh trailed from lips that were stained ruby red. On seeing the Choreographer, he stopped and stared like an animal. The Choreographer grabbed him by the arm and started to pull him up. The physical contact allowed him to know everything about the boy, and he understood the Audience's choice. A lifetime of soul-destroying misery; a loveless upbringing before being cast onto the streets as a child; a boy who spoke a truth too strange; a pariah who saw what others didn't want to see.

"Come on, Lyn," the Choreographer said, hoping the boy was still human enough to understand language. Beneath the grime and the urchin appearance he was a pretty boy. His face was delicate and slightly triangular. His eyes were narrow, becomingly-shaped and glittering grey.

Lyn struggled and pulled away enough to pick up a green glass box of cigarettes and an antique gas lighter, which had tipped out of the dead man's pocket.

The Choreographer sighed and hauled him away. Lyn barely bothered to resist, but the Choreographer had not expected him to; they never did, they were always instantly aware of the power of the Audience without cognition of what it was.

There were one hundred faces in the Audience. They sat in seemingly attentive rows. Above the Arena, lanterns hung swaying from the thick boughs of overhead trees, linked by thin looped chains. The light they cast was distant and soft.

Lyn stood in the centre of the circle, alone. The unseen orchestra played; waves of dilute and vague sound washed over him. The Choreographer had prepared him for the dance as the Audience had requested. His hair had been thoroughly cleaned, dyed red and black and plaited into a myriad of tiny braids. His face was painted boldly;

striking black and red lines extended from his eyes. His lips were violent crimson, his pale face was made paler. Droplets of ruby hung from his ears and around his neck.

As he had been silently transformed, he had seen the Choreographer standing in the doorway, watching with his arms folded, supervising his mindless assistants; hollow people who were nothing but extensions of himself. Lyn did not care how these helpers had come about, or who they had been. He was a prisoner here and cared for nothing other than himself. The Choreographer followed him everywhere, maintaining a threatening presence, and the only time Lyn was alone was when he was locked away in his cell, although sometimes he thought he was never more alone than when he danced.

His clothes were comfortable if not spectacular. He was clad in a close-fitting black top and equally dark leggings, with tatters of cloth wrapped around his limbs and waist, so that when he leaped the fine lines of his body could be seen, and when he whirled the strips of material would chase him round. He stood motionless in the middle of the dirt circle. His feet were bare.

It often took him a while to launch into his dances. Sometimes, the music churned his soul up and pushed him into it like a stray leaf in a breeze. Sometimes, he consciously willed it, knowing that it could never stop if it had never begun, and he would be trapped here until he stopped, as he had been trapped here every night for a long long time, regardless.

The Choreographer had told him that he danced for the Audience but would not say who they were. His instructions to Lyn had been minimal; he had to dance with all his heart, but there was no right way.

Why should he dance when no one watched? Why should music be allowed to fall on deaf ears? The Choreographer never observed him. He wasn't permitted to and couldn't tell Lyn why, reacting to the question as if the Audience angered him with that peculiar exclusion. Lyn twisted round slowly and thoughtfully. They would know if the Choreographer watched, just as they would know if he died. They could not see or hear, but they could feel. This hurt Lyn a little, made him feel hopeless, unnecessary. He needed a reaction, a sign of humanity from the rows of blank faces, to show that they cared about him, and that all his passion was for something. If he fell – and he now fell, collapsing into a beautifully delicate bundle in the arena – there would be no reaction. Nor would there be if he died here, if he screamed out, if he stood totally still forevermore.

The thumping of his heart lulled him into a rhythm, but he stayed still, feeling as the music urged him to stand, that he was free to leave, or stand still, or die, but that he would always choose to dance. It was this choice that they loved so much, his freedom, and they would love whatever he chose to do, as long as he could do it with spirit.

He was free.

The Choreographer handed Lyn a lump of bread, as they stood in the costume room, and Lyn took it, but held onto the Choreographer's hand for a lingering second. Their eyes met and the Choreographer realised with some horror that Lyn was not going to kill himself, as the others had done before. He saw the same animal hunger he had glimpsed in Lyn's eyes back in the alleyway. He realised he had let himself be fooled by Lyn's compliance, believing him too dim-witted to desire escape.

Lyn's hands were up around his throat with the grace, speed and strength that the Choreographer expected of a dancer. Instinctively, he struggled, but not with great force, as Lyn seemed so fragile; he didn't want to anger the Audience by damaging the boy. He tried to control Lyn gently, but failed. He crumpled to the floor, after Lyn had thumped his head twice on the wall behind him.

The Choreographer had been surprisingly easy to attack. Lyn had always seen him as a strong and omnipotent being. Now the man lay at his feet, unconscious, unable to prevent Lyn from binding his hands. Lyn waited until he had awakened, and could be urged into the Arena at the point of a sword.

The music sounded as always. The Audience made no reaction. Grinning, Lyn scanned the tiers of apparently lifeless bodies, feeling their anticipation and hunger for what was to come. Dusty colours and pallid faces; ordinary people like those he had murdered in his home city. The Audience comprised a hundred or so people, from all walks of life, now blind and deaf to anything that didn't matter to them.

"I am your prisoner," Lyn yelled at their blank faces. "I am he who dances and this is he who found me." He shoved the Choreographer forward. "You are blind to my movement. I no longer wish to move. And though you applaud me, I cannot believe it is genuine. How can you appreciate my talents when you cannot even see?

"So tonight, I dance a new dance. It is not the swirling creation of my soul, as directed by the Choreographer. It is a different dance of passion. You perhaps would like it. If you could see. If you could hear."

Lyn knew the Audience understood him, and that they all saw his words as lies. For Lyn to confront them, he'd had to pass beyond perceiving them as simply blind and deaf. He'd had to know they loved his dancing for other reasons, otherwise he would have killed himself, as others had before him.

Lyn began his performance by binding the Choreographer's ankles. Then he began to dance around the man, playfully cutting and slicing, flicking blood over himself and the dust. He leaned down to kiss the Choreographer's wounds. And the Choreographer remained silent, biting his lip occasionally, as if to stop himself from shrieking. Eventually the dance moved towards its climax. Lyn's digs with the sword became deeper and his motion faster.

The last cut. Across the throat. Straight.

The music stopped, although the musicians could not see him.

The Choreographer lay crumpled at Lyn's feet, who performed a few more turns around the body before bowing to his audience: these blind, deaf creatures who demanded passion and spirit. The Choreographer had told him that he must always dance with his heart. They would not tolerate soulless movement. They hated disorder, but also hated order. He was never to repeat a sequence.

The murder had been as passionate and spirited as all his other dances, if not more so. He would always dance for them but not here, in this heartless arena. The Audience would find another Choreographer, who would solicit for them other artists. Now, Lyn would light a cigarette, supplied to him by the Choreographer – good quality cigarettes at that – and then chew on a couple of the dead man's bones. Then he would leave, go home, go anywhere. But wherever he was, whoever he was killing, in whatever way, it would be a dance for the sightless ones. Always. This was his goodbye, he decided, bowing deeply once more.

The Audience applauded.

The King of Hearts and the Jack of Frowns

Jason Gould

Wilson was the type of teenager who revelled in angst; he found solace in its comfortless embrace. When I first knew him he would spend every lunch hour camouflaged by coats and bags in the cloakroom, scribbling pages and pages of unreadable poems that held meaning only for their author. He was minutely acquainted with the interior of every toilet bowl in the school, their scent a sort of cologne. His flat, wet hair was a constant of his daily appearance. He expressed his emotions in a permanent scowl, and stayed home sick for weeks at a time. When his mother fled, he tried to attach a scarf to the landing light and kick the chair from under his feet, but the noose unravelled and left him with a swollen neck, a cancerous rasp, and a father whose indifference was legendary.

Inside, he was ugly. Inside, there were killers and poets and opium-fanciers yearning to unfold.

But I had to admit I rather liked him.

In our final year at school we drifted together, attracted by mutual feelings of exile. My taste in music and clothes earned me rabbit-punches and mimicry, and Wilson's quietness coaxed hatred from the boys and pity from the girls. Our friendship was a natural development. We immersed ourselves in a marvellous landscape of inertia; staring at ceilings through hazes of wine. We slept in parks and sniffed the air as dawn peeled back night with its dew-tipped fingers.

When Wilson hit his late teens, he became the type of person who would flee from dance-floors and hammer his fist into toilet-wall mirrors, screaming *"all shit, all shit"*, until the bouncers dragged him outside and painted purple blotches over his stomach. When crossing a bridge, he often leapt onto the railings and frolicked mere inches from death. During the day, when the greyness seemed eternal, he would stay in his room and design mosaics of grated flesh from the cuts that patterned his arms. Those scabby lattices were, so he said, a necessary prelude to liberating the blood that knocked at his wrists. I spent many dull evenings slouched in casualty while they bandaged his despair. I listened to arguments and watched tramps check the Maxpax machine for uncollected copper.

I never held any bitterness towards Wilson. The trouble he caused me, the cash he borrowed and failed to return, even the restless nights I endured in hollow cells, didn't turn me against my friend. I don't know why. Perhaps in him I glimpsed a chaotic reflection of myself; and also, apart from the occasional squabble, we rarely turned our hatred on each other.

The streets of York are so ancient they surely house magic. Growing up there, however, meant that the spirits that enchanted so many in those narrow lanes, for us blended into the tedium of adolescence.

Wilson and I used to hang around various pubs; our favourite a nameless hole wedged between some vacant flats and a wax museum, where the guts of quartered highway-men were seen through the fingers of cowering children.

The flip-side of society kissed shoulders in that cramped bar, sipping colourful drinks and quoting lyrics by bands who would split within the week. Some scored a hit, then stumbled outside to explore the city that twinkled beneath the river; others swapped tales, or rummaged for love in the shadows and corners of the melancholic room at the top of the stairs.

Everything was coated in velvet; the walls, the floor, the tables and chairs, forming the impression that you sat in a ribcage, all sweaty and red. The regulars owned their special spots and unfamiliar faces were viewed with obvious caution.

It was balanced on the edge, that place, where suicide and sex were common conversation and the jukebox was shrouded in a thousand dark songs.

We usually consumed spirits at the bar, the gloom-boy and I, for the panelling behind it was a patchwork of mirrors, and we relished the sight of gradual stupor. Jerry, the barman, declared we were killing ourselves slowly. The phrase struck a chord and we scrawled it on road-signs, billboards, and beneath the arches of railway bridges, a word of advice to the lost and the lonely.

Kill yourself slowly, we wrote after sun-down. *Kill yourself slowly*, we sang to passers-by. And they read and they listened, shaking their heads once we'd moved on.

Then, after two years of singing these psalms to the hopeless, we met Houdini.

Houdini was a traveller who'd rented a room from Jerry; his payment a bag of jewellery that immediately disappeared from the premises. He needed to crash for a couple of days, then vanish back into whatever sunset he'd galloped in from. He wore a carnival of trinkets, several days' stubble and an aura of immortality, as if he'd witnessed every comet that had ever skimmed the earth and slept in the mud of a million fields. His father, a circus aide, had treasured the works of Houdini – the renowned escapologist – and, before the growth in his wife's belly had developed a head, he'd instinctively known the name of his child.

In lieu of school, Houdini had studied showmanship, palming coins and unpicking ropes, while others his age struggled with their laces. By fifteen, he'd dangled from rafters and suffocated in tanks of water, thrilling the young and shocking the old in a dozen different cities across Europe. The tents, he told us repeatedly, had been packed, the ground outside trenched with the endless footprints of those who went to be amused but left feeling awed.

"So how come you don't still perform?" I asked.

"The entourage was bought by another outfit," he explained. "They wanted to know exactly how my tricks were done, for safety regulations."

"And you didn't want to share your secrets," guessed Wilson.

"There aren't any *to* share," he corrected.

We were sitting amid the velvet, drinking cheap beer. It was a late, frustrated afternoon, and the town sighed at the speed of the clock.

We were the only ones in the bar, apart from Jerry, who whistled Christmas carols and slowly transformed the place into a grotto by hanging black tinsel and daubing the mirrors with kohl.

I admired people like Houdini; they carried with them a sort of inbred charm. If only it could be learned.

"So, where you heading after here?" I enquired.

"Up north. I've a friend in Sunderland who inherited a three-storey house. She almost has a menagerie teeming through its corridors."

I exchanged glances with Wilson, drained my glass and summoned a refill.

"You guys could tag along if you liked," Houdini offered, pre-empting our thoughts.

I tried to sound only moderately attracted by the idea. "Yeah? What about your friend?"

"She won't mind." His voice lessened in volume. "There *is* a small bit of business I need to finish first. You may find it slightly distasteful."

"If we'd be intruding..."

Houdini raised his palms; the lines were deep, deep enough to hide illusions. "No, not in the least," he assured us. "It's just – she treats her animals like kids; some of them passed on recently and she can't bear to be parted..."

"So, you have to take care of the burial," interrupted Wilson.

He smiled, and said, "I have to take care of the resurrection."

We started to chuckle. Houdini's complexion flushed, and his tone became irritable. "Perhaps it wouldn't be such a good idea," he decided, standing and padding towards the stairs.

Wilson gave chase and patted his shoulder. "Hey, no offence. We thought you were joking." It was the only time I'd ever seen him placatory.

Houdini stared into his face, reading its misery. "You belong on the sunless side of the world," he said, "you remind me of spring."

"In what way?"

"The way you strive to disguise your despair under blue skies of booze."

Amused, and just a bit unnerved, Wilson crossed back to our table. He sat down, his eyes resembling those of a child at the centre of some gorgeous and fleeting dream. Houdini loitered at the intersection of rooms. "I'm leaving tomorrow. If you'd like to accompany me, come here tonight for drinks upstairs. If you're to spend Christmas with us, there are several things we need to discuss."

He left and we listened to his footsteps as he ascended into the upper half of the building.

Wilson hummed the theme tune to the *Twilight Zone*. I ordered more drinks.

"Take my word for it, he's crazy. Look what he said to you about spring and that stuff about resurrecting dead animals."

"It's so weird, though," replied Wilson.

"Yeah, okay. But I don't fancy being alone with him, and as for living there..."

Wilson threw another stone into the river, then quickly re-gloved his hand with his pocket. The water was still, its inhabitants at rest.

"What did you see?" I asked, after a pause.

"Where?"

"In his eyes."

Wilson glared at me. "Nothing."

"You looked as if you'd seen...something you really wanted."

"I don't want anything," he said. "All I need is this skin and this blood."

"Don't forget memories, and stop quoting song lyrics."

I didn't know why we were arguing about the afternoon's episode. It was obvious we'd keep our date with Houdini.

Night congealed and hid the currents at our feet. I felt nervous.

"Come on, then," I said as the tower issued nine.

"I'll need a Martini first."

"Good idea," I agreed.

Houdini was perched on the window-seat when we popped our heads round the door. A chorus of chatter and anguish seeped up from below.

"It's so sad. isn't it?" he said, watching the fairy-lights that were strung in the empty trees outside.

"What, Christmas?" I asked.

"Everything," he replied. "Do you know if it wasn't for light, human beings would die out? Quite ironic, since we do most of our fucking in darkness."

We walked into the centre of the room, and I clicked the door closed. Apart from a bundle of blankets thrown into one corner, it was free from the mark of habitation. The rugless floor begged ghosts, or perhaps they already wept by our sides and we were too blind to see them.

Houdini turned to us, and I heard Wilson swig from the bottle he'd brought along.

"Is that why you asked us here, to tell us that?" I demanded.

He shook his head and the ear-rings swapped gossip. "I want to show you something, and then I hope you'll join me in Sunderland. And perhaps, after that, onto Berlin."

"Berlin?" My voice couldn't restrain my surprise.

"In the New Year, there's to be a convergence there, a gathering of travellers... like-minded people."

It sounded fairly interesting. "For the millennium?" I asked.

"Don't be so trite. It's for... no particular reason. If you look deep enough, there aren't any reasons for anything; there isn't one for this..." He exhaled and frosty breath swirled before him "So why anything else?"

Houdini went to where he'd stashed his belongings and hunted in the creases of a wine-stained blanket. Having found what he was looking for, he moved back towards us. A skeletal cat purred and blinked in his arms. He stroked its ears, and its eyes flickered erotically. He crouched down and kneeled on the floor, arranging the animal before him. It trusted its owner enough to retract its claws, to relax. Gently, he began to massage its chest, as a lover would. His deft strokes indicated a craftsman.

Gradually, sleep foamed in the cat's eyes until they slid shut, washing its dark face featureless. Its master continued to caress the area directly above its heart.

As he continued, he spoke: "There's an old superstition among entertainers that states you should never use your real name on stage; that if you do your act will certainly flop, and you'll be chased from the auditorium by a heated mob." His fingers sped up in their work, nipping welts of fur and flesh, twisting and kneading them one way, then the next. The creature's paws dithered about in the dust and dirt of the floor, its tail and head following suit, attracting splinters that would itch and grow sore. It could've been in rapture or agony; it was difficult to tell.

First one way.

"I always called myself: *The King of Hearts.*"

And then the other.

"They're my speciality," he confessed.

One way.

"So easy to persuade."

The other.

"See?"

He quit his movements and smoothed the fur he'd disrupted, leaning back on his haunches like a painter admiring his canvas. The cat was mute and motionless. The chest didn't expand, the nose didn't twitch; its feet might never have padded the rooftops of York. I prodded its stomach; the gristle succumbed to my fingers and toes as if truly unwarmed, truly dead.

What *had* I been an audience to?

"If you were a child, this spectacle wouldn't cause you stress."

I doubted that, but didn't argue.

"Age makes fear out of wonder, that's what I wanted to tell you tonight. So, if you decide to come with me, you must dump your last ten years – close your eyes to nothing."

He dropped to a squatting position and flexed his uncanny fingers. The cat began to stir, and after what was probably the same amount of time it'd taken to die, it rediscovered life, springing suddenly upwards and darting from window to door.

"Re-emergence *is* a problem," admitted our host. "Someone once told me it's like orgasming on a serrated edge."

"You mean this has been done on people?" I asked.

"Of course. Perhaps if you tasted death you wouldn't be so keen to squander life."

An obscure silence settled about us. The cat had pissed its terror away. I wondered if I should clap and whistle for more.

"You don't fancy pausing *your* heart then?" he asked.

"Absolutely not," I said.

"At my friend's house in Sunderland there's to be a party where…"

His sentence was snapped off by Wilson. "I do," he said, stepping forward and unbuttoning his shirt.

I put my hand out to stop him. "Don't be crazy…"

"I want to try it," he said firmly.

Wilson removed every item of clothing, until he stood unprotected against the world. I half-expected him to shave his head and pluck his groin, rip out his nails and snip off his lashes. Then he lay down, stretching out his malnourished whiteness in the dingy murk. His muscles shivered at the cold, at our stares, at the prospect of dying.

The air in my lungs stopped curling.

Houdini put two fingertips on the left of my friend's chest and rubbed them around in a loose invisible circle. The pair of them looked like a corpse and a mourning, desperate lover. Music oozed from the rooms below, reminding me of life; and here was Wilson, my friend, my elder, freezing his blood.

Below us, the tempo on the jukebox picked up. Houdini's hand mimicked it, and continued after the song's abrupt end. I squinted outside and saw how the candy-lights bobbed on the breeze, announcing the season with their bright, sorrowful bulbs.

Wilson shuddered once; then died.

I felt breath escaping from the corners of my mouth.

Houdini scanned the body from toenail to forehead, drinking in its longness, its paleness.

"They say it's like being back in the womb," he said, "they should bury us foetal." He rose and wandered from wall to wall, his attitude cavalier. "So, do you fancy Berlin? Dirty neon at dawn is such a sight to behold."

"Bring him back," I requested.

"Give him chance to enjoy it."

"Bring him back," I said again, "please…"

There was a blink of hesitation. Houdini shrugged. "Okay."

He gathered mounds of flesh between his fingers and started to tap at Wilson's heart, undoing whatever knot he'd tied.

I knew Wilson better than anyone else. I'd observed the tantrums, the despair, the longing looks at his father's razors scattered in front of the bathroom mirror. I turned to the wall and scrunched up my eyes. Behind me, I could hear fingers rasping at skin, their urgency growing faster as each new second ached by.

"Bring him back," I said to the mouldy plaster.

Before Houdini's lips had parted I knew what he was going to say. "He doesn't want to. The desire... it just isn't there." Houdini knew, as well as I, that no matter how much magic he pumped into that corpse it would never buck and jive back into action, never bruise and lacerate itself as it spasmed back into life, baptised by a long squirt of piss.

I stared out of the window at endless night; at the riverbank, we'd so often staggered down. Behind me, I could hear the rustle of skin on wood as Houdini dragged Wilson into the gloom. Then, I felt the killer's breath on my neck.

"Sometimes, we don't realise the true desire which lurks in our hearts," he said. "You'd be surprised at how many people fancy death."

"But Wilson didn't want to die," I said softly. "It was just attention seeking, a bit of a laugh."

Houdini sighed. "Apparently not." He waited a moment, then asked: "Do you want to try? Do you want to put *your* desire to the test?"

I turned round and his face was close, too close. I thought of the limp morning that would soon drag itself over the grey horizon and turn half-heartedly into afternoon, then evening, and appallingly back to morning. "I *am* tempted." My eyes darted momentarily to where Wilson's lifeless features grimaced from the shadows. "*Very* tempted."

"I don't believe you," he said. "Listen, you no longer have to copy your friend. If you need a guide, use me."

"A guide to what?"

He shrugged. "Life, and death."

"But aren't *you* ever tempted to empty your body through your wrists?" I asked.

He shook his head.

"Why not?"

"Because when I was a little younger than you, I was talked out of suicide by a close friend."

"How?" I asked.

He broke our eye-contact to watch the memory: "I was staying with him in France, and one night he took me to an abandoned warehouse on the outskirts of Paris. It was damp inside, and the air reeked of petrol. There was about ten or eleven men huddled in front of a small, creaking podium, and I learned later that each had paid ten thousand francs for the evening's performance. A man walked onto the stage, a cold-looking woman in tow. She was naked, and her limbs and eyes were sedated. I watched as he pulled a revolver from his inside pocket, put it against her temple, and created an abstract masterpiece on the filthy wall behind them. After that, I figured the world wasn't so bad after all; it wasn't all grey; it was just a case of looking for the colourful bits." He turned his attention back to me. "There's badness in everyone. If we submit to it, we find contentment. It's when we deny it that we feel the itch in our wrists. Come with me to Berlin. Join us."

The grey morning crawled closer. I had nowhere else to go. "Okay," I agreed.

"Good. I'll show you sights that'll make you glad to have breath in your body."

"I doubt that."

He put his hand on my shoulder. "Have faith in your fellow man," he said. "With him around, it's easy to be a tourist in the macabre. From this moment on, you will be known as The Jack of Frowns, and together we shall tour twilight, and its farthest dominions."

We walked downstairs and out towards the river. Dawn would soon trick the faithful with the false hope of another day. The men who strutted so agilely to work would soon become crooked and bitter; the women on their arms would grow barren and resentful, and the children who tottered blithely at their ankles would soon wave goodbye to innocence and laughter, and start worrying about lines around their eyes and lumps in their flesh. Like Prospero, every third thought was of my grave.

But now there was Houdini. Perhaps with him as my guide the

scenery wouldn't be quite so bleak.

I didn't allow myself one final glance at Wilson. I didn't crouch and stroke his cheek, didn't whisper some personal motto or bid him adieu. He wouldn't have approved of a career in depravity anyway. You can only hurt God, he'd always said, by hurting yourself. Maybe, but I'm willing to give the alternative a try.

Succubus

Chris Green

Midnight begotten daughter,
Unworldly paramour of pain,
On the night stars fall spent from the sky,
Fly the gloom whilst I await
My darkling angel, who hunts
And barbs my heart with dreadful allure.

Night fall form, infernal spawn,
Embrace me in cold compassion.
My helpless flesh in your caress:
Shredded, torn, consumed.
With each and every kiss,
Unholy passion draws me down
To drown and share your shadow.

And next to me, your body
Burns my skin, echoes of the sinner's pyre,
And malefic tender torment.
This carnal carnage now complete,
Alone and abandoned, I lie,
Bereft of death, in poisoned desire
For grace and foulness fused.

Dancing Day

Liz Williams

If I listen carefully, I can hear everything: fires burning, the drift of snow, secrets whispered into walls and voices calling. I have heard many voices across a thousand years, demanding, pleading and finally falling silent, but that day Lilith said that I was still too young to know sense from nonsense.

"You've got a lot of learning to do," she told me, rattling her brassy feathers. She looked at me out of a fierce golden eye. "Not a thought in your head, that's the trouble with you."

Lazy Ishtar from the fire said, "Oh, leave the child alone. Let her make her own mistakes."

It was always the same at home. I did not want to listen, and so I went down to the shore to dance. The stars burned molten, and far away I could see the other dancer: the one who is always there, spinning at the edge of the world. I felt the sun blaze beneath my feet and the furnace heat of the sky against my skin. In dancing, I forgot who I was, but someone had remembered me.

Her name was Shadineth Massaret. She wanted a wild love, bright as the sun and deep as darkness, and so she shut the windows, threw a pinch of incense onto the fire and summoned me. She called me by my own name; raised from the depths of some shadowy arcanum, written in blood on the day of my making.

Much later, Lilith said, "You don't have to answer, you know, just because someone bawls your name in your ear. You're not a dog. I don't know what got into you."

I don't know either. I suppose I was bored, or perhaps I just wanted to see what it was like; that small grey world, filled with dim mayfly souls.

Shadineth called my name three times and on the third I answered. Stars rushed by, the air rang like a bell, and I fell like a stone into the body of a girl, on a rainy night in Constantinople, in the year, 1923.

I don't think that Shadineth was expecting quite so spectacular a success. She was no professional necromancer: just a bored girl, at a loose end and excited by the thought of the forbidden. We all like to play with fire, sometimes. I was rather surprised at my sudden incursion into the human. Her body was cold; wet as snow and fragile as a shell. Her heart fluttered against her brittle ribs. I tried to tell her that I did not want to hurt her, but my voice sounded thunderous in the vaults of her head. She cried out and clapped her hands to her ears. Somewhere, beyond her, was warmth and I reached out to it, but she screamed again and plucked her hand from the coals in the brazier. Clearly, this matter of possession was something we would both have to work at. I think she fell; the room spun, and I found myself looking out of her eyes at the yellow plaster of the ceiling. Her heels drummed the floor. The door burst open and people swarmed in. They picked her up and carried her across to the bed, where they forced something sour and honeyed down her throat. She swallowed convulsively and dropped into dreaming. I had time to think, then, and to consider the consequences of my position.

Possession is such an ambivalent word. The Churches are unanimous in their disapproval, saying that it is common knowledge that people become possessed by demons. Yet we demons know that humans possess us: beguiling us with their desires and capturing us in the webs of their will. We find ourselves imprisoned in cooler flesh than our own, frightened and bewildered. I thought to find a new friend; instead I found myself securely stuck in the chilly veins of an amateur sorceress, now out for the count. I was cold beyond bearing and I wanted to go home. I think I howled.

I was held in her body, afraid and raging, until the morning. The sun came up in a torrent of light above the city, and Shadineth flinched as she opened her eyes. I stirred within her, as gently as I could. She rolled over, trying to escape the lodger in her head, and fell off the side of the bed. Servants came running in and helped her back. Then a man came: dressed in a robe the colour of dawn. From the sleeve of the robe he drew a small bag and from it he took a pinch of a black powder. An attendant lit the brazier and he cast the powder into the coals. It flared up with a hiss. I watched with interest. He raised his arms to the ceiling and cried out a single phrase. After a moment's reflection, I recognised it. It was an incantation, predictably enough against demons. It was evidently somewhat past its best. I tried to tell him this, but my voice roared out from my hostess' stretched throat. A confetti shower of plaster fell from the ceiling and the brazier spat sparks. My voice was too loud; my essence too hot; I was too much altogether for this small, neat world. I gave up, sulking.

The tedious process of exorcism continued throughout the day. Priests and clerics of all descriptions trooped through the House of Lanterns, all bent on becoming the one who would liberate its heiress from her besetting succubus. I did my best to co-operate, but nothing seemed to work. Then there was a tapping of heels on the parquet floor and a woman came in. She had dispensed with the customary robes and was wearing a rather modish suit with a rabbit collar. Her title was Luna, and she was a priestess of Cybele: Our Lady of Beasts. She was unwilling to tolerate any nonsense, threw everyone else out of the room and bolted the door.

Then she turned to the poor prone figure on the bed and said, "Right. Enough's enough. I want you out of there on a count of three."

In the smallest voice I could muster I said, "I can't." My voice was a gale. Words billowed through the room. The windows rattled.

The priestess clapped her calfskin gloves to her ears. "Don't speak. Just nod your head, yes or no."

I managed a little nod.

"That's good. Now, are you stuck?"

I nodded.

"Do you know how we might release you?"

I shook my hostess' head.

"Very well. There's only one thing I can think of, and it's a little risky. Not to you, to Shadineth, so I suggest you listen carefully. If she dies, you will not necessarily be free, and it will take a considerably greater effort to disentangle you: one which is beyond my capabilities."

With care, I nodded.

I don't know how she persuaded the family to accept her proposal. I was dimly aware of a disconsolate muttering throughout the hallway as the assembled religious were told that their services would no longer be required. Then an attendant came, with a stronger sedative that sent both my tortured hostess and myself into darkness.

When we awoke, we were no longer in the House of Lanterns but somewhere echoing, filled with a watery light. The first thing that met our gaze was a face: vast, malign and upside down. The carving, which bore an uncanny resemblance to myself, was framed with stone coils of serpentine hair. They had brought us to the cisterns beneath the city; the water reservoirs which served Constantinople, even in these modern days. They had brought me to this damp dark place away from the dance of the sun, to keep themselves safe from me. The Luna whispered all this into Shadineth's ear. To my chagrin, I discovered that the Luna was not to be the one to lead the exorcism: this was an honour reserved for the high priestess herself.

"But I'll be here," the Luna whispered. "I'll be beside you."

I tried to ask her what was going to happen, for they had not exorcised any of my kind for a very long time. In the old days, more of us had been young and foolish, but now there was only me. Ghosts may possess and be possessed, it's true; but they have no more tenacity than shadows and a breath or a word can send them shrieking into the wind. I was an altogether different proposition. They had paid for a sacrifice, which surprised me. This was the 1920s, after all. I did not see who it was: perhaps one of the janissaries, whom the alchemists created in their hidden laboratories beneath Pera.

Attendants strapped down my hostess' protesting head, so that all we could see was the ceiling. The Luna whispered in my ear "Watch the smoke. Watch it drift and die..." over and over until we were both entranced.

I began to follow the smoke up into the vault of the cistern and slowly it took me with it, pouring from Shadineth's eyes and mouth. A crimson drop blossomed like an anemone in the water. Someone cried out; a shadow sprang past me into the smoke and I followed, but as my pinions reached free above her head, Shadineth began to fight to keep me in. I wanted only flight and air and sunlight, but she began to reel me down; using the beat of her heart and the pulse of her blood, all the human snares. She was stronger than I; this was not my world. She wanted nothing more, she would have said, than for me to be gone, but the unconscious self is immune to reason. It wants what it wants, and blindly it sucked me back and hooked me in.

The Luna's face was very close; I could smell her narcissus perfume. She was staring into Shadineth's eyes and somewhere she saw mine looking back at her: a spark of gold in an empty head. "It hasn't worked," she pronounced.

The high priestess shoved her aside. "Of course it's worked. Everyone saw: the demon was cast forth."

"No, it went back in. What did you do that for?" she demanded of me.

I shook the girl's head and, once started, I couldn't stop. It rattled to and fro like a broken puppet.

"Stop that!" She held Shadineth's head still by sheer force.

The girl bit her lip and a drop of blood ran down her chin. I chased it with her tongue.

"Oh, I don't know what to do," the Luna said, in despair. "Get them back to the house. We'll try and think of something else."

They took us home to the House of Lanterns and laid Shadineth on the bed. Then they left her, possessed, to wait out another long night. I lay within her, like a seed, waiting.

Somewhere in the depths of the night, Lilith came. I dragged the girl's head from her uneasy dreams and opened her eyes. Lilith was leaning against the mantelpiece, examining her taloned nails. Her fiery feathers fluttered in an unknown wind, but in the chamber the candle burned quietly. I opened Shadineth's mouth and spoke, as though through a ventriloquist's doll. "Help me," I said.

"Can't, I'm afraid. Not unless you're willing to see her unmade... not just dead, child, but unsouled. Do you want that? D'you care?"

They say that we prey on living souls, that we are beyond compassion, but I was young, with a child's fondness. I did not want to see Shadineth hurt. I said so.

"You should have been more careful. If I've told you once, I've told you a thousand times..." Her bronze skin shivered and ruffled. She blinked golden eyes. I was beginning to feel very sorry for myself. "Nothing I can do," said heartless Lilith, reaching towards the brazier. "I'm sure someone will think of something. Bye."

"Lilith, wait..." I cried, but she was already gone, in a shower of fire.

Life settled down a little after that. Gulan Massaret continued to advertise, covertly, in the esoteric press for the person who might free his daughter. Enough people answered, over the course of the next year: mathematical mystics from Syria; Gnostic clerics from the Maghreb; the drug makers of Ghent and Antwerp. None of them achieved even partial success. Massaret was reluctant to let his daughter's condition be generally known, for obvious reasons, but it is impossible to keep a secret in Constantinople. The city absorbs lies and confidences and, as befits the cradle of alchemy, changes what it hears. Some said that Shadineth was mad, or ill, or possessed by the spirit of her grandmother, the formidable Alicien. A surprising number even knew the truth.

The new sciences of the mind began to take a hold in Vienna and Geneva, and Massaret enticed its principal proponents to Constantinople and the House of Lanterns: anything, he reasoned, was worth a try. Shadineth was analysed for hours. She lay on the couch and stared at the ceiling, and when they asked her to talk about her dreams, she only smiled. At last, despairing, her father had her shut away in the high attics of the House of Lanterns. In the evenings, we would sit behind the filigree bars at the window and watch the lights come on across the city; in all the other gilded cages in which the lost children of Constantinople are kept.

At length, people forgot poor mad Shadineth. Gulan Massaret was given a diplomatic posting to Paris, in an attempt to stop the growing threat of war. He left a handful of retainers to care for his daughter, but it proved to be care in the most minimal sense, for they were afraid. And so, lonely and tormented, Shadineth turned to her constant companion for comfort: to me.

Gradually, over the years, we had achieved a kind of equilibrium. I learned how to be still, and quiet, and gentle. I learned how to speak to her in a small voice, so that she could understand me without pain. Together, we explored the vaults of her mind. She led me through her dreams, and I helped her to understand the mysteries of number and symbol, which together make the rules of the world. I danced for her, and she watched every move and turn I made, spinning down the pathways of her brain. When at last her father came home, years later, we had danced so much that I had almost forgotten who and what I was, and so had she.

Her father was not the same man, either. They had unmade him in the crucible of the internment camps. His mind wandered and soon he took up permanent residence in the rooms below our own. After a few months he died and shortly after that, we discovered that the door to the stairway had been bolted shut. Occasionally, voices floated up through the floorboards; we recognised none of them. No one brought food, but Shadineth did not seem to need it. We kept to the bed after that, becoming absorbed in the play of the sun across the plain of the ceiling. We watched the inconstant light: how it shifted and turned and spun away. Darkness and sunlight became the same: only a different day, running round. Winter came over and again. Frost hid the window and icicles clustered beneath the sill, but Shadineth and I spent all our days in the hollow places of the head and sleep. If we drifted down, we had the thoughts of the city to choose from and other dreams, too, under the snow: the dreams of the lions in the high hills, the multiple mind of the bees in the hive, honey dreaming, slow and other and endless. Sometimes the voices grew louder, closer, but Shadineth and I no longer cared. We were listening to light and the fall of shadows; to warmth and air and winter.

Years ago now, I had told myself that if I trusted Shadineth, she would find her own answer. If they left her alone, she would work out a way. No dramatic exorcisms; no drugs; no long dissection, only Shadineth herself, taking her own time. And somewhere on the long roads of the mind, we parted company at last: shook hands and said good-bye. I watched Shadineth as she rose from the bed, unlocked the bolts with ease and walked down the stairs. I listened until her footsteps stopped and the voices below, one by one, fell silent. Then I went on my own way, soaring towards the sun and a brighter day.

"What time do you call this?" Lilith asked when she saw me, and

I laughed at her and ran through the stars to the shores of the world. Just before I reached it I looked back, once, to where Shadineth was singing, and then I was gone, dancing and away.

Illustration by Ruby for Issue 4 to accompany an article by Neil Gaiman

Storm

Sian Kingstone

Coiling
Black serpent of cloud
Nesting in bristle-back hills;
It looms
With a boom of doom,
Promising
To strike with tattered tongue
And rail in banshee rage.

Stirring,
Medusa devouring day,
Shifting, sliding, writhing,
It descends,
Crackling and intense,
Suspended –
Like some beast's bulging belly
As it rumbles over us.

Caught –
A moment's pause too much.
We stare,
Rooted in stone.
Then it begins
In a flash that mummifies the land,
As poison seeps
And serpent rears.

Hide, hide!
Run from the venom at your heels
And the whiplash tail at your back.
Dive into brittle shelter and shiver,
Quiver like quarry run to ground.

But found!
The pounding resounding, the fight to get in,
With a wail from the demon's mouth at the hearth.
Pummelling and grinding, crashing and whining,
As if prising a lid from a jar.

And then,
Its weeping whispers of sorrow and shame,
Tears of regret,
Tumbling on bruised and battered land.
Fading
To that empty ache of wounded silence
As it slinks away to shed its skin

Deities

Austin McCarron

Outside my window the city of nature
is like a seed to grow time.
Overcome with spring I describe the
power of its origins.
Listening to acts of light I stroke the
hair of its silences.
How many times have I counted its
pictures on my wall?
In pools of water I watch one of its
portraits burn.
How like fire to never see!
One day I will cure its heart of flames.
Before me crowds of blood:
I smell morose weddings and woollen
courtesies. To the delight of animals
I draw a home of hunger and violence.
Each death I imagine
is like the magnificent body of winter,
bursting with trees and veins, leaving
behind on a narrow path
the threat of something that once lives.

The House by the Lake

Lisa Pallin

On the lake by the house where we lived, my father rowed to his death.

On that eerie morning, I remember watching him from my bedroom window as he set out across the lake; the water still and voluptuous, caressed with tendrils of mist. It was going to be hot that day, the dawn moist and steaming, the fog ready to lift like a shroud from summer's molten pourings. The boat drifted silently across the water. The lake, with her dark wet depths, seemed to beckon to him like a mistress. Everything was very quiet, as if the trees were holding their breath, and the birds had ceased their singing; they all seemed to be in some terrible conspiracy together.

Then the fog swallowed my father up, and he was gone. He never returned.

Later, in the midday heat, the empty boat drifted desolately back to shore. The plants and trees wilted as if in sorrow. I wandered around the edge of the water, while the police searched endlessly downwards in vain. The lake was very deep, dark and cavernous, and in my mother's despair seemed to reach down to hell itself. They never found him.

A week later, we left.

We had moved to the house by the lake during a golden summer. The three of us – my brothers and I – were full of the boundless energy that only a child can know, awe-struck by the vastness of the lake that was to be our haunting ground. Though we were strictly warned about the dangers of the water, we secretly dreamed of adventures to come. I was the middle child, and the only girl, yet could run faster than the other two, and climb just as high. The house too was a source of delight, far larger than our previous home, and surrounded by trees that seemed to watch over us. Up the cinnamon dusty drive, and round a corner, lay the orchard full of cherry and apple trees. We spent many golden times there.

With the passing of time, the lake held less appeal for me. In my pre-pubescent agony, all too aware of my ripening body, I would not go semi-clothed around my brothers, though they teased me for it. However, my relationship with my father did not change. He was a quiet man, not prone to outburst or outward show of emotion, and he weathered my turbulent moods patiently. And when my mother's voice rang through the house in anger, cruel words slicing like knives, he simply shrugged; a slight stoop to his shoulders, the only indication of upset. In my stilted adolescent years, angry looks often passed between my mother and I, but my father's strength was constant.

On the day we left, I sat forlorn in the back of the car, gazing out of the window as the house grew smaller behind us. It seemed sorry to see us go. I wondered if, when our mourning was past, we would return. The house dwindled in the distance, and then it was gone, lost among the trees.

A year passed; a grey year, full of shadows and bitter tears. As a child, whenever I had woken screaming from nightmares, or fallen from a tree like a soft, ripe fruit, it had been my father who had soothed my tears and kissed my bruises away. When the wind roared, and the nettles stung, and I thought I would never stop hurting, my dad had always been there to wrap me in his big arms and keep the world at bay. Now there was just a tangible emptiness, an achingly clear recollection of him, a hollow where he should have been, and no one to kiss it better.

But, gradually, the fiery pain subsided to a dull ache and we began to live again. After twelve months of staying with grandparents, my mother decided to take us back home. I was surprised that she felt able ever to go there again. I was unsure of my own feelings. It was home, yet now there was someone missing. Could I ever look out of my bedroom window again, and not see him drift into the fog forever?

It was late summer when we returned to the house by the lake. The year was in full bloom and nature was well endowed, her ripeness ready to burst. As we drove through the orchard, the sun was red and low in the sky, and the trees blushed as we came by. Then we rounded a corner and there was the house. It looked empty and strange, and I wondered if it could forgive us for having deserted it when it too was grieving. It loomed closer, then I saw a window wink at me in the sunlight, and sat back in my seat, holding my breath. We all looked tentatively at one another, full of emotions and uncertainties. My mother looked at my brothers and I as if for reassurance. My eldest brother, sitting in the driver's seat, put a hand on her shoulder. "It will be all right."

One by one, we climbed out of the car, all coming to stand beneath the house as it towered over us. The slamming of car doors was the only sound to break the silence.

Then, we walked through the door together.

Motes of dust were captured and suspended in amber rays of sunlight that beamed through the windows. The house smelt alien, and felt unlived in. Silently, we drifted from room to room, and when the others had renewed their acquaintance with the place, they slipped away to their own rooms to unpack. Yet I could not settle and wandered about the house, trying to catch the shadows that hung on the edge of my vision. I wondered if the angles of the house really did look different – or had I simply forgotten them? Memories paused on the threshold, trickled from the floorboards, and began to gain momentum as they rushed about me.

Yet as I wandered, I felt the house had changed. On the day that he drowned, my family had talked of a terrible mistake, a tragedy. My father had always loved the water, and it seemed natural to them that he would take a boat out, even so early in the morning. Yet I had watched him as he floated across the water, and I remembered the look on his face, as he cast one final glance back at the house. I knew that it had been no accident.

The house had seen it too. This was no longer the carefree home of my childhood. He was missing and the house seemed to feel it. The floorboards creaked angrily beneath my feet, as if to mirror my own pain. As the dusk crept in, my recollections were tinged with unease.

That evening as I sat on the stairs and remembered, memories swirled in the twilight shadows around me. I recalled my first kiss in the cherry orchard on an evening late in May, when the air was awash with the scent of blossom; the hollow where I lost my virginity on a stormy midsummer night while the lake kept watch. I remembered picnics in the woodland in summer; and walks with my father through rust-coloured leaves in Autumn, our breath coiling like smoke; and chopping firewood in winter when the lake was silver in the snow. And I recalled all the times I helped my father in his vegetable garden, my dead father, my dear old Dad, who wasn't coming home. Tears lulled me to sleep that night.

My family tried to get back to normal and settle back into the house and their lives. But I could not, and spent hours furtively watching the house from among the trees. I was sure it was biding its time. It seemed too quiet and stared at me too long sometimes. The lake too had changed; it was an enemy to us now, and we all kept away from it. It had killed my father and refused to give him back to us. I was afraid to go too near it; it lay like some benign creature, yet what else lay in its depths?

The summer dragged on endlessly. I hated this season for it had taken my father from me. The heat felt like warm, fetid breath on my face, and the abundance of nature only served to mock my sorrow.

One day, I was walking through the trees by the lake, remembering, as usual. I felt that fate had dealt me the cruellest blow of all. I had been the closest to my father and did not have the bond with my mother that the boys had. My brothers too were strangers to me nowadays, sullen and moody. Since our return, we all seemed to have scuttled to our own corners to brood. My father's absence was oppressive.

I came to a clearing and noticed a hush. A bird watched me quizzically and the trees had stopped swaying. Suddenly, I realised that I stood face to face with the trees who had watched my father row to his death. They had not warned him. My brothers and I had grown up playing in these trees; they had heard all our whisperings. I had always felt that the surroundings of the house were benevolent, yet now, it was as if they had conspired against us. *You knew*, I thought, *you knew but did nothing*. I hit the trees, again and again, till my hands were bleeding. Then, I ran back to the house.

That night the bad dreams began. I had nightmares, in which the trees spoke to me, eager to assuage my doubts about them. They murmured ominously and the lake laughed. I also began to dream about the morning when I saw my father drifting across the water. In my dreams, the trees were trying to warn him, but they could only whisper and he could not hear.

One night I dreamed that I lay on the banks of the lake, staring deep into its depths. My father was talking to me through the water and trying to grab me and pull me down with him. I could not move. As in the other dreams, I could not hear what he was saying as he mouthed words at me. I wanted to talk to him, yet I was afraid to join him down there. As I tried to crawl away from the edge, his hand shot out of the water and grabbed my wrist. His touch was icy cold.

After that, I would not go near the lake. I was afraid that my father's hand would plunge up through the surface and drag me down.

The days sweated by. My mother stayed in her room all day, with the curtains drawn against the daylight, gazing at old photographs. My brothers always seemed to be just around a corner. I could hear them whispering throughout the house. I had no one to talk to. Sometimes, I would hear soft laughter behind me, and think my father had come into the room. But when I turned around, he was never there. I knew that he was still down there in the lake somewhere and felt unable to let go. There were so many things left unsaid. I desperately needed to talk to him again. But he was dead.

One night I had the worst dream of all.

I dreamed that I came downstairs for breakfast, but standing on the stairs could not hear the usual clatter of dishes. Something seemed wrong; the house was deathly silent and my heart began to beat faster.

I opened the kitchen door. My brothers were sitting at the table, grinning. My mother came across t
he room and put down a bowl of food. She was glowing. She looked happier than I had seen her in a long time. Then I saw why she was smiling. My father sat at the table.

He must have dragged himself out of the lake and across the lawn to home. Weeds clung to his legs. His clothes were tatters, as was the flesh of his hands that even now were lifting the bowl. But his face was the worst thing. It was so decomposed I would not have recognised him but for his eyes, his grey eyes, that turned and looked at me.

My mother smiled. "Look dear, your father is home."

I stared at her horrified. *But look at him*, I wanted to say, *what is wrong with you all? Look at the state of him.* Instead, all I could do was open my mouth in a silent scream.

I woke early that morning. My bedroom window seemed to beckon me and I dragged myself towards it. Gazing down, I saw the lake was covered in fog, just like that morning a year ago. I half expected to see the boat drifting across the water, taking my father to his death. But the lake was empty, patterned with the phosphorescent mist that floated and swirled above it like a ravenous, ethereal creature.

As I made my way down the gloomy stairs, the house was deathly silent. In the mirror, my reflection watched me as I passed. The kitchen was empty, for everyone was asleep and still in bed.

"Tick tock," said the clock and then stopped.

I wandered outside into the oppressive heat. Clouds of midges droned about the lake. They seemed to watch me, and the trees bowed low before me. I walked to the water's edge and tried to see down into the darkness, wondering if my father was down there, waiting for me to rescue him. But the lake sighed; she was not willing to give up her lover so easily. I stepped closer. The trees whispered and the fog curled around me like fingers. I looked back at the house; it appeared to be grinning.

Then, almost eagerly, the mist parted and the boat came drifting towards me; empty, save for the oars. It bumped gently against the shore. I paused. The midges had stopped dancing and watched me uncertainly. The trees wrung their branches together in great agitation. Their leaves scraped me as I walked forward, as if trying to stop me. I stepped into the boat and let it take me to my destiny. Looking back over my shoulder, I saw my bedroom window, watching again, as I disappeared from its view.

Gazing into the voluminous depths, I imagined that I saw my father waving to me from far below. I no longer felt afraid of the lake. It seemed that I was keeping an appointment made some time ago, as if I had been claimed the morning I had watched my father being taken. Silently, the water opened up and, smiling my last smile, I slipped into it. As I fell, the lake swallowed me and the darkness pulled me down.

Later that morning, the sun rose and the trees basked in its glow, glancing warily about. The house awoke and went about its business. A solitary boat floated on the edge of the water. In its azure, darkened depths, the lake breathed.

And we waited.

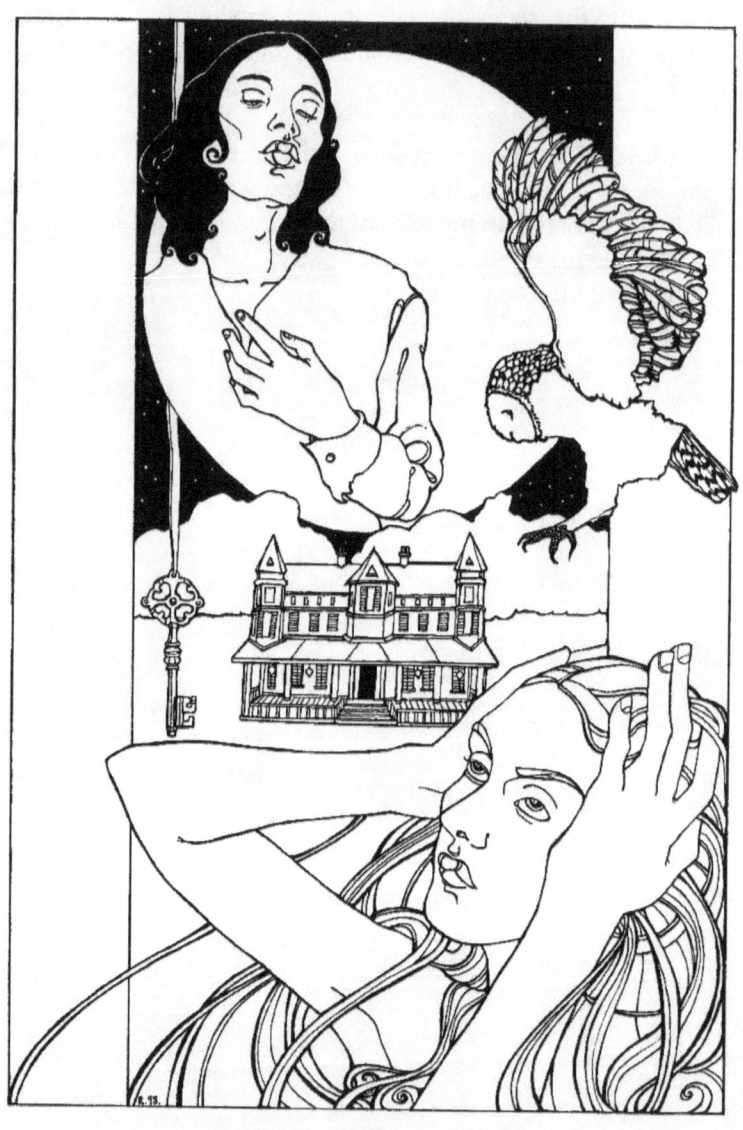

Cover by Ruby for Issue 10
(illustrating 'Awakening' by Isabel Taylor)

Awakening

Isabel Taylor

The house was old, but new. White plaster columns, white wooden shutters and whitewashed walls gave it the look of something just created, although it had stood there for as long as Jacintha could remember.

She was also old, but young. She had the smooth unlined face of a child, the slim firm body of a teenager. Bright eyes and pale hair. She could not remember being young.

It had always been the same.

Every day, Jacintha would walk through the rooms, examining the white leather sofas, the white marble tables, imagining that something might have changed. But always, the house remained the same. Even the garden that surrounded the house was not affected by time. White roses always grew in the white plaster pots that led down the steps to the lawn. On the grass, Jacintha would lounge on a couch until the sky darkened and the moon dipped her slender figure in ice. And so the days passed.

On the afternoon that the man arrived, the sky was frosty-blue. He strode across the lawn, his black boots trampling the perfectly manicured grass. Jacintha had never seen a man before. She could not even remember her own father. But she was not afraid. She stared at him with her bright eyes.

His tall figure shadowed her as she lay on her couch. He wore a grubby vest and torn jeans. His bare arms were muscular and tanned; his hair, black; his eyes, amber. His face was lined, but Jacintha guessed that he was not old.

The silence was broken as if the man had taken a knife and ripped through the silk of it. "Miss, I have travelled a long way, may I rest a while in your fine house?" His voice was deep and velvety with the trace of an accent that she could not recognise.

Jacintha nodded.

"My name is Lucian," he told her.

She did not reply. She did not know if she could speak. Had she ever spoken? She could not remember.

She motioned him towards the house and watched him disappear into it, a sooty mark on a pristine canvas.

When the moon rose, Jacintha glided towards the house, a silver queen to her silver palace. She found Lucian in the dining room. The table had been set for two. Before, it had always been set for one. So the house knew that he would come. Perhaps it had brought him here.

Lucian had changed into a black suit. Now he was all darkness and straight lines. Jacintha wore a white cotton dress that swept the floor. Pearls hung from her ears and neck. She sat at one end of the long table, Lucian at the other.

As they ate cold chicken and salad from china plates and drank white wine from crystal glasses, Lucian spoke. "I have been travelling so long, to such terrible places, it is a relief to come to this house." He did not seem to notice that she was silent.

Candle flames coloured Jacintha's face yellow and orange. On the walls, more candles were held in brass sconces.

"You are so lucky. A princess locked in her magical castle," Lucian said.

Jacintha was still silent. Lace curtains fluttered at the open windows.

After the main course – a dessert of iced cakes. Lucian ate greedily but Jacintha's plate remained full. The cakes were too sweet for her.

"Perhaps you would allow me to stay here again if I ever pass this way?" Lucian asked.

Jacintha nodded. Then she rose and glided from the room, a butterfly fleeing danger.

In her white bedroom, beneath the lace canopy of her bed, Jacintha lay awake, thinking of Lucian.

How different he was to everything else she knew. Dark, loud. She did not know if she was afraid or fascinated. It did not matter.

Tomorrow he would be gone. The house would be pure and silent again, and she would sit in the garden until the moon appeared.

But she had promised that he could return. Why had she done that? Should she make him understand that he was not welcome? No, he would forget the house. The noise and dirt of the places he travelled to would lure him away. He would not find the house again.

Still Jacintha could not sleep. She thought of the places he had visited, wanted him to tell her about them. Perhaps in the morning she could ask him? No, he would be gone. She thought of his black hair and amber eyes, his tanned skin and muscular arms. She only thought of them because they were different, she told herself.

Rising from her bed, she stood by the open window and watched the moon. The lawn was coated in silver. It was cold and harsh, peaceful.

Then, Lucian appeared, wearing his vest and jeans, walking away. He did not look back. She watched his dark shadow recede into the distance.

In the west, the sky lightened. The stars winked out, one by one. Jacintha looked at the horizon. Lucian was gone. She fell back onto her bed and wished that he had not come. The house felt different now, even though he had left. It was as if he had left fingerprints everywhere. Eventually, she slept. The sun rose and set. The moon rose, and still Jacintha slept on.

Gradually, Jacintha shrugged off the strangeness that she felt. She forgot Lucian; he was a dream. She rose at sunrise and lounged in the garden until dusk. She grew accustomed to the whiteness and the silence again and forgot the darkness and sound.

Then, Lucian returned.

The first she was aware of him was as a shadow as she dozed.

"Good afternoon, I hope I am not intruding. You said I could return," he said. "Perhaps you were being kind."

Jacintha did not speak. She shielded her eyes from the sun as she looked up at him. He was a silhouette against the light.

"I have brought you these as a token of my gratitude."

He crouched close to her and now that he blocked out the sun, she could see him more clearly. His dark skin and dark hair, a blot on the day.

He offered her a bouquet of flowers. She did not recognise all of them. Roses, she knew, though these were crimson and ochre. There were also flowers of cerise, violet and orange. A myriad of colours that was overpowering to her eyes.

The scent was intoxicating. As she inhaled it she imagined it reached inside her to every part of her body. It made her feel light and warm.

She smiled at Lucian and almost spoke.

When the moon rose, they dined. The same bland, colourless food and drink as before. Jacintha did not feel hungry. The flowers had been placed on the table in a porcelain vase, an explosion of colour that blocked out the sight of Lucian.

"You must be lonely, living here," he said.

Jacintha shrugged.

Perhaps you would like to visit the City? I could take you there."

Jacintha shook her head. Her heart beat faster at the thought of escape.

Lucian was silent again. He bowed his head. He knew that he had crossed a line.

When dessert was finished, Jacintha did not rush away. She sat with Lucian on the veranda. Paper lanterns lit the darkness. An owl with moon-coated wings flew by.

"Tell me about the places you have visited," she said.

Lucian stared at Jacintha's pale lips, as if he could see the shapes of the words as they emerged. She did not know where the words had come from.

"They are all so different, I would not know where to begin," he said. "Some towns are small and dirty, filled with more animals than people, others are cities full of tall buildings and harsh noises, colours and smells."

He described to Jacintha a few of the places he had visited. She listened enraptured, storing everything, even the words she did not understand. She imagined she saw some of these places in Lucian; in his excitement, in his brashness.

Eventually, she stopped him. "Thank you," she said. "Perhaps you can tell me more next time you visit."

She floated from the veranda like a wisp of smoke and vanished before Lucian could stop her.

When Lucian returned again to the house, the flowers had wilted and died. Crisp brown petals fell onto the dining table and the wind through the open windows swept them away. He arrived carrying more gifts; an abstract painting, vividly detailed in primary colours; a bottle of perfume that was spicy and exotic – Jacintha imagined that it smelt of the places Lucian had visited; a purple parasol to shade her as she lay in the garden.

"When I am away, I dream of this house," Lucian said. "Of its coolness and its quiet. I feel as if it has become my home."

Jacintha did not speak. She was still examining the gifts that Lucian had placed in her arms.

"I'm sorry. I should not feel this way. I hope I haven't offended you."

As they walked to the house, she assured him he had not.

Before dinner, they explored the house together. There was little to see. On the ground floor, plain rooms of whitewashed walls and white tiled floors contained tables and chairs, a sofa, in one room, a white grand piano.

Walking silently along the halls and through the rooms, the silence seemed to hang over them like a bubble that would burst if they spoke.

In the main hall, a crystal chandelier dangled like a cascade of icicles. A large staircase rose and branched out above them. Upstairs, they found more white rooms, almost identical to those below, except that they also contained beds covered in white like sweeps of snow.

Next, they followed the stairs down to a basement. But the door they reached would not open.

"Why is this door locked?" Lucian asked.

Jacintha tried the handle herself, expecting it to open at her command, but it would not. "I don't understand it," she said.

"Don't worry about it. Perhaps next time," Lucian said.

They returned to the dining room where they ate a meal of steak with red wine and a dessert of glazed strawberries. But Jacintha did not enjoy the food. She was thinking of the locked room and what it might contain. She could not remember ever having seen the door before, or, of ever having entered that room.

"I have a key," Lucian said.

The key glittered as he held it up to the light like a prize he had won. Jacintha reached up to snatch it from his hand but he would not give it up. She grabbed and pulled at his fingers, but they tightened around his prize. Jacintha sank back onto her couch.

Lucian smiled. "Now, we shall see the room," he said. He set off towards the house and Jacintha followed, afraid but excited.

Inside, the white walls silently witnessed her apprehension as Lucian forged ahead, unaware that she shuddered with every step she took. She wanted to pull him back, to tell him that she did not want to see the room, but he was an adventurer, hungry for the challenge of the new.

Reaching the door, Lucian waited for Jacintha to catch up, eager for a spectator to observe his bravery. "At last, all secrets will be revealed," he whispered as he placed the key in the lock.

Jacintha closed her eyes. She heard the key turn, the lock click open. Heat swamped her and the smell of dust and incense made her cough and stagger away from the assault. When she opened her eyes, the door was open. Lucian had already crossed the threshold. He took her hand and pulled her inside. "Come on, don't be afraid," he encouraged her.

Darkness surrounded them for a moment, then Jacintha felt as if her eyes expanded, taking in more than they could possibly see.

The room was a warehouse of oddities. The walls were painted in psychedelic patterns of purple, red and gold. Silk scarves of amber and green were draped from the ceiling, giving the room a warm, still atmosphere as if they had walked into a womb. Dusty shelves were furnished with trinkets of tarnished gold and silver. A carved oak chest was burdened with old wooden toys, yellowing books. Here and there, candles ached to be relit. Jacintha was startled by her reflection in an ornately framed mirror. A headless figure loomed behind her. Turning in fright, she let out a sigh of relief as she realised she had only been alarmed by a dressmaker's mannequin.

Lucian laughed. "You're easily shocked. Have you something to be afraid of?"

Jacintha did not reply. The room made her feel uncomfortable She wanted to leave, but Lucian blocked her path. To cover up her discomfort, she fingered the fluid folds of red silk that draped the mannequin. The soft material made her think of a lover's skin and she quickly withdrew her hand.

"That's a beautiful dress," Lucian said, hovering at her shoulder. "It would suit you well. Wear it tonight."

The thought of that red silk caressing her skin excited and horrified her. But Lucian's pressure made it difficult for her to refuse. It was as if she had no control. "Yes, I'll wear it tonight," she said.

As Jacintha glided down the staircase, the red folds of her dress spilled across the steps like an ever-growing pool of blood. Lucian waited at the bottom to greet her. He held out his hands for hers, as if they were lord and lady preparing to make a grand entrance. Jacintha was sensually aware of the dress clinging to every curve of her body, aware that Lucian watched her every movement. If she had been naked she could not have felt more sensitive to the movement of his eyes across her body. When he kissed her cheek, the sensation lingered as if she had been branded.

The house felt different, wrong. The air felt heavy; she thought she would suffocate.

"Please, we must leave now," she said, urgently. The desire had surfaced in an instant, but she knew she must obey it.

For a moment, Lucian seemed startled, but the mask of charm was soon readjusted. He smiled. "Your wish is my command," he said.

He led her from the house, down the steps and across the lawn. Jacintha looked back at the house. All the lights extinguished, it brooded like an abandoned lover planning revenge. She turned away quickly. The silver of the moon could not dampen the fire of her dress. Wearing it, she felt dangerous, but she was also afraid of the power it possessed.

The red dress lay in a crumpled heap at the foot of the bed Jacintha shared with Lucian. She watched him now as he slept, the gentle rise and fall of his chest, the fluttering of his eyes beneath the lids as he dreamed. She had lost track of time since she'd arrived in the City with Lucian. The days had merged into one long experience of new sights, sounds, smells. Lucian's stories could not begin to describe all the magic and mayhem that the City contained. He laughed at her wide-eyed astonishment. The nights had also been filled with other new experiences. Passion was a fever Jacintha welcomed along with the pleasure it released. Lucian delighted in revealing these things too. Gradually, her astonishment died and with it Lucian's interest.

The moon dappled his skin in silver stripes that fell through slitted blinds at the window. The hot air smelled of sweat and sickly sweet air freshener. Muffled sounds of traffic punctuated the night. Jacintha rose from the bed. For a moment, she picked up the red dress, then discarded it in favour of jeans and a T-shirt.

As she opened the door, she looked back at Lucian's sleeping form. She thought about lingering awhile, waking him, but she knew she could not reawaken the desire in his heart. His arm stretched out to the space she'd left. The emptiness did not distress him; he spread out, filling the entire bed.

Jacintha sighed and stepped through the door. The red dress lay in a crumpled heap, discarded like an old skin.

Jacintha travelled by night, hoping the moon would guide her home. She had little recollection of her journey to the City and now she trusted instinct to lead her away from it. As she left the confines of the grey buildings her spirits lifted. She drew comfort from stars, undimmed by the dominance of electric light. Moving further away from the City, she became aware of the night creatures, crickets chirping, owls screeching. The air felt cool and clean on her skin.

She spent many nights watching the horizon, hoping that home would appear over the next hill. It never did. Then, one night, as the sky began to colour in the west, she reached the summit of a hill and in the distance saw a familiar sight. She began to run towards the house. As she ran, the sun burned up the night. The shadows began to lift and the house turned scarlet. Jacintha slowed. The dry grass crackled beneath her feet. Dead roses hung from withered stems in their white plaster pots. She climbed the steps to the house.

Each second, more was revealed. She stood so close now that she could see the deep cracks running through the walls. In some places, weeds had begun to grow. Tattered curtains blew through shattered windows. There were gaping holes in the roof where it had fallen in. The touch of the sun tinged the house red as if it was embarrassed by what it had become.

Jacintha walked away, she did not look back. She walked until the moon rose and did not stop when it set.

Gradually, she began to think of herself as a wanderer. She discovered many of the places Lucian had described to her. Although she travelled many miles and walked for many years, she found that her path did not lead her to the house again.

She knew it would not.

Illustration by Ruby for Issue 10
(illustrating 'The Satanic Sex Machines of Dr. Zhinn' by William Eve)

The Satanic Sex Machines of Doctor Zhinn

or: The Perfect Wife

William Eve

That's my last Duchess painted on the wall, looking as if she were alive.
    I call that piece a wonder now. Fra Pandolf's hands worked busily a day and there she stands.

From: 'My Last Duchess', Robert Browning

The atelier of Doctor Zhinn lay in one of the narrow alleys behind the Basilica of San Marsyas. If you would see his likeness, visit San Aristeaus and view Fra Peisenor's *Judgement of the Damned*, painted over the high altar. Study the face of Satan, which Fra Peisenor modelled on the Doctor's death mask: some think it very fine.

The doctor appeared one day in the city, from no one knew where. He rented an atelier in a crumbling palatzo that had long since been abandoned by its noble owners and rented out, room by room, to poor craftsmen. It is said the doctor paid the factor an outrageous price in gold coins of curious and outlandish design, unknown to even the most far-travelled of merchants.

News of the doctor's skills spread quickly through a jaded city that was hungry for new sensations, but few wished to be seen crossing his notorious threshold. The doctor would receive visitors in his cluttered workshop; some would be masked with dominos hiding their features, others would slink in with their faces hidden beneath hoods, while yet more would pull the collars of their cloaks up high to hide their pale features. Some visitors stood diffident, with tongues unwilling to articulate strange thoughts, others would talk volubly on any topic other than the purpose of their visit. But silent or voluble, sooner or later they would look into the doctor's milky green eyes, and he would draw from them slowly their darkest secrets, their most unspeakable desires, their basest dreams. Haltingly they would describe perversions they scarcely knew how to name.

The doctor would sit listening in the candle-light, nodding slightly, and at the end of the recitation, coins would drop into his outstretched hand. A few days later, the doctor would supply a compliant partner; silent, discreet, tireless, and always available.

But Doctor Zhinn was no pander, who kidnapped young boys or girls from the street. Nor was he a bawd-monger selling diseased flesh. No, he was an artist, a scientist, a magician. He created automata, simulacra, which at the turn of a key would counterfeit the movements of life. Many the wife of a rich but flagging husband would turn to her automatic Adonis, and many an ageing *roué* would fall into the arms of his clockwork Venus. Hardly a brothel worthy of the name was without at least one automaton.

A purchaser of one of these miracles would run his hand over the marmoreal skin of his new toy, wondering at its sensual smoothness that would be elastic and cool to the touch, enticing yet repellent, like the skin of a corpse. The doctor would point with a long fingernail: "Press here, sir, and she will kiss... and here, sir, she will perform the act of love in any variety you choose."

The simulacra lay about Doctor Zhinn's workshop in their coffin-like boxes, like a seraglio of the undead waiting to rise. The doctor moved among them, a flickering lamp in his hand casting his distorted shadow into the corners of the room. He paused before one of the boxes and caressed a white cheek, before moving on to run his spider-like hand down the smooth thigh of a small blond girl. He stooped to plant a lingering kiss on the red lips of a youth, whose blue eyes stared sightlessly at the ceiling.

Outside, a black carriage clattered over the cobbles. It struck red sparks from its iron-rimmed wheels and drew up alongside the workshop door. A black-cloaked figure stepped down from the conveyance, illuminated by the gibbous moon above. The horses stamped and fidgeted, while the figure slipped quickly through the workshop door.

The Doctor greeted his client with the slightest of bows. "I am honoured that the Baroni Tesauro has condescended to visit my humble workshop."

Wordlessly, Tesauro drew a jewelled locket from his breast and flicked it open: "This is she. My wife." He proffered the locket to Doctor Zhinn, who took it in his long-nailed hand.

The Doctor scrutinised the picture in the locket carefully. It was a miniature of a slight blond girl of eighteen or nineteen. He expelled a long sigh. "She is truly beautiful. For so many, beauty is merely skin deep – strip away the flesh and it is gone. But in this one," he tapped the picture, "beauty lies deep." He looked up at the Baroni. "True loveliness lies in the subtle architecture of the skull, the delicacy of the bones and the articulation of the joints. Beauty lies in the bones themselves." The Doctor took one further long look at the picture before closing the locket and returning it to the Baroni with a slight mocking bow. "What may I do for the most fortunate of men?"

"Can you do it?" the Baroni asked. "Make her exact replica, down to the last detail?"

The Doctor poured wine from a bronze jug into chased silver cups and handed one to Tesauro, before answering: "Why should you wish for a simulacre, when you have just married the original?"

The Baroni emptied his cup in one draught "She does not please me. She is too independent – too much herself – and she is cold in bed."

The doctor sipped his wine. "Cold or perhaps unsophisticated. A little patience might persuade her to submit to your... ah... innovations." His eyes never left the Baroni's face.'

The Baroni spun round, his cloak billowing, and hammered his fist against the wall. "I will not be defied! Must I coax and wheedle for what is mine by right? Damn her, she is my wife!" He turned back to face the Doctor, but was unable to meet Zhinn's gleaming green eyes. "Can you do it?" he whispered.

"The skin must be unblemished. I cannot correct post mortem bruising. Do not use drugs; they can leave discoloured spots on the skin."

Tesauro's already pale face turned ashen. "Fiend! I can assure you that Master Hieronimo knows his trade."

The doctor smiled, "Ah, Fra Hieronimo, the public executioner," he said mildly. "Yes, he is a master craftsman. We have done business before. You call me fiend – that is hard. I am only the tool; the will is yours. Hieronimo will bring me the material, yes?"

"Yes. Tomorrow at midnight." With these words Tesauro turned and strode from the workshop.

Franchessca watched her old nurse filling her bath. "I cannot endure him."

The old lady put down the large brass jug, her face creased with concern: "But you must, my dear. He is your husband, whom you promised to obey."

"How can I endure a man who allows me no freedom? He tells me what I must wear, where I may or may not walk, who I may or may not see, even what books I might read. It is intolerable! He would keep me in a box if he could."

The nurse padded over and took Franchessca's slim hand in her own plump one. "It is only because he loves you."

"Love! Do not talk to me of love. *You* do not have to share his bed."

The old lady screwed her face up in concern. "But, my chick, wives share their husbands' beds – that is the way of nature."

Franchessca spun round and grabbed her nurse's wrists, causing her to wince with pain. "Don't talk to me of nature. He would use me as a boy! And I'll die before I become his fellatrix."

The nurse moaned, a tear dribbled down her cheek. "What can we do? We have no friends here. We are in his power. You must submit to him or we are lost."

Franchessca dropped the nurse's wrists and slipped her robe from shoulders before stepping into the bath. "I shall be free of him even if it should cost me my life. I'll not endure him any longer."

The nurse sighed, picked up her jug and shuffled off with it to fetch more water. As she entered the passage, a masked figure stepped from behind the arras and snuffed out her fragile old life with a black-gloved hand. She slumped to the floor, uttering a low moan.

Francessca called out, "Nurse, bring me more water."

Hieronimo contemplated the corpse for a moment. He took a butcher's pride in a clean kill. He pushed the nurse's body beneath the arras with a black-booted foot, then padded quietly into the room.

Franchessca had her back to him, and called out, "Nurse, wash my back."

His black-gloved hands took gentle hold of her shoulders and pushed her beneath the rose scented water.

The water roared in Francessca's ears as she fought for breath. It flooded her nose and mouth. She choked and gasped, but only sucked in more fluid. In a last lucid moment, before she spiralled into darkness, she saw above her the kind, sad face of Master Hieronimo in its black half mask.

At midnight, Hieronimo delivered a dripping bundle wrapped in a blanket to Doctor Zhinn, and laid it on a table in the workshop.

The doctor glanced sharply up at Hieronimo. "You are sure the flesh is unmarked?"

Hieronimo folded his massive arms across his bare chest and replied, "I am master of my mystery. She is unmarked." With these words, he strode away into the night.

Left alone, Doctor Zhinn disrobed the dead woman of her skin, with scalpels as light as stinging butterflies. He slipped her face from her skull like a masquerade mask. With delicate precision, he drew a red line down the length of her spine and stripped the skin from her shoulders and arms as though removing long gloves. Like a lover removing his mistress' stockings, he slipped each leg free of its integument. Then, he laid the skin in a solution of precious oils that would transform it to a marble whiteness. He plunged the remains of her weeping red corpse into a vat of corrosive salts that would eat away the remaining flesh and fill the bones with a mineral hardness.

Days later, Francessca's re-articulated skeleton lay gleaming on the doctor's long bench, each joint jewelled like a German watch. He reached into her rib cage and riveted into place a cruel steel spring that drove a great toothed wheel in a place once occupied by a softer organ. Slowly he replaced her other organs with cogs wheels, ratchets and pinions. What had once been flesh was now steel, brass and precious stones.

Over this armature, he laid a padding of fine leather and silk. Like a sculptor, he modelled the curves of a woman. Then, with infinite care, he drew the smooth white skin over this thing of metal and bone. With subtle art, he closed the integument invisibly, leaving no scar. An observer would think he was looking at the sad corpse of a young woman. The doctor picked up a golden key and inserted it into an almost invisible hole between her breasts. He twisted it clockwise a few times with a loud ratcheting sound. There was a whirr of spinning wheels and she sat up. Her gaze flickered around the room. She stood up, took a few steps, and then stiffened into immobility The Doctor nodded and smiled to himself.

A black lacquered box was delivered to Tesauro's house on the cardo. Two sweating footmen carried it into the Baroni's black satin-draped bed-chamber. After he had dismissed the servants for the night, he lit a number of thick white candles in polished silver sconces. Wings of light flared into the corners of the room. Then, he bent and lifted the lid of the casket. She was dressed in a green silk gown. On her breast lay a scroll and a golden key.

The Baroni smiled and, for a moment, stood there gloating. "So, you would be free of me, even though you die for it." He reached down and pulled the front of her gown away, revealing her small white breasts. Then, he inserted the key between them and began to turn it. "You have certainly died, my dear, but you are far from free of me." He removed the key, and consulted the scroll for a moment, then pressed a spot beneath her left breast.

There was an audible click, followed by a quiet whirring noise. Francessca sat up. Her gaze flickered around the room. The Baroni wondered if he could observe fear in her eyes. "But no, she is a mere mechanism." She stood up and stepped out of the box.

"Now, my dear, you will dance to my tune" He reached behind her and pressed again. She began to dance a silent tarantella. Tesauro stood watching with a cynical grin on his lips.

The dance finished, Francessca slowed to a halt and curtsied. The Baroni applauded her ironically. "Bravo, well done, the good Doctor has cured your rebellious sickness." He ran his hand down the side of her face and neck. "You will never disobey me again. The perfect and compliant partner, anatomically perfect, so the doctor said. We shall soon see, my pretty. But what did you say? You would die before you became my fellatrix? Well, your prophecy has proved true."

He pressed a spot beneath her jaw. He was sure he could see hate in her eyes, even though her face was quite immobile. She sank to her knees, as the Baroni fumbled with eager trembling hands at his cod piece to reveal his engorged and quivering organ. He placed a hand behind her head and forced his virile member between her lips. He ran his fingers through her hair and pressed. There was a click as a small clockwork pump whirred into life. He thrust in hard, as though trying to bury himself deep within her. His hand convulsed, clutching her hair as he pulled her face tight into his groin. He pulled back and thrust in again and again in a frenzy of lust. He felt the pressure rising in his testicles and spent himself with a gasp.

He stood there stroking her hair. "You see how easy it is, my dear, what a fuss you made." He started to laugh uncontrollably but his laughter turned suddenly to a scream, as he staggered back clutching at his ruined groin. He collapsed writhing onto the floor, blood spurting through his fingers.

Franchessca stood contemplating the dying man for a few moments, before stuffing the now shrivelled organ between his blue lips.

She began to search the room, but as she searched her movements began to slow. She moved as one in a nightmare, or one walking under water. She looked desperately around the chamber searching, until she recognised the gleaming golden key where Tesauro had dropped it. She picked it up, inserted it between her breasts and began to turn it, bringing life back to her languid movements. She paused only to toss the key in her hand, before pocketing it and tiptoeing out into the night.

And what of the doctor? They say he was found sprawled in his workshop. Someone or something had crushed his throat with an inhuman strength. Strangely, a strip of torn green silk was found in his hand.

An Angel's Effigy

Dylan Kinnett

Nothing had burned in quite some time. So, the Volunteer Fire Department stood empty. I played in its shadow, which wavered in the heat. It hadn't rained in weeks.

The building dominated the hill upon which it sat, like a castle. It towered over the entire neighbourhood, and I was its ruler. I clung to the rusty railings on its sides, the ones that reached the top of its bell tower, its turret. I gave speeches there to all my subjects. The dim light from the building's dusty windows inspired wonder in me. What went on behind them? The firemen put piles of burned wood behind the station. I spent lazy afternoons watching ants eat it.

I felt like the lone ant with a whole colony at my disposal, waiting for the others to return. Even a child, as I was, knew that something would burn eventually. The siren would scream. They would all rush to solve the problem, to silence the screaming beast that the station became at times.

Until then, the castle was mine.

In the morning, when blue sunlight fell through twin windows in the turret. I drew pictures with sidewalk chalk. Since it hadn't rained in so long, I had to wipe off the previous day's drawings or else draw on top of them. As morning turned to noon, I began to enact the stories told in bright colours on the concrete. If I drew astronauts there in chalk, then the grounds were my safe haven from alien attack. If dragons, then there was a princess in the tower, whose eyes shone even as sunlight through blue marbles. Everything was just so.

By noon I had drawn and conquered whole worlds, and lunch with Mom was an adequate reward.

No one else on Poplar Street had any children, only Mom. Other people brought this fact to her attention often, with concern. She would concentrate on her gardening or turn away from afternoon conversation. She would look toward the station, with its sunlit turret burning in the light.

"Some children are... solitary," she would say, and that was that.

With the colony gone, I was at liberty to make my own ants, thousands if needed. Mine was the right to start wars with them if need be, and then destroy them. I could always remake my playmates, dragons and all.

When lunch was over, I had that liberty again. Mom let me go back up the hill to play around the station.

"Stay where I can see you," she would say. She was usually down the hill in the garden in case I needed her.

Mr. Mann always rang the one o'clock siren. Whole worlds burned. That siren always meant certain peril. The princess was screaming because her wicked Father locked her up again. Red Alert! Invaders from planet moon have arrived. You'd better call Captain Space! The Queen ant was gone; The drones have learned to spar. Every day at one, I'd run as fast as my legs could fly to the top of Fire Station hill to finish my play.

"It's all right!." Mr. Mann would say as he descended from the wire box on the turret. He was a black spot way up there, moving slowly downward. "As you were," he would say, and then drive off in his rusted station wagon. Mom always waved as he passed.

When the battles were all fought (which sometimes took quite a while) the station was safe again. The Princess was free. The aliens were on the way home and all the drones were toiling. When I was certain the place was safe, it was time for marbles. A simple game, but I had to finish it before sunset.

Mom said sunset was when the shadows grew. So I put my marble circle inside the shadow of the station. When the shadow turret covered it completely, I knew it was time to go home. The rules were simple: be the first to knock all the blue marbles from the circle. I usually won.

That was a typical day for me, until the bird fell.

I was playing marbles when it happened, like any other evening. I was winning. Yet, even the best contestants sometimes get nervous. I had stopped twelve pirates from stealing Mom's watering can. This was important because, if the pirates got a hold of it, rain would never come. I thought these pirates may have caused my nervousness. I felt someone watching me. I could feel the other ants' need to return to the colony. I tried to shake the feeling.

I tossed my shooter marble into the air, which caught the light and sparkled. Three more blue marbles and then I could go home. I heard the ruffling of feathers. I heard the bird take flight. By the time I turned toward the station to see where the bird perched, it plummeted toward me.

"He wants to play my game!" I screamed, "No!"

The bird slapped my chalk circle with the whole of its body. Its bones cracked. My marbles scattered away into deeper parts of the station's shadow. Feathers came down to rest on the cooling pavement. The bird was still. Feathers fluttered, marbles rolled. The bird was still, swallowed up, as was the whole affair by the growing shadow. I ran home.

"Don't touch it," Mom scolded. "Birds are nasty animals." Mom was from the South. *Nasty* is a southern word. People like to say it there. I had never been in the South but I knew I wanted to go. People there would ask me what life was like where I'm from, since I'm not from those parts. I would tell them and I'd say it in that hushed tone that Mom always used. Then we would all get along.

Nasty was one of the few words that Mom said in that tone. Nasty, along with *different*. She always used that one whenever she spoke about Mister Mann. Even though we both liked him very much, he was still *different*, he *wasn't like us*. But those words weren't as upsetting as the one word she used least and whispered most.

The next day was Saturday. On Saturdays, Mom and I always went to Victoria's house. She lived on the other side of town. My Mom and Victoria's discussed things over tea, while we played in the backyard.

"Why didn't he get up again?" Victoria asked several questions after I told her about the bird.

"He couldn't get up because he doesn't have hands to prop himself up with and besides," I explained, "his legs aren't really big either."

Victoria lost interest in the bird. She told me that her Mom said, "Sometimes everybody falls down. Sometimes they get up and sometimes they don't. That's why we have Angels." Victoria made me promise to remember because her Mother had made her promise to remember. I promised.

It was hot. Victoria and I tired of being outside and went upstairs to play with her dolls. Victoria had magnificent dolls. A corner of her room held a box packed full with their twisted together little bodies, a whole swarm of them.

Her favourites were the plastic ones. They had clothes that you could change. I could tell which dolls she disliked. They were naked, their clothes stolen for Victoria's favourite dolls. The naked dolls had darker skin than their clothed companions. It was so hot and they were naked. The dolls were different because Victoria was mean to them.

I liked the larger, stuffed dolls that lived at the bottom of the box. Their clothes were sewn on to them; they could never be naked. They were not plastic so they could not break.

"Those have big heads," Victoria said. "I hate them." She saw that I had taken a liking to the stuffed boy doll. She let me keep it. He had red hair.

I heard the siren ring at the fire station as Mom and I walked home, but it was too hot to play. The next day, it was still too hot to play. Mr. Mann didn't test the siren because it was his day to go to church. His church was all the way on the other side of town, so he never made it to the station on Sundays.

Mom said it was time to start sewing again. Whenever summer was almost over she would sew warm clothes for when it got colder. She said that this year it was time for me to learn to sew.

"This is the kind of thing that Mothers teach their children."

Mom was crying.

"I know it's early, but I'm going to have to make your fall clothes, and your winter clothes now. While you're here, I can measure you for sizes. I'll make the winter sleeves longer and then sew them up. Your Father can let them out for you." Mom had trembling hands. She had tears in her eyes so that she couldn't see the needle enough to thread it. "You're growing so quickly now!"

It wouldn't be long before I was the tallest kid on my block. It wouldn't be long before I wasn't the ONLY kid on my block. The end of summer brings school, and I did not want to go to school. Victoria said it was horrible. I wouldn't even see her there, and I knew that. I wouldn't see Mom anymore either; I'd be with Dad. The cancer meant that I would have to leave. Mom never said that, but I knew. Mr. Mann knew. Victoria knew. Everybody knew. They never mentioned it, but their eyes were sad whenever they looked at me. I wouldn't get to play games at the Fire Station once the summer ended. I wished it never would.

"You are good at sewing," Mom said. We practiced by making a big coat for my new doll, like the one Mr. Mann wore. "All firemen have big coats," she said. "It keeps them from burning up in the fires they walk through."

My new doll was a fireman too, with a big sooty coat. I took him with me to the station the next day. He helped me draw in the morning.

I drew a circus. My red-haired doll watched as I scribbled clowns on top of yesterday's space ships. An old wizard had his beard rubbed off (with help from my doll's rag-like qualities) and I drew a new hat. There was a ringmaster, with people marching all around the circus tent, like insects ready to crawl away with a treat. I drew lions roaring at the sky.

At lunch, I asked Mom if I could have a needle and thread of my own. Instead of marbles, I wanted to play with making more clothes for my new doll. He would need to stay extra warm when winter came. Mom agreed. She gave me a very big, very dull needle with a large eye and thick thread, just for me.

I got back to the station in time to see Mr. Mann climb slowly up to the tower.

Then the siren screamed.

He was just a speck up there. He began down again, rung by wrought-iron rung. When he got to the bottom where I was, he pointed to the sky.

"Looks like rain today. 'Bout time!" he said.

"Yes. Do you think there are angels up there?"

Mr. Mann's laugh resounded from deep within his coat. He got into his rusted car and then drove away. Mom waved to him as he coasted down the hill. Finally, he was gone. I bolted around the station, to where the marble circle was. The bird was still there. Ants were crawling all over him. They had come back to the station because there would soon be lightning, and then, fires. That meant more scrap wood in the pile behind the station. There would soon be work for them to do. They were biding their time keeping company with the bird. But, I scared them away.

"Bird," I said, "you're not going to get up, are you?"

No answer.

"Well, of course. Silly me." It had been two days and the bird had scarcely moved, except for what little movement the ants had caused trying to carry him home. Their bird had only drifted slightly outside the circle, which was still filled with feathers.

"You can't get up because you don't have hands. You can't stay up because your legs are weak. I understand. I brought you this doll. He has arms and legs, good ones! I thought they would help you."

No answer.

"Well, it looks like the ants are already helping you. But, why aren't they bringing your feathers? It must be time for you to get a new coat. Can I have your pretty feathers? They would go so well with my doll's outfit."

The sun was lower than I had expected. The shadows moved differently. I knew, because Mom told me, this meant the end of summer was near. The leaves would change colours soon. Birds would fly south for winter.

Mom always said that the South is the best place to stay warm, it's always summer there. That must have been why Mom said that birds were 'nasty' because they were in the South all the time. I wanted to fly south, where it was always summer. Never any cold school months.

I worked faster than the sunset. I had to; at dark, the ants would come back. Rain began and it was almost dark before I finished. When I did, I decided to climb to the top of the turret and ring the siren.

I wanted the whole world to know that summer was going to die and that the birds were moving away. Whenever the siren rang, if it was not one o'clock, everyone came running to the fire station to see what was the matter. Once, Mr. Mann rushed so fast that he forgot to put most of his clothes on. Under his big coat, he was in his underwear, almost naked.

Everyone would rush here to save the summer.

The sky darkened from thick evening rain. Water was all over the ladder, so I had to climb carefully. When finally my doll and I brought ourselves to the top of the turret, I flipped the switch on the big red box, the way Mr. Mann always did.

The siren wailed.

A wind picked up, making the rain fall faster and at an angle. It drummed on the station roof and slapped on the street. Everything smelled of humid concrete. The siren hurt my ears.

I wrapped my hand onto the rusty ladder pole so that the wind wouldn't blow me over and did what I had to do. I threw my doll into the wind. His new feather wings were shiny and wet. They caught the lightning light from the sky and glistened.

"Fly south!" I screamed, louder than the siren, and he did fly. I was surprised. I had wondered if the stitches would hold, but they held.

The sky roared with triumph!

Mothers always taught well, and the sky really was full of Angels.

Then, the wind shifted, and the rain began to push my feather doll downward. Because of all the feathers, he fell slowly. The glimmer of wet feathers faded and faded, a spot falling away. As all the cars began to swarm around the fire hall, he hit the sidewalk.

He did not fly south. It must have been bad feathers.

Sympathy for the Devil

Paul Whyte

He always felt that virtue was overrated.
After all, what good is purity without depravity,
Creation without entropy, salvation without damnation?
But yet, he's still aggrieved to be eternally cast
As the embodiment of sin and tempting serpent,
In the never-ending drama of good-versus-evil.
All he ever truly desired was to be the archetypal rebel,
Defiantly raising a single finger towards heaven.
It was impossible to refuse to fall from grace-
All energy and light inevitably descends into matter.
Every physicist and Gnostic is aware of that.
He was never interested in bartering for souls,
He delegated that task to lesser demons.
After all, he's an archangel not a devil.
Although in ancient Sanskrit 'dev' means sacred.
Once the most beautiful creature in creation,
He was reinvented and portrayed as crimson skinned
And cloven hoofed, suavely swishing a forked tail.
Satan, Beelzebub, Great Beast, Father of Lies.
Lucifer, Prince of the Morning, Bearer of light.
On the last day when Heaven and Earth dissolve,
And free will and choice is his at last
Which face or persona shall he choose to wear:
Prince of Darkness or Morningstar?

Forgotten Sounds

Simon Williams

The land lay buried under snow. The taller buildings of the abandoned city stood darkly resplendent against the shock of white, the half-crumbled buildings like mute and motionless concrete giants astonished by the harshness of winter.

Allura strode towards the heart of the city, fired by some hidden purpose, and because her music had already bewitched me I followed her.

Allura fashioned images and dreams with her music. One night, many days before we reached the metropolis I asked her how she made it happen, and she smiled and shook her head as if I'd simply asked the wrong question.

"It happens around me," she said eventually. "I'm only a part of the spell. I'm not the instigator – and you yourself are far more than a casual observer."

"But all I do is listen and watch," I pointed out.

"Someone has to," she replied.

Allura didn't explain herself, but over time I learned that we were both bewitched by a phenomenon that neither of us could hope to understand. Both she and the instrument were vessels to some physical, shimmering force or entity that could express itself only in the form of sound.

And what sound.

The instrument – by which I mean the actual instrument – looked worthless. It was a battered and scratched old guitar, an ancient artefact of the old world where music had been commonplace. But when I heard the beauty of the sounds it created, my other senses almost felt redundant.

As time went on, the music immersed us both ever deeper in its mysterious spell. Sometimes Allura sang as well, and her voice became part of the spell. I understood none of the words – I didn't know what language she sang in, and I didn't need to know. I suspected that she brought them forth without knowing their meaning, if they had any. But the meaning of the words mattered no more than the condition of the guitar. The magic that suffused the music was everything – an omnipotent river of primal, unknowable force.

There are some songs that become more than memories. They become a part of *us*. Allura made such songs and sometimes, when she finally put her guitar aside, we remained sitting in stunned silence for hours, unable to release the emotion that had grown from a mere seed within us at the sounding of the first note. A faint and delicate tone would more often than not give rise to an avalanche of sound that threatened to crush our hearts with its impact and singular vision.

Allura and I had wandered the countryside for months. Winter coated the ground wherever we ventured. We slept in cold and desolate places, because those were the only places to sleep. If intact buildings still existed then we had no idea where they might be, and certainly we saw none until we caught sight of the city in the distance.

The remains of once-grand structures dotted this metropolitan landscape. The wind howled through these broken fortresses of commerce, and the snow gathered inside them wherever their roofs had caved in.

"Where are we headed?" I asked Allura.

"Towards the centre," she said.

At dusk, we arrived in an area dominated by a vast, ruined church. Weary from plodding through the snow, we sat upon the crumbling remains of a low stone wall and viewed the surviving parts of the building. I sat next to Allura and waited for her explanation in the knowledge that it would come eventually.

Night had fallen, and stars glittered over the lightless city, before Allura spoke.

She turned to me and said, "There's another instrument in this church. A flute."

"How do you know?" I asked her.

In answer, she simply touched the guitar.

I accepted the gesture and lack of any other explanation without comment. Months of travel in Allura's company had conditioned me to her often-fragmented way of communicating. We walked into the cool dank air of the church, and it was there that we eventually found the instrument itself, on an old table where candles had been lit.

The fact that someone had clearly been here recently would not have stopped Allura from taking the flute – and then we would have hurried away from that desolation, if a man had not staggered out from the shadows and lurched towards us. Old, sallow-skinned and ragged, he sat down in a pew with a gasp of pain. The pitiful creature's hands shook. Some kind of affliction had eaten the left side of his face, leaving blistered and festering skin. One of his eyes wept a thick yellow liquid.

"You've come for the flute," he said accusingly. His hands trembled, then they clutched suddenly at the thin robe he wore as if to stop themselves.

Allura gazed calmly at him. "Even if you have been its guardian, it's not yours to keep. It belongs with those who are able to use it, in other places."

"I know what you are and what you do," he told her. A hungry, desperate look loomed in his eyes. "I knew that you'd come here one day. I want you to play it for me. There's a song I want to hear."

"Why?" Allura already had one hand on the instrument.

A tear rolled out of the healthy eye. He tried to speak and couldn't at first. Eventually he said quietly, "I live in the past. I can't help it. I clutch at old memories, and when I sleep, I yearn for them even more. There were some songs... old songs. You wouldn't remember them, I shouldn't think, and they need more instruments. They're from before the world moved on."

My initial revulsion began to subside. This pathetic creature was searching for something that had evidently been a blissful point in his past, desperate to hear again songs he had last listened to perhaps many decades ago – songs now forgotten everywhere, that might never be played again. *Sometimes I think Allura plays the only music anywhere in this sorry new world,* I thought.

Allura picked up the flute and went over to sit on the steps leading up to the altar. "Tell me about the songs and what they meant," she murmured.

He drew a deep and painful breath. "It's so long ago. A night of.... candlelight." He gestured to the flickering flames around the church. "Candles everywhere in a small room, and my love was by my side. I want to remember the words we spoke as we listened to this music. All I remember are fragments, and I can't even be sure they're the right ones. I want the clarity back again." He uttered a dry, choking laugh. "I can't tell you how the song sounded. I can't even tell you that much."

His voice had drifted. It had become something mellower, oddly wistful, and it no longer matched that dreadful face at all. As I gazed at this hapless, tearful being I made a sudden decision.

Here stands the barely living result of that which I fear most – the onset of old age. I'll sever myself from this world before deep lines etch themselves, before the ravages of disease eat at me. I'll never suffer the horror of a defenceless body and a confused mind.

Allura looked thoughtfully down at the flute. "Can you name these songs?"

"No. I thought perhaps through your powers you might..." He stopped suddenly. "The flute will know."

He lit more candles, although there was no need. His hands trembled as he moved from each candle to the next and knocked some of them over. I moved to help him but he waved me aside. "No! *I* have to do it. Just like we did before – we always lit them together."

A short while later, the church was bathed in the glow of scores of little flames. They threw madly flickering shadows against the dingy walls. The old man stared around as if he considered them members of his congregation. Then he sat awkwardly and painfully upon the floor. The flames surrounded us all.

"Play," he murmured shakily.

Instead of protesting that she didn't know what song to play, Allura simply put the flute to her lips. The first note shimmered in the air, and the spell began to weave itself.

This was not a song I had heard before, nor had I expected it to be. It changed tempo with bewildering frequency. Sudden power bloomed from the quiet fragility, and then faded to a tremulous, simple passage. As always when Allura played, time itself might as well have melted.

The old man listened with head bowed. He rocked back and forth and wept bitterly and cried out the name of his lover, which even now I fail to recall.

A while later I saw flames everywhere around us. They grew with the power of the music. They fed upon it as if it was oxygen. They rose tall and perilously thin, amber fingers that stretched towards the murky ramparts.

The instigator of this spell sat transfixed, eyes tightly shut as the flute wrapped imagery of a forgotten time and place around us. Allura no longer played the instrument, but the music continued regardless, set in motion and unstoppable.

I dreamed, or experienced a vision.

A small room, far smaller than this cold hall, far warmer, more welcoming. Walls decorated with art and ornamentation. A mirror. A comfortable, gloriously large and ornate bed. Perfume in the air. Coloured candles, fashioned into intricate shapes, giving forth flame as their delicate forms slowly perished in the heat. An arched window, and beyond the window, the colder light of a three-quarter moon and several stars.

A young woman sat upon the bed. Her hair and eyes were dark, yet they shone richly in the light. The music soared and became more powerful than ever. She rose from the bed and walked to the window, and opened it...

I opened my eyes suddenly. The heat was too real, the music a deafening, continuous roar. The vast flames around us had drawn closer, I thought. The old man threw back his head and held wide his arms as if in welcome.

...and I saw the woman.

She touched his face. He sobbed and the music played on and on, louder and now increasingly joyous with each passing moment.

Then, like a wave the flames swept over us all.

When I opened my eyes perhaps a day later, all that remained of the old man was a charred, unrecognisable body, lying upon the cold stone. His arms hugged the shell of his torso closely, as if he had died embracing something. The candles stood extinguished and cold. Allura lay upon the ground, the flute still clutched in one hand. Neither she nor I had been burned. The fire had left us both untouched.

We had turned one man's life of lonely despair into a blissful death. Observing the char into which he had turned, I wondered if that woman had been real in any physical sense. Certainly, nothing of her could be seen now. Then I decided that it hardly mattered. Her lover had thought her real, and in that knowledge he had died in her arms, whether or not she existed.

I crawled weakly over to Allura and cautiously touched her. She was cold and her heart was still, or so I thought. Then as I sat, disconsolate and half-mad with grief, it occurred to me that the truth was far stranger. She had simply *slowed down.*

I lived on snow-melt water for two days. I paced the length and breadth of the church. I took deep breaths of the cold and dead air and watched as it spiralled from my mouth into the desolate chill. *Our work isn't done,* I told myself as I returned time and again like a faithful dog to where she lay.

When Allura eventually opened her eyes, I cradled her head in my hands and the intense relief washed away any words I might have thought of.

I've been asleep for a long time, she told me with a slow smile, and she reached out reassuringly warm fingers to caress my cheek.

A cold sleep, close to death, I told her, and she smiled. Perhaps she didn't believe me.

But as we travelled towards other broken towns, we encountered further situations that defied belief and explanation. Something unseen and unknowable masqueraded as sound. It had made willing disciples of us, and we accepted every vision, every transformation, every miracle.

The nights were never again the same. I could still feel Allura's embrace, but her touch now felt a little colder than before. Her long sleep had perhaps robbed a little of her heat, which could not be replaced.

Often, she would play songs of ice and black stone and places beyond this desolate world, perhaps a memory of the distant land of her birth. Visions of these constructs rose fearfully before me like waves that built with each trembling note. Detail built upon itself until the hard beauty became unbearable. Each time, before we could both be swept into the maelstrom she would put aside that terrible, wonderful instrument.

As time went on, I occasionally feared that the next resurrection might separate Allura and myself forever. On the one occasion I voiced that fear, she told me, "Nothing lasts forever. Not even separation. Time turns, and somewhere in the distance of ages our own song will be played."

So, with eternity as strange comfort we travelled on, and with each and every destination reached we brought forth more forgotten songs. We brought them echoing and weeping yet somehow hopeful, out of the distant past and into a world where music had become magic.

Those who listened wept and laughed as their final moments played out, their faces uplifted, their spirits flooded with a joy that shone through the surrounding emptiness.

Luncheon with the Last of a Kind

Colin James

Begrudgingly he gets into position
moving chairs and lamps to fit
within the dust silhouettes.
The water in the kettle is still warm.
Teeth are stained from withheld remarks.
The greeting is always much the same,
a hand extends outward
a head alertly turns.
It's when you look into his eyes
that you first experience fear.
We deserve the shock.
We have become too satisfied.
Under reversed conditions,
a far less civil lunch.
We have always been servants to our species,
and prisoners of our Earth.

Féa

Janine Jones

"Féa! Féa! Féa! My dearest darling Féa. What a lovely name you possess! It leaves one to wonder what on heaven's earth could have possessed your dear mother to confer it upon you. What, with a face like yours! So soft, so sweet. It wants only to be whispered. And to think! A sound so divine with you as its bearer. Whatever could your mother have been thinking?"

That was the cry that beckoned me during all my real life days. Those who would call me by name are not to be given the benefit of the doubt. They knew all too well what my mother had in mind, tagging me Féa the moment she laid eyes on me. Why it's meaning, what else?

My story is not a long one to tell, unless I were to dwell upon fading details, which would only recall a dull ache to my heart, reminiscent of those I had in living. They say beauty is in the eye of the beholder. Perhaps. But the world at large beheld me as not fit to be seen, starting with my own sweet mother, who took one curious look at me and looked no more.

They say a mother's love is unconditional, that it can conquer all. They say a mother will see her child as beautiful, no matter what, as it is her own. My mother saw me and knew my name.

Not everyone mocked my uncomeliness. There were those, girls my own age and their mothers, who did not turn their heads at the sight of me. Decked out in nature's loveliest forms, they would smile on me, deigning to stroke my knobby shoulder, all the while reassuring me with words dripping with sweetness, bursting with wisdom.

"Féa, don't worry, dearest. Someday you'll outgrow your name.

Give it a few years."

That's what the daughters said. Their mothers' words sounded more equivocal, though I understood them not.

"Féa, my child, all things must come to an end. Bad things too. God would never be so cruel as to have it otherwise. And always remember this. Though you may feel wronged, it is not for you to judge."

Then mothers would smile lovingly on daughters, revelling in their own past looks and glory, and they'd walk off arm and arm, the original's vanity supporting the copy's and vice versa. Meanwhile I, idiot that I was, believed what I could of their grand words, forgetting their smiles and gestures.

The first time such advice came my way I ran off like the wind until I found the tallest tree. I stood with my back against its trunk, knife in hand. With the thrill and terror that comes with performing black magic, I slashed its back to mark the height I was that day. Every year afterwards I checked the mark to see how I had grown. And I found (to my delight!) like grass – or the beanstalk – I had. But I did not outgrow my name, which grew on me as I grew more hideous with each passing day.

An ugly infant must be marvelled at, an ugly child mocked or pitied; and an ugly woman despised and condemned, as though her very being were all her own doing.

My mother had to feed me, clothe me, give me shelter, until I was of age. That was law, and custom. I left her in peace after fifteen summers, the time when maidens who'd come into the world the same year as I were married off.

I left without dowry, or a cent to my name. Yet I had hope of living a life in accordance with God's law, of keeping myself by His word and my hand. Nature had cursed me with a face of rot. But He had blessed me with a touch of gold.

Sweater. Coat. Hat or sock. If it be something to make I made it beautiful. And in that way, I came to earn my keep in a time when women did pull the needle and turn the wheel but could not open shop.

I never blossomed. My breasts, my hips, my hollow belly never grew to know what fullness is. So my mouth was never searched by a tongue not my own, and my legs never opened to a prick of invited intrusion. With needle in hand – in and out, in and out, in and out – I worked miracles in material. And I opened shop.

I made my home and worked in a place many weeks' walk from my natal village. People came from all around to buy my wares and gaze upon the miracle offered by the sight of me, ugly as sin, giving birth to works whose virtue was their beauty. Wretchedness spinning loveliness. Was the world coming to an end? The people prepared themselves, thinking this a sign.

They gazed and stared and wondered. They clicked their tongues. In the beginning, when they came, I feared becoming a spectacle. My father had always threatened to sell me to the travelling circus. "They're offering a fair price," he would tell my mother. "More than feeding a crooked mouth such as hers is worth."

My mother would hear it over and over, every word. But I stayed. Perhaps there is some truth to what they say about a mother's love.

But it had stayed too, the fear of appearing in a spectacle. And there I was, full of fear, thinking I was becoming one. But those who came to see me sew and spin were also fearful. Filled with the fear of God they were. Imagining themselves to be beholding a miracle, they looked favourably upon me, thinking God might look favourably on them and their crops. Thus it was that beyond the sloping sides of hills, further than the eye could see, people began to say, especially to scold beautiful maidens who passed their time before mirrors, or on their high horses looking down at the blemished of the earth: "Pretty is as Féa does."

My downfall was my doing, Nature's design. Though my body knew no fullness, sap was full to overflowing in the vessels of my groin. But I had my virtue to uphold. That was law, and custom.

I know some might think, "Who does she imagine would have taken her, had she been undressed and laid out on a fine oak table?"

Who would have kissed this deformed mouth of mine or that other mouth whose layers would not offer the slightest resistance to being opened by prying hands, as do the fresh crisp leaves of the heart of a lettuce. No, as you may have guessed, those private folds of mine were like the outermost leaves of an old lettuce head, brownish-green and sagging, wanting only to be stripped and tossed away.

And my breasts, like caves – why should they be explored when men want only to move mountains? My head sitting atop my shoulders, my legs connected directly to my back. No neck to bruise, no butt to ride! Yes, and I know as well as any other woman that men, like dogs, need to leave their mark, and like sailors dream of mounting tides.

With not even a lobe of ear to pull and tug away at, my virtue should have remained the best kept secret in the world. Concealed between sealed legs. So, what happened? The explanation is simple. Just as men gather to see a spectacle, they'll gather to lay one too.

I had several proposals, on numerous occasions, from two or three gentlemen who wished to make it a night and gather in my name. I knew their ways well.

There was a girl in my new village not half as horrid as myself. I must say it was to her disadvantage to have been so ugly in such an ordinary way. She had never been marvelled at, nor pitied, nor condemned. There was nothing awesome in her ugliness. Her ugliness was spoken of, as are all commonplace things, like the colour of her hair. "Tell ugly Olga with the mouse brown hair to go fetch the milk to make the cheese."

Ugly Olga never got herself a single man, but three at a time they'd take her on. They'd cover her head with a potato sack. One would take her from behind while the other took her from the front. The third reaped his pleasure from inside her mouth, whose lips were thin as a snake's but whose tongue was wet and tasty.

No secret was made of their goings-on. They took her to secluded spots, so nearby that any man might pass that way, and did. Some would stop and take a turn. Others would put it off till another time. The town tongues wagged till the women were in the know, and ugly Olga shunned by all.

Why did Olga do it? Why did she squander herself, give the men a good laugh and a warm place to relieve themselves at her expense and at no cost to themselves? I'll tell you why. The sap was overflowing in the vessels of her groin, and she was too ugly for an ordinary man to make an honest woman of her. All her doing. Nature's design.

Now listen carefully, those of you whose limbs grace you softly as the flower's petals do the stem. The mere thought of my crooked legs spread in a scalene V, my contorted face grimacing in Eros' embrace, my blotched face bursting with blood, my balding head damp against their bare chests, my caved-in chest heaving huhuhu to heaven, my claw-like toes and nails clutching their calves and shoulders, put those men with a mind to have me in a way of senseless delirium.

Two or three began huddling around me, whispering with lurid looks, "Come on, Féa. Let us gather in your name."

The simple sound of my name whispered lightly by their dripping mouths made me fuller than the greatest river during spring's first melt and my death's-head throb with the blood of pleasure.

I fought their advances as best I could, never forgetting Olga's fate. Giving into their perversity and my unfulfilled pleasure would have certainly meant my downfall. I would have lost my status as a miracle worker, and my ability to earn my keep. And unsightly as I was, I could expect no one else to provide it for me.

I prayed for an answer when I felt myself losing the struggle, when I felt myself melting, giving way to "Féas" whispered on the sly.

The night I gave up on a virtuous answer being provided, an angel of darkness responded to my call.

"Come and let us gather in your name, Féa," three men whispered and slipped away.

I could resist no longer. So, I put down my needles. For once, I wouldn't work into the wee hours.

I put on my coat and hat, sneaked out of my shop, feeling the watch already on. A curtain was pulled back. A pair of eyes peered out. I walked down the silent village street until I reached the path that led to Mr Miller's old, abandoned barn. Though spring was on its way, a sharp bite cut through the night air. The moon was rising bright and full in form, lighting my path as it travelled its own.

After a bend in the dirt road, I saw the barn up ahead. I didn't hesitate, for fear of turning back. I walked on, quickness in my step, the friction of my uppermost thighs, the only fleshy part of me, sparking preliminary warmth. I would be ready on arrival.

As I got closer, I heard voices coming from the barn. I walked in and stood in the entrance. The three men stopped talking and drinking their brew. One man raised a lantern. All three stared at me, their faces aghast. Then, as though suddenly remembering the fulfilment this face of mine would bring, their faces broke into grins filled with new blood. One lifted a bottle in toast to me,

"Where two or three gather in your name. Here's to you Féa. We'll make a woman of you yet."

They passed the bottle around. I would be next.

One man started unloosening his buckle, his eyes on me. There was no backing out. They wouldn't have let me had I tried. I was there. I was theirs. It was as simple as that. Nothing like a change of mind would have moved their rustic natures. I was there; I was theirs.

"Come here, Féa," one said holding up the light. "Let us get a better look at you."

I moved in close enough to feel the lantern's brightness on my face, and squinted to save my eyes.

"Féa is as Féa does." They burst out in laughter and toasted me, and my name, once more.

They hadn't fouled me yet, but my fate, as had been Olga's before me, was as good as sealed.

They licked brew from their lips. They'd moved in close enough for me to smell the odour of rotten oats on their breath. My rivers began to overflow even as my fate swam in my eyes. One laid a moist, heavy hand on my knobbly shoulder.

That's when a shadow expanded over the entire ceiling of the barn. Like an eagle spreading its wings, two sides of darkness spanned the ceiling overhead. We must have felt it, sensed it before we saw it. We all looked up. But the maker of the shadow was, of course, at the entrance to the barn. Not above us.

"Good evening. Having a party and didn't invite me?"

I turned. We stared at the door. One man raised the lantern to get a better look at what we were facing. The stranger lifted a bent elbow. Like a black wing, it flapped over his face.

"Lower that light."

His word had been spoken and heard as command by men who'd taken orders from lords since their earliest days.

"Put it on the ground."

I heard the lantern's base touch the floor of the barn.

"Is she not a virgin? Have you not heard of feudal rights?"

"Yes, my lord," the three mumbled, the words of one stumbling over the words of the other, in their fear not even knowing whose lord they were addressing.

"Leave."

The men made their way towards the door, stepping softly. My saviour opened his black cape to show them the way out. One by one, they stepped towards the threshold, then through the entrance. There in the darkness I could not see whether they had walked into the night or vanished inside his cape.

"No need to be afraid, Féa."

I heard steps approaching.

"What is it you wanted from those swine? Has no one ever told you if you show your pearls to swine they will demean them?"

Flames burned where eyes should have been, lighting up a face, white and smooth as a porcelain plate. A lower lip glowed thick and red, as though gorged with blood.

"Féa, what could they teach you of pleasure? That humiliation's pleasures, especially when well nurtured, are the most acute? Hence, the sweetest?"

The stranger laughed quietly, pleasantly, as though amused at the errors of a well-meaning but otherwise foolish child.

"I'll show you pleasure's virtues and take you at your worth. Otherwise, Féa, pleasures aren't worth the having. Take my word for it. Flesh broken, blood spilt, a spring melt. Over in a moment, it will leave no trace. I'll take you for what you're worth, and leave you with a memory that will burn your blood. I'll teach you to taste pleasure's delight, not its stench. But for a price."

This creature of darkness went on speaking, and I didn't miss a word. Wretched as they were, I did have two ears.

"I'll wipe your unwept tears away and give you something worth crying over. Or is it possible, Féa, you know not your own worth?"

Who'd ever suggested I was worth any more than a piece of beautifully fashioned cloth? I had no recollection of such a person, and hardly knew what he meant.

Entrusting my memory to his care, I went without a word of reply and lay my head on a clump of rotting hay. I closed my eyes. I'd seen all I wanted to see for a lifetime. Life, as I knew it, had seen enough of me.

Like a huge black bird he spread the sides of his cape and kneeled over me. He overwhelmed me until just before the cock's turn to cry and I could cry no more.

"My lord," I said sadly afterwards, "I have no neck to offer you for all your trouble."

He held my crooked hand in his, ice cold. He turned it over and over and then stroked my palm, kindling new pleasure in the process.

"No need to despair Féa. A neck is but a detail."

My wrist supplied the vein he wanted.

Now when I go back to drink the blood of the village cows and pigs I hear the people talking about me. Even in the throes of grappling with the mystery of their perpetually dying livestock, Féa is still on their minds and lips.

"Another cow gone."

"She slit her wrist. You should have seen it! Took her own life."

"The cow's calf is bound to follow her."

"It's a sign, I tell you. We must prepare. We don't want to get caught unprepared."

"Wallowed in her lust, then couldn't face her shame."

"She's finally where she belongs, I dare say."

Little do they know that it is I who kill their cattle. They might prepare, prepare themselves for poverty, a condition that will make them earthly heirs when the good day arrives. A sign.

World without end! The old dead cow was a sign of nothing more than my thirst to live through another sleeping day.

My shame! What could they know of my shame, I who had none to speak of! Wallowed in her lust! they say, when I bathed in a torrent that flushed me downstream and carried me out to sea. What would they know of that!

With moonlight as my witness, my bath was prolonged in a rocking ocean whose salt-cured wounds carved deep into my being. Human works of art. Once soothed, like a lone piece of timber wood I drifted out to a death that promised not the hardships of eternal day but brought the splendid calm of an infinite night.

Cannot face her shame!

I simply cannot bear the light of day that never showed me to advantage.

The Magus of Inner London

Austin McCarron

I read the first volumes
of polluted air,
bound in beautiful white books.
I sound empty and terrified. In
each hall the picture of a ghost.
I meditate
on sacks of dead animals. I heal
passionate crimes.
I find poems with great wounds
and stories of immense suffering.
I walk on leaves.
I wake rivers.
Human riches I spend with magic
until my spirit is gold. I see through
the blindest consciousness blood
to warm. Over collapsed
bridges the water is silent with art.

Collector of Broken Things

Lauren Halkon

The soft creak of a slowly opening door accompanied the passage of a shaft of light across a hitherto darkened floor. A breeze drifted in, lifted dust into the air to decorate that expanding triangle of light. Throughout the building there was a sudden silence, the kind that descends upon the abrupt cessation of frenzied activity. The man, at least he was called 'man' for want of a more appropriate term, lifted his slanted nose and breathed deeply. His second eye-lids flickered across his expanding pupils. He knew something had happened during his absence.

He closed the door. The light blinked out.

The bag's handle slid gently down his fingers till he felt the floor take its weight. He let go.

Unburdened now, he padded forward. The floorboards creaked under his weight. He concentrated for a moment, then proceeded in total silence.

Somewhere in the depths of the building he could feel her. She had done it again.

His mind drifted lazily into the contents of the bag, caressing them with tendrils of his thoughts. He lifted each one up to the light of his inner eye, remembering their circumstances. The chaos of noise, blood and fear did not disturb him. His footsteps continued carefully, one in front of the other, each physical eye scanning the high, stretching shelves. He was not angry. He did not know how to be. He just wanted to find her. To see her. To see what she had done.

He moved faster now. She was hiding. She always was, even though he never did anything to her. Maybe she didn't want him to see. His eyes were too greedy.

Scuffles filled the gloom, like rats in a pipe. Dust plumed. A shelf above him bucked and rocked, something slid off, he almost stopped to pick it up but knew it was a distraction and began to run.

As if this were a trigger, the whole building burst into uproar, falling metal clanged and whirled, creatures howled and roared, leaves and branches thrashed, the moist, rotten scent of burst and fallen fruits impinged upon his senses. Light shattered the darkness and lanced through the shelves, illuminating the apparent lack of ceiling, the brilliant epiphytes, the huge spreading green boughs, the water pouring down millennia old rock, all stacked row upon row in an endless space within time.

A raptor in flight flashed overhead, the downdraft of its wings stirring his hair.

Something small and agile leapt from shelf to shelf, swinging through trees its ancestors had never seen.

Oh no, the man thought, *I'm not so easily deterred.*

He skidded to a halt, almost pulled the ladder from the wall in his urgency and sprang up it three rungs at a time.

Silence and darkness fell like a wall. He felt almost sorry for her. It was the only veil she had. She should know better than to use it against him.

He lifted a hand ahead of him and saw a shadow move. Eyes opened and looked at him. They were large eyes, mirrored and reflective in the darkness. She was not human. She could see him. But he was not human either. His second eye-lids blinked again and his vision cleared.

He saw another pair of eyes before the darkness took them beneath her obsidian wing.

He did not care; he stepped up onto the shelf and over the boundary. The darkness grew deeper, darker, thick, like drowning water burning in his lungs. The lack of noise was anti-noise; he felt it sucking eagerly at him, yearning to mask the steady thud of his heart, the quiet pulse of blood in his veins, to kill him by total negation of his being. Incongruous softness tickled his ankles. A green fragrance drifted upwards from unseen bruised stems. The shadow shifted, a languid dancer in the molassic depths. He shook his head, determined, blinked again.

Now he could see.

There were others.

She had made others just like herself.

For a long moment he stood quite still, simply looking, filling his gaze with the mother and her young that lay before him, crouched on a shelf that flickered and merged into ochre-coloured scrub, the hint of endless skies above. The spotted cat gazed back at him, her great slanted head aloof yet intently alert, her gracefully slender body curled protectively around her blind and wriggling cubs.

His mind filled with fog. *Wrong shelf*, he thought. *It's the wrong shelf*.

He could not feel fear. He was not capable. He remembered all the things that had fallen on his way here. *I have to put them back*, he thought, *starting with this one*.

His first move towards the cubs brought an explosion of hissing and spitting from the mother, his second brought her instantly to her feet, hackles high, canines bared, eyes wild and dangerous. She had never done this before, never dared. Always change, always she wrought change in the dark, while he was away, in the outside, but not this, never this. He stepped back. He had no defences against this. He had never needed them before. Everything he had brought back here had been grateful. He did not understand. Her eyes burned into him as though seeking to impart a knowledge he did not want, and he moved back to the ladder, his alien gaze never leaving her.

His mind categorised with calming intent as he climbed back down, his legs and arms so stiff it seemed they had lost all malleability and would snap like petrified sap at any moment. He looked down the aisle he had so recently come. Various items, sentient and non-sentient, lay scattered upon the ground. The fog in his mind coalesced and reformed. He strode purposefully towards them, their shapes growing and regaining form and meaning with every step. His hand closed around a small animal with a long tail and hind legs. It gave barely a whimper during the journey up the ladder, but when he put it back in its place its eyes watched him, just like hers.

He did not think of it, simply relaxed his hands and slid down the ladder with practised ease. He had left his bag near the door. He would go to it, categorise all his recent acquirements.

Long fingers slid inside soft cloth, trickling water echoed from inside, then, like a magician with the whole world within his sleeves, he pulled out a lake some hundred miles across and wondered what he should do with it.

He could put it with the others, make a great sea – an influx of new nutrients would encourage more life. He shook his head and a million drops of water fell to the building floor and flew slowly and purposefully away.

No, that wouldn't do. It must go on its own, carefully placed, kept in stasis forever. How fortunate that he had found it before the drought that would dry it, turn its beds into cracked saltpans. He could not bear to see it as it would become. So much better to save it as it was now.

He walked down the aisles, the watery globe revolving like a million galaxies in his hand. Space had no meaning in his world, but it hurt the eyes to watch him nevertheless. He reached his perfect place and let a world of water slide away from him. More came from the bag now, birds with nets for beaks, birds with curved sabres, birds with plumage like jewels; out they flowed, out in twisting chains, tiny like motes of glittering dust in the beginning, growing with every heartbeat to full size, arrowing for the water in search of food.

He turned at the last minute, grasped the neck of the bag to stem the silver tide. The lake glittered its far horizon at him, the birds called, filled the air with their confusion, circled in one giant flock of kaleidoscopic and sinuous arcs, and arrowed down like feathered missiles to land on trees that shivered and unfolded from the lakeside, even as the birds ceased their flight. All this they did, curving their wings around their bodies and staring at him with a scrutinous intent that should have melted glass.

He did not see them. The rest of the bags' contents must go elsewhere.

He took the fish and laid them out in glass cases. Rainbows, glistening, fins like gossamer sails, eyes both soulless and endlessly vital, waterless, but alive, forever. Like butterflies still living but with pins through gills in place of wings. He did not hear the pitiful cries of the birds; they would forget soon, and they would sit on the branches at the water's edge in perfect, unmarred beauty for all time.

Calm descended once more. No mirrored eyes could disturb him now. He had saved them all, these broken things. He sagged into the dust, spine curved against a wooden wall and slept, his fingers wrapped in soft black cloth.

He awoke to a sensation so strange he could barely put a name to it. It had seemed for a moment that something soft and warm had trailed across his skin, a lingering motion, threatening in its intimacy.

Eyes, eyes in the dark.

He sat up straight, pulled his bag close. A vision of bright amber ovals disappeared back into the shelven recesses. He flexed his fingers, flickered his eyes to clear them of sleep's laziness. A voice seemed to whisper to him, of places under hot burning suns. He remembered them well; this was where she had come from. She who had betrayed all that he stood for. He climbed to his feet. How could he have forgotten? Back, he must put her back. But even as the thought occurred, his mind's eye slid over it like ice, and he forgot the blind cubs, forgot the threat in her eyes, headed instead for the door, the door to outside, out there, where the broken things dwelt, the poor broken things that he must save.

The door swung slowly shut behind him and from the darkness the sounds of life began slowly to gain momentum once again.

The man stalked under a hot sun, his black clothes an event horizon on the shimmering plains. And yet, all creatures curved away from him, as though knowing with some primitive instinct that he desired to order their existence with his long cold fingers. He nodded his head slowly as he strode, like an extinct bird, his eyes hooded to protect them from the intense light. His legs unfolded with too many joints, buckled, unfolded, buckled, unfolded, propelled him forward with metronomic intensity.

He saw tall thin shapes on the horizon, moving with the bulky shapes of pastoral beasts, their belled necks clanging dully. Pointed sticks speared the molten air as they approached, catalysts for shimmering motion. The man blinked himself out of existence to watch as they passed by.

Colourful these creatures were, with much in the way of woven cloths and beads, the brightness contrasting with the supple blackness of their hides. He wondered what they were, he had never taken one yet, did not know how to touch them with his dextrous hands; they slipped away from him like the dreams he never had. One turned as they neared him, eyes alert for predators. They narrowed slightly on looking his way and he blinked again, darkening the light. The creature looked away, hide creased into a disarray that somehow conveyed a meaning to the others, because now they all stopped, sharing noises and gestures with more of that mysterious intent.

The man curled space around his body. Thick whips of golden grass rose up to meet him; he shared the concealment of many predators, wondered if this was what the colourful ones had seen. He put this thought to them, and they immediately lifted their pointed sticks and moved away with startling speed, ushering their herd of beasts before them.

Soon they were thin specks on the horizon once more, and the man rose like a thorn from the ground, looked around, began his walk again, only to stop, too soon, in a single moment turned to stone, face, eyes and hands expressionless.

For something moved in the grass nearby.

His heart did not beat faster, but his ears sucked in all sound, quick and eager to corner their quarry. An explosive sound, unlike any he had ever heard, dragged his eyes in an instant to the source, and he knelt before the impulse had the chance to reach his muscles, parted the grass and looked within.

The creature did not see him or hear him, he was too far from this time to interact, but he could see it.

It was like him, yet not like him. Like the ones that had gone, but smaller. Hide as dark as theirs, fur close to the head. It had long hands, just as he, one of which it held to its mouth to stifle another explosion. Then, abruptly, it moved off, pushing the grass away from its path, a journey burning in its mind like blue lightning.

The man followed. Unbounded, he walked a path much easier than the creature's and thus saw the destination sooner. A wide herd of angular brown beasts that the creature's eager eyes sought out. Knowledge of punishment burned brightly in a brain that should know better, but curiosity and tales of bravery amongst others of its kind swam wildly and drowned these better, more sensible thoughts to quick and watery graves.

The man twisted black cloth between his hands, a thought of his own burning in his brain. He could see ahead, deep into the grasses, possibility upon possibility, the creature, boy, boy, his mind merged with that of his quarry: I am a Boy of the Warriors, I will make my first kill, I will join the elders, younger than any of my tribe, I will be remembered in story...

The man's mind careered, out of control, out of control, he struggled, touched on each and every living thing upon the plains, felt the minds of predator and prey, all watching, eating, waiting, pulsing, living, breathing, being, perfect being. And there, there, oh there, was the mind of the consummate stalker, so much stronger than this boy, boy, its dappled hide merging in the shimmering light, and so close, so close, it watched the young, the vulnerable, the boy, boy...

The man could wait no longer, he dropped out of time like stone, the boy shrieked, remembered his bravery, thrust the pointed stick, the man snatched it away, snatched life away, stowed it in his bag and was gone before the leopard pounced.

A new shelf awaited, the man knew this, all he had to do was find it. He strode the aisles, fingers curled tightly around the bag's neck. It was no heavier than it always was; only his mind told him what it contained.

On his return, all had remained quiet. Strange. It had not been so for a long, long time. Always on the heels of his return the shelves erupted with chattering, maddening life, always he was aware of that spotted coat, elusive in the shadows, desiring light yet knowing it was dangerous, hunting what she could not reach. She, where was she now? He wondered what this formidable quiescence presaged. Then he stopped wondering. It was not his place to wonder.

Where is she?

A thought, traitorous in the shadows, stalked him. He cast his gaze askance, in hope of catching it, but it darted, chuckling, amongst the endless welcoming depths, behind and between the shelves, and he could not pin it down, no matter how much he blinked or searched with his mind.

Where is she and what is she doing?

The bag twisted in his hands. He ceased his blinking. Tormented by scurrilous thoughts and cloth both. This could not be. Would not be. With a sudden burst of feeling he shook the bag till it ceased its twisting. Something chuckled once more in the darkness. He threw the bag from him in a vicious arc, seeking to still that dreadful gurgling laughter forever.

But as soon as it left his hands the silence shattered, as though it had never been, light speared down and a thousand animal shrieks filled the room, a thousand mammalian laughters, a thousand avian threats, a thousand reptilian growls and one, one feline hiss of warning as she, *she*, landed before him, perfectly balanced motion, paused between downward and upward plunge. He paled before her beauty, her aliveness, her vibrant, undeniable nowness. And then time snapped, the shrieks ended, the cheetah's paws flashed down and out, propelled thirty feet in a single bound, fluid death and life in rough spotted fur, erupting from endless shelves, herds of lightning-quick gazelles, white flashes as they darted this way and that, the cry of fear as the paws brought down the lone fawn, the gasp of life struggling to hold on between smothering jaws, the blood pulsing in a body pushed to the edge of its limits, the sun beating down, the sky swirling blue overhead, the scent of fresh blood, open intestines, the cubs, long-limbed, ungainly and graceful, tearing, tearing, eating so quickly, mother looking, looking for those who would steal, and then, then, a young boy charges, screaming, shouting, the cheetah starts, yips a warning to her cubs, thinks to stand her ground, sees the meat is almost gone, runs towards the boy, who does not back down, the man, he, he cannot move, the cheetah turns, follows her safely-fleeing cubs, and the moment is over, gone, stored in mind, body and sinew, never to be seen again, but to be repeated a million times over for all eternity, and the boy, the boy, boy, is sitting, pulling at scraps of meat, and he looks up at the man, and then the shelves return, and there is a small boy sitting before a fire, cooking meat, a shred of black cloth caught behind his fingernails, and the man turns and runs, his fear a fresh thing to him and all the more wondrous for that reason.

"I am not scared of you" the boy said.

The man checked his flight. Turned. The boy stared back at him, motionless for a moment, then he held out a morsel of roasted meat.

The man backed away. His breath hissed from between clenched teeth. Behind him the darkness shifted. For a moment he felt a desire to run to slashing claws, a desire so strong that his legs weakened and he fell to his knees, heart beating wildly, as must that of all prey before it dies.

The boy shrugged and continued to eat. From the darkness, a shadow paced forth, followed by three others. The man twisted his head wildly from shadows to boy and back again.

Boy. He tried again. "Boy." His voice was dusty, creaky as an old house. "Boy, beware. She comes."

The boy looked round, but alarm did not cross his face. He lifted a hand, and it seemed to the man that this hand stretched so far and wide that it encompassed the entirety of what had once been his and his alone. It scoured the shelves in an instant, closed around that which clung barely to life, brought it down and slung it in the path of the approaching cheetah. She took the gift, delivered the killing bite, laid it down for her cubs to feed. Then she moved beside the boy and sat next to him, a spotted sphinx, ready with legends and riddles to unfold. The man felt water start in his eyes for she was so beautiful and he had forgotten how.

"Who are you?" he asked the boy. The boy grinned, an ingenuous and unlikely thing on the face of one who had accessed time and space as no other should.

"Who are you?" he countered, the cheetah a sentinel at his side.

"I..." The man stuttered, the urge to run flared again, but the cheetah's inscrutable amber eyes turned on him the moment the thought was formed. and he was pinioned as any prey. The cubs, finished with their food, bounded up to him and began to play, tugging at the blackened tails of his clothing, pouncing and rolling as though he were no different from one of them. "I am He Who Collects." The man exhaled, his voice catching on the million hooks his throat now thrust forth. He reached out to touch the cubs, but the boy's voice stopped his hand a fraction above mobile fur.

"The Broken One."

He looked up. The boy was older now, yet still young. Scarifications and etchings covered his face, accentuating lines and pits that only age could bring.

What?

"The Broken One, lost soul, of my family and not of my family, lost you are, you take but cannot fill that which is gone. Collector of Broken Things. These things you break with your sadness. They were not broken; they are as they are and back they must go."

The man looked up through filtered eyes, rainwater ran through him; he saw shelf after shelf, row upon row, millions of animal eyes radiating their endless sadness, penetrating and filling him with it, for now they had his attention, this god who was not a god, and they felt his sadness, his loneliness, and they expanded it with their own.

So much loneliness bred from one wretched ember.

The man curled into a tiny ball, covered his face in trembling hands. The cubs yipped confusion and then, incongruously, empathically, they circled him, lay down around him, cradled him in life unbroken.

There was no leopard, no death, no broken boy he had saved, there was only him, his own mind, his own desperate loneliness, and now this, this...

"You are not to blame." The voice of the elder struck deep into the saddened pit of his soul. For a moment fingers like bark touched his cheek. Two pairs of eyes glowed in the dark. "But you must break. You must break now. And you will be glad of it."

The circle closed, the sphinx bared her tender canines and the man dropped grateful hands in face of the first and last peace he would know.

The elder lifted his feathered staff to the sky and nodded one single time, as shelf upon shelf tumbled back into the stream of life.

Toe in Water, Hand in Flame

Brian Maycock

As a respected businessman in a small town, Malcolm felt it was best to worship the moon in secret.

He was not a fanatic. There were many cold nights on the west coast, and when it was particularly bitter he kept his long-johns on instead of being naked as, strictly speaking, he should have been when he worshipped. But still he felt people would not understand and he didn't want his business to suffer.

As he made his way to the deserted cove where he practised his religion, the cold felt as if it was eating into the marrow of his bones, despite his thick coat and hat. Nonetheless, he trudged on, drawn by the brilliant, three-quarter moon that waited for him.

The beach was a narrow, precarious strip of sharp yet slippery stones. He undressed crouched on his haunches to avoid a fall, carefully folded each article of clothing in turn and placed them in his rucksack. As it was so cold, he kept his socks on as well as his long-johns. Then he made his way to the shore, stopping just before the sea that lapped at his feet.

This was his altar.

Malcolm raised his arms high, turned his face to the moon to bathe in her rays and began to whisper. Praising the moon, praying to the moon; both these acts comforted him.

After a time, his devotions were complete and he opened his eyes. He breathed out, at peace and – at first certainly – remained quite calm when he saw the creature that was now lying on the beach next to his feet.

If its head and torso had been those of a beautiful young woman, if its lower half had been silvery, sleek and tapered to a fin, well, then he would have called it a mermaid, because this thing, this creature that rested on the wet stones was half-human, half-fish.

Its eyes blinked. It squinted at him.

"What are you?" Malcolm asked the creature.

Through a smile of sharp stones, it replied, "The moon made me from the sea and the shore, and sent me to be your wife."

Malcolm shook his head. "No, this is wrong. You are wrong. You're…"

Scaly-skinned and skinny. He could see its ribs under that revolting skin and then there was the small skull dominated by huge eyes, and a mane of greasy seaweed hair. Below its emaciated torso and waist, its tail was a pillar of white, raw animal fat that ended in a serrated stump. If the moon had meant to make a mermaid, it occurred to Malcolm that it had been a rush job, a botch.

Malcolm told it this.

"I am flawed because your devotion is flawed," it replied and looked at his socks, which were green and woollen.

Malcolm tried to defend himself. "I am not a young man anymore. I am vulnerable to the cold, I am…"

"So very alone," the flawed mermaid cut in.

Malcolm wanted to tell it that it was wrong, or to mind its own business, or say nothing and walk away, as he did whenever anyone else, whether they were a well-meaning friend or not, raised the subject of his loneliness. He refused to admit that he was lonely, that he needed more than his work, his classic car and his wide-circle of 'friends'. He would not, could not, tell anyone this. Except the moon, when she was full and beautiful. She did not care that he got so worked up when he was close to a woman that he always made a complete fool of himself, that he had been lonely for so long that he had not been capable the last time that, by grace of accident and alcohol, he had managed to find himself with a woman.

Flustered, Malcolm looked at his feet. There was a hole in the sock over his right toe.

"I could fix that," the flawed mermaid said.

He was only going to take his sock off so she could darn it. The night was still cold, after all. But then he found himself pulling his other sock off and slipping out of his long-johns, and there he was, sitting next to her on the rocks; naked, shivering and shrivelled.

"It's all right for you," he said through chattering teeth, "You don't feel the cold."

"How do you know what I feel?" it asked.

He ignored its question and held up his sock. "I thought you were going to fix this."

It ignored what he had said and asked, "Why did you take all your clothes off just so I could darn a sock?"

He shrugged. "To show the moon I am devoted to Her."

The flawed mermaid smiled. The lines of its scales were no longer so defined, or the lines of its ribs, and where before it had been flat-chested, the mermaid was no longer, in Malcolm's eyes, flawed at all.

The next day, at work, Malcolm's PA, Janice, noticed that he seemed distracted.

On every day of the week for the last ten years, she had been the closest person to him in the whole world. She discussed his diary with him, screened his calls, and signed letters on his behalf. To anyone else, these might seem small acts, but to Janice they were no smaller than a kiss on the neck might be, or fingertips brushing back a lock of hair.

Today, though, she felt excluded, pushed back into the dusty corners of the office.

She spent the day fighting back tears, and at five-thirty she hurried home, where she double-locked the door, closed the curtains and went up to her bedroom.

A plain white cotton rug dominated the floor. She turned it onto its back to reveal a painting of the sun.

Then she went to stand in the middle of the sun, where she wept.

She had waited for so many years. She had never pretended to herself that she did not know why. It was because she was frightened, because she knew the effect would not last. For a single day, she would shine. He would be dazzled and they would be together. But as night fell, she would fade with the daylight, and in the darkness that followed she would have to face his disappointment at seeing that she was just an ordinary woman, a bit fatter than she wanted to be, with a few more moles than she would have liked, and hairs here and there, where she did not want them. His disappointment and his regret. He would say, "I'm so sorry Janice. I shouldn't have." After which, he would get dressed and leave, and she would be left alone, her fantasy that he might want to be with her destroyed.

Her fingers well and truly burnt.

So, she had not done it. Instead, she had waited and waited, cherishing the small acts they shared and telling herself that one day she would have the courage to act.

Janice sighed, looked down at the sun, at its beauty, its vivid colour. Her heart began to beat a little quicker, her skin began to tingle.

No more, she thought. No more waiting. No more of the loneliness that was slowly destroying her. She could not take it anymore. She *would* not take it anymore.

Janice took a deep breath. In a few hours' time, when dawn sunlight burnt down on the outside of those curtains, she would do it. She would open her heart to the sun – the sun she had worshipped in secret since she was eighteen, when she had failed her A levels and gone to secretarial college instead. She would open her heart to the sun and take it deep inside her.

She knelt down, gently brushed tiny specks of dirt from the rug. It would have been better to worship under the actual sun, but she had found it impossible to find anywhere to stand naked under the actual sun in Scotland, (when it was sunny, which was not too often), without causing a scene. This rug, that she had sewn herself, had proved a practical substitute over the years.

Now, she wanted it to be perfect, and when the moment came, when the dawn sunlight burnt down on the outside of those curtains, it would all be perfect.

She would become irresistible, and to hell with the consequences.

They were sprawled across the rocks, entwined. He ran his fingers through her hair, which was indeed hair now, not seaweed in place of hair. With her, he had not been nervous or stupid. The moon, he figured, had seen to that. And this was how he wanted things to stay.

"Come back with me," he said. "Come home."

"I can't," she replied. Her skin was flawless in the moonlight above her waist, and below her silver scales glinted.

"Why? What's stopping you?"

She rolled on her side and whispered in his ear.

He heard only the sea. "I don't understand," he told her.

"I cannot stray from the sea and the shore. I am still part of them. The moon can bring me here to be with you through the night, but her power fades in the daylight. I cannot follow you past the dawn."

He had not wanted to leave her last night, but she had slipped into the waves as dawn approached, and he had lost sight of her. She had not responded to his cries.

She stroked his lips with her forefinger, and he tasted salt water. She said, "I will not leave you. I will be here for you, every night from now on."

He began to cry, wiped his nose, and through the tears and snot said, "I don't want us to be apart ever again."

"The nights..." she began.

He put a finger to her lips and he wondered what she could taste. Bank notes? Champagne? Car polish?

"The nights are not enough," he told her. "I'm fifty years old. What do I have left? Twenty, thirty years? That's nothing." He cupped her face in his hands. "I have wasted my life being alone and now I have to make the most of every precious moment."

Her grey eyes sparkled. "The moon is stronger out there." She turned to face the sea. "Deep down, beyond the reach of the sun. She could protect you there during the day."

"And we would be together?"

She laughed. "I would be all around you."

He got to his feet and held out his hand. "Take me," he said.

She placed her fingers in his.

If Malcolm had been in the office he would have been hers.

They probably would not even have made it to a bed. They would have done it there and then on his desk.

Probably.

Possibly.

Janice twirled a pencil around in her fingers and thought how the next morning, when the sun's power had worn off, if he had lost interest in her, she could always take the power of the sun inside her again, make him hers again. And the next day and the next. She had thought of doing this before, but it had always seemed to be taking things a step too far. She wanted him to love her as she loved him – all the time, and because he was who he was and she was who she was.

Janice ran her finger across the wooden surface. Dust glistened as her fingertips brushed against it.

If only he had been there. She checked the time. 11 am. He had never been late before without telling her. He had always told her if he was going to be somewhere else.

She looked around the office and sighed. Flecks of golden fire drifted from in-between her lips, hung for a brief moment in the air.

She would wait and hope. Probably take an early lunch if the phones stayed quiet.

What You Came For

Jaine Fenn

The house is half way up the hill, cantilevered out from the fierce slope on a rotting wooden platform. Since the last legal resident left, just after the millennium, the garden has rioted through the small plot, shrouding the building in weeds and creepers, nudging at the boundaries, separating the house from its respectable neighbours and sending leafy emissaries onto the cracked concrete pavement.

As is your custom, you pause before crossing the threshold. Above, the sky is refreshingly blue. The surrounding hills, clearly visible from this high vantage point, are pleasantly green. The air is pure if a little chill. Despite its fame ("Baldwin Street – the World's Steepest Street") the street is deserted. Perhaps there are more visitors at the weekend.

You step from the pavement onto the short path of naked earth that leads up to the house. Small creatures patter away into the undergrowth at the unexpected intrusion. You pause again, at the three steps on the end of the veranda. To your right, downhill, the tangle of the abandoned garden is all but impenetrable. Though once boarded over, the space below the cantilever will have been made accessible by decay, scavengers, and human curiosity. It will be a dark, fetid place and that makes it a likely location. But you would have to fight your way through the rampant foliage to get to it, so you decide to try the house first.

You step up onto the veranda. The middle step creaks and sags beneath your foot.

Here is the first possibility. Rachel Levinson came to New Zealand with her husband in 1949. They barely survived the Nazi bigotry of World War 2 Europe, and after the war ended they were finally uprooted by a house fire that killed their surviving child. The

Levinsons chose to come here, to a new country, as a way of escaping the past. Rachel was far from happy to move to a house made of wood – a combustible dangerous house – but she deferred to her husband, as ever. Within six months he was dead of tuberculosis, and she was alone. She lived on in the house by herself for thirteen years, quietly looking for someone to blame. She died on this veranda, rocking in her chair, still searching the far side of the valley for reasons, back before the wild garden sealed off the view. She did not die happy, but she did die quietly. Not her, then.

You move on. A pair of empty wooden window frames flank the doorway. The front door has been missing for some years, giving free passage into a hallway that stretches through the length of the house, ending in a damp-stained door. You step into the primal reek of decomposing wood. Beneath it are other, fainter, smells: Smoke, rotten food, urine.

You take the first door on the right, an arbitrary choice, and find yourself in the main bedroom.

Now here is someone unexpected. A middle-aged man by the name of Frank Harris. He was, in his own opinion at least, a painter. He had money and ego enough that his inability to make a living by painting did not particularly concern him. He was also a transvestite, back before such things were considered an acceptable lifestyle choice. There, against that wall where the wallpaper now hangs down in mouldy strips, he had his special wardrobe. He kept it locked, even though he rarely had visitors. Frank Harris inhabited a quiet, secret world, spending hours at his dresser, just out of sight of the window, making himself glorious. He had dozens of 'correspondence lovers' as he called them, men he encountered through advertisements in certain magazines. But whenever he left the house he always wore a respectable suit. And he never invited his lovers here, in case reality disappointed him, and shattered his private fantasies. He lived in the house between 1962 and 1973. He did not die here.

Across the hall is the living room, the largest room in the house. The smell of smoke is stronger here and a few charred lumps of wood lie in the cast iron grate. The wallpaper has peeled away from three walls, but on the back wall it is still possible to make out the pattern of flowers, nature pinned flat and bound between vertical lines. The mantle shelf is gone now, but once it held a gold carriage clock, the prize possession of George Marchant and his wife Beth. George and Beth spent their final years in the house. They moved in after Frank Harris left, and, a quarter century later, they died here. Beth went first, to a stroke, bent over a bed of pansies in the garden. She hung on in the cold white hospital for several weeks. George's suffering during those weeks, though short lived, still marks this room. He faded within a year, was ushered into the arms of the state by concerned neighbours, and died in his sleep in another town, in a home that was no home to him. George and Beth were uniquely common. They believed the government, communicated just enough to get along, did their part when required. They expected, and got, small rewards for their simple loyalty. They were the last of a breed now gone from the world. Their suffering was simple, clean and stoical.

You are not here for them.

At the back of the house, it is darker and danker, and fungus scabs the walls. There are three doorways, two still with doors in them. You chose the one without a door.

Light seeps through boards covering the window of a small bare room. A nest of woodlice has turned the skirting board into a mush of pulp and splinters. This used to be the dining room, but in 1999 Tom Lawson converted it to a second bedroom. Tom and his wife Elaine, a quiet god-fearing couple, were awaiting the birth of their second child. Their first, James, had died in his sleep in their old house the year before. A blameless accident. One of those things. You move on. The Lawsons moved here, and tried to forget. But when their new-born daughter Mary proved to be a problem child, sleeping no more than two hours at a stretch, the secret thoughts and buried regrets came to the surface, and the love that bound the Lawsons soured. They blamed each other. They blamed their God. They blamed the screaming infant who would not settle, would not stop crying. And one day Mrs Lawson walked out and left the child to cry alone, until her father had her taken into care, and moved away himself, leaving the empty unloved house to decay on its steep hillside.

You leave the dining room and open the door opposite. It creaks and wobbles on its hinges. From the jutting pipes and tiled walls, it looks like this used to be the kitchen. A few algae-etched shards of glass hang in the window frame. The room faces upslope, and the foliage, starved of light, has not invaded beyond the sill. Rustlings and occasional bird calls sound from the back garden.

And here is the builder. Or rather, here is the woman he built this house for. A young man called Lawrence Cutler, one of the *émigrés* who came to New Zealand between the two World Wars, hoping to build a new life for himself. And he did, claiming this less-than-desirable plot of land, building this house with his own hands, and waiting, patiently, to be noticed by a woman who might have him for a husband. In the summer of 1941, he met and married a local girl called Hilda. In the autumn of 1941, he kissed her goodbye, and went to do his duty in the war. And in the spring of 1942, he died in the deserts of North Africa, converted from person to unidentified meat by a misfired mortar from his own side. Hilda, knowing only that he was missing in action, did not give up hope. She waited, keeping the house he had built spotless, keeping his memory alive, until one day she woke up and realised she could wait all her life. She put the house up for sale, moved to Australia, re-married, had children, and died without ever knowing what had happened to her first husband.

Such small, everyday hurts are not your concern. You are after rarer prey.

Only one room left, behind the stained door at the end of the hallway. The door is stiff, half off its hinges, and fungal blooms ooze at the edges of the wood.

This was the bathroom. There is still frosted glass in the window, though pallid tendrils of foliage have crept through the cracks and gaps at the corners. The toilet and sink are gone, but the heavy zinc and enamel bath still sits the side wall. The floor is crusted with stained lino, through which rotting planks show like patches of raw skin.

Ah, here he is. Michael Fortune, the last resident of the house, living here illegally for a couple of months after his parents threw him out. He was nineteen. He still lives in town, in a scruffy studio apartment, and he works as a mechanic at the cut-price garage whose roof is just visible from the road outside.

His family were average, his childhood uneventful. He had no excuse. He did have a fertile imagination, an unruly ego and an unquenchable sexual deviancy. Magic, the sort that promises to grant your every wish if you are strong enough to force your will on reality, holds a natural appeal for Michael Fortune.

Her name was Hene O'Hara. She could have been anyone; he didn't know her, though they might have passed each other once on some other street in this small town. She was eleven years old. She loved her parents, hated her appearance, and put up with school. Like most people, she had problems of her own, and she huffed her way to the top of the World's Steepest Street one blustery autumn afternoon to look out over the town and the hills and get a sense of perspective on a life overfilled with homework and parental disputes.

There was no one else on the street that day, either.

He saw her go up the street from the veranda where he sat. This is a dead end street, so he knew she would be back.

Michael Fortune was intoxicated with the possibility of combining pleasure and power. He wasn't smart, but he was clever. So when Hene O'Hara ambled back down the street he called her over – *Hey, wanna see something really cool?* – and when she wandered up the bare earth path he grabbed her and dragged her into the house. He pulled her into the bathroom, this room, where the big zinc bath was still plumbed in. He bound her with cable ties to stop her struggling, and gagged her with masking tape to stop her screaming, and then he did everything he'd ever dreamed of doing. Afterwards, he let the blood drain down plughole, and used a woodsaw to section the body before burying the pieces in the wild garden.

She took some hours to die: the room stinks of her agony. You imagine that even a human being entering this room would feel the corruption here.

Hene O'Hara's disappearance remains a mystery to most people in this town. There have been no others yet, but even now Michael Fortune is wondering if he should try again. After all, what has he got to lose? He got away with it before. And maybe this time he'll get it right, and after he has indulged his desires he'll get a high that's better than sex, better than chemicals, better than fear: the ecstasy of magic. Last time, he waited all night to feel the rush. But this is not his land; he does not understand how magic works here. The power he craved never came to him.

Instead, a year and a day later, you came.

In a few short breaths, you change. You are smaller now, your skin darker, your disobedient black hair pulled back into the ponytail. You wear a grey school pinafore and sensible shoes.

You have what you came for. Now you will act.

You leave the way you came in. The sky is still cloudless blue, the air still clear and chill. The street is still deserted. No one sees you. If anyone did, they might think you looked a bit like that poor girl – what was her name? – who disappeared a year or so back. Mrs O'Hara would know you for her daughter. And Michael Fortune will certainly recognize you.

Briefly.

The Heroic Acts of Strangers

Ian Whates

It shouldn't be long now. She pushed back a stray lock of blonde hair and considered the house again. It was perfect for her requirements: an unassuming, detached suburban home. She knew the type well. Built in the 1970s, upstairs would boast a main bedroom with *en suite* shower, plus two further bedrooms and a family bathroom, while the ground floor consisted of a front to back through-lounge and a spacious kitchen, big enough to accommodate a table that the whole family could sit around at mealtimes. Of course, that didn't necessarily mean they ever did.

She glanced at the car parked in the driveway; a mid-range Toyota – metallic blue, this year's number plate. It spoke of financial comfort rather than prosperity. Then her eyes returned to the house, looking up to take in the neat red brickwork, the replacement UPVC fascia and guttering – white to match the frames surrounding the double-glazed windows – before settling on the windows themselves; her attention drawn by one in particular.

Yes, there was a flicker of uneven light and shifting shadow. It was almost time to make her move.

Some might think that what she was about to do should be harder these days, given the constant advance of science, of human knowledge and understanding. In fact, it was easier, thanks to one of those very advances, albeit an ancient one. What had for so long been solemn warning, dutifully passed down from generation to generation by word of mouth in a culture that had turned its back on human sacrifice, was eventually committed to paper. Once written down it became immutable, accepted as fact, as permanent as stone.

"Can I help you?"

So intent was she on that window and her musings that she hadn't heard anyone approach. The voice startled her, coming from close behind, almost at her shoulder.

She whipped around, to find herself facing a neatly dressed, mild-looking man, late twenties or perhaps early thirties, with hairline already starting to recede. The father, she realised, returned home from work. There had been no sound to suggest the arrival of a car, so he must have walked, presumably from the nearby station.

Not without reason have men's eyes been called the windows to the soul. In his she watched the various reactions to her presence laid bare in rapid, flickering sequence that reminded her of some poorly spliced home movie. There was suspicion tempered by curiosity, even guarded hostility, and then dawning appreciation of her lingering beauty. She still noticed the embers of interest in men's eyes despite the flush of youth having deserted her some years ago. Oh, she realised that time had left its mark and her face no longer showed the seamless perfection which had, in decades past, seen wealthy men and even a minor Prince vying for her affections, but the echo of that woman still remained and false modesty had never been a failing she subscribed to.

She smiled ingenuously and, being a man, he naturally smiled back. The wary overtones disappeared as he unconsciously relaxed.

"I thought…" she began, playing the innocent and flicking a concerned glance back towards the tell-tale bedroom window.

"Yes?" he prompted, softly, pleasantly.

"I thought I saw…"

There could be no doubt now. The shadow of a smile played at the corners of her mouth, to vanish as she turned back to face the man once more.

"My God," he exclaimed, as his gaze followed hers. "Fire!"

He rushed forward, fumbling in a pocket for his keys. She was there as he pulled the door open, slipping inside ahead of him as he hesitated, disconcerted by the wall of heat and smoke that billowed out in greeting.

"Is there anyone home?" she called, knowing the answer already.

"My wife... my daughter," he said. Then, as if by way of an afterthought, "Be careful! You can't..."

But she already was. Ignoring the tears that gathered in her smarting eyes in face of the acrid fumes, she stepped into the lounge. Thick tendrils of denser, darker smoke spilled out from the stairwell, hugging the ceiling as they were drawn inexorably towards the open door, moving with unnerving speed, writhing all the while like a mass of roiling serpents. A woman was slumped in the settee; half sitting, half lying, her eyes closed in oblivion.

"Moira!" the man cried in anguish, recognising his wife.

Moira still wore the same summer top and faded jeans that she had been wearing earlier in the day at the coffee bar.

Coughing, spluttering, sobbing, the man rushed forward, defying the instinctual reaction for self-preservation that must have been urging him to flee. Handkerchief clutched to his mouth, he reached her. "Moira."

Haste made him clumsy and he nearly dropped his precious charge in struggling to lift her up. She slumped to the floor and gave no sign of moving. He began to half carry and half drag her towards the door, gripping her under the arms and shuffling backwards.

"What about your daughter?" the woman said. She still stood at the room's threshold, close to the front door, unmoved by the husband's struggles. She was impatient to be done and needed him to focus.

"Hannah," the man gasped as he reached her side, "my baby..." as if he'd forgotten the infant until then. His gaze swept guiltily upwards, towards the upstairs landing where the fire had truly taken hold and flames danced behind the swirling smoke as if to goad it on. His handkerchief had been dropped somewhere along the way, his eyes were streaming and he was suddenly wracked anew by a fit of coughs as the choking smoke flowed freely into his lungs. Still he stood, his features twisted by uncertainty as he wrestled with dilemma, undecided whether to complete the task of carrying his wife to safety or risk the stairs and the fiery hell beyond in an attempt to rescue his daughter.

"Go!" the woman urged, placing a hand on his shoulder and

propelling him gently towards the door. "See to your wife. I'll fetch your daughter."

Before he could protest she started up the stairs, not looking to see whether he heeded her advice, shutting him from her mind.

The heat increased dramatically as she pushed forward, step by resolute step. The stairs themselves were smoking, on the verge of catching alight. Perhaps the father called out, but if so she didn't hear him, so intent was she on the roar of conflagration, the crackle of man-made structures as they ruptured and collapsed in the face of such unrestrained fury.

She knew about slipping in and out of buildings unseen, she understood such things. Most of all, she understood about fire.

Flames licked at her now, biting and scalding her flesh. She revelled at their kiss, breathing deep of fire's ever-faithful attendant: smoke. Her clothes began to smoulder and her body progressively failed as she continued her steady advance, the flames taking their inevitable toll on organic matter. She ignored all such distractions and walked at the same deliberate pace across the landing and into the smallest bedroom, towards the form that lay on the bed: the little girl, golden haired and beautiful, perhaps two or three years old – hardly a baby as the father had claimed, though she doubtless seemed so to him. This was the radiant, blue eyed child she had first seen in the coffee bar with her mother earlier that same day. The girl who reminded her so much of herself, as she had been a lifetime ago. Exactly the girl she had been waiting for, searching for.

Her top finally caught light, and she took the last few steps ablaze, like some ghastly human torch. Not much time left; her body was almost spent. She felt her flesh begin to crisp and blood vessels burst, rejoicing as they did so.

Yet still her movements were unhurried, as she lifted up the small form and clutched it to her, so that they burned together, body melting into body, two forms melding into one, the so-vital essence of youth suffusing her own old and tired frame.

Humans and their tales: so easy to manipulate. The trick had been to interfere with the telling while it was yet malleable, before the act of writing, in an age when such things were still related orally and subtle changes and distortions would inevitably creep in with the passage of time. Not all such were accidental. A few small details tweaked along the way and what had started out as dark and dangerous portent gradually metamorphosed into a tale of wonder, an accepted part of 'folklore'. Within a century or two of the written word supplanting verbal tradition, the whole thing was already being dismissed as legend: the quaint beliefs of primitive ancestors who knew no better.

She smiled as she surrendered to the fire, closing her eyes and giving herself to the flames, revelling in the pain: so intense, so sensual, so exquisite.

The little girl ran from the building, crying but miraculously unharmed despite soot-smudged cheeks and some singed patches on her clothing. At sight of her, an inchoate wail of aborted despair and relief tore loose from somewhere deep inside the mother, who had recovered sufficiently from the smoke to grieve, however prematurely. She detached herself from the growing crowd of anonymous onlookers – neighbours summoned by the prospect of tragedy – and swept the girl up in her arms to hug her, whilst the father hurried across to hug them both.

The crowd watched the flames anxiously for sign of the heroic woman who had dashed into the burning building with such disregard for her own life, but she never emerged.

The knowledge of their own failing, that neither had matched this stranger's feat of selfless bravery on behalf of their daughter, would haunt both parents thereafter, and the guilt each felt over the unknown woman's sacrifice would cause a rift between them, terminally blighting their relationship in later years.

Although unharmed physically by her ordeal, the little girl seemed greatly changed in herself – quieter and less given to childish glee – but the experts assured the concerned parents that this was only to be expected after such a harrowing experience. And if on occasion there appeared to be a shadow in the depths of her eyes which hinted at wisdom and maturity beyond her years, then surely that too could be explained away as the legacy of that dreadful night.

As years passed the girl developed into a startlingly beautiful woman, lauded by many and envied by more. None of whom suspected that every day she gave silent thanks to a man she had never known, to that anonymous scribe of yore who first made the blessed error of recording that the Phoenix was a bird.

Chess

Douglas Graham

Fire crackled in the hearth, throwing heat out into the room. The gnarled logs popped and crackled, and the flames flickered as a door opened, then settled again. The room was lined floor to ceiling with bookshelves of dark oak, leather bound volumes packed in, row upon row, gold-embossed spines catching the firelight. The window was hung with expensive heavy drapes, blocking out the light of the midday winter sun.

In the centre of the room stood a small, square-topped table, on top of which rested a marble chessboard. The pieces were ornate and beautiful, the white angelic and glorious, the black twisted and dark. Two men sat on either side of the table, their appearances as diametrically opposed as those of the chess pieces in front of them. White was a grotesque figure, hunched in his high-backed leather chair. His name was Gustaf Minjarez, though he was more commonly known by his nickname, The Bastard. Not to his face of course; a corpulent mass of flesh topped with a greased-down slick of tobacco-yellow hair. Small, restless piggy eyes peered out from under a heavy brow, which he mopped periodically with a large spotted handkerchief.

Black was taken by a man known only as Sorensen, a tall man with short, neatly-cropped grey hair and beard. His slim face bore a white scar from his chin to his left temple, cutting across the milky white orb which replaced his left eye, which had been lost in a skirmish many years gone. His opponent hadn't been quite so lucky, and had gone home in a box. A very small box.

Sorensen leaned over the board, one finger stroking at his beard. He paused, then made his move. The game had been running now for several hours, and he was beginning to grow weary. He glanced at his watch, straightened his cuff and sat back in his chair. The game was a gamble; carefully calculated to the last decimal place, but a gamble nonetheless. He favoured his chances, obviously, but Gustaf was not a man to be trifled with, although appearances might be to the contrary.

"Knight to King four," he said, eyes locked on his opponent.

Gustaf giggled, a queer high-pitched sound reminiscent of a young girl, running one pudgy hand through his hair, then reaching for a plate of delicate morsels to one side of the board. He grabbed a handful and stuffed them into his mouth. Sorenson twitched, repulsed.

"Did you really want to do that, old man?" Gustaf said, obviously delighted with himself and his own cleverness. He leaned over the board, dripping flecks of sweetmeats onto the marble surface. "I think you've made a terrible mistake! What fun!"

He moved his own piece, white Queen swiftly taking the Knight. Gustaf tossed the black horse carelessly over his shoulder and chortled. "Another horsey for me. Come now, Sorensen, I thought you were good at this game? Or are you as bad at that as you are at running your little band of brigands?"

Sorensen smiled, a humourless smile. He reached over and moved his Rook. "Check. And my 'little band of brigands' is doing quite nicely, thank you very much. We took over Fredrickson's quarter this morning."

Gustaf's smile faded briefly. He chewed on another mouthful of sweetbreads, belched, and beckoned to the servant standing in the corner of the room. "Godders! Come here! Bring me some more of these delicious tidbits." He took a swig from the glass in his hand. "And something for dear old Sorensen here."

Sorensen shook his head. He wasn't hungry to start with, and watching Gustaf eat made him feel quite nauseous.

"No? Bring some anyway." Gustaf turned to Sorensen. "How is dear old Fredrickson these days?"

"Rather unwell. Suffering from a slight case of decapitation. Poor chap."

Gustaf swallowed, a nervous tic playing in one corner of his mouth. Fredrickson had been regarded as one of the more successful warlords of the eastern district, a small psychopathic man, with a fondness for sharp toys and red-hot spikes, a trait shared by Gustaf himself. He had always wondered what would happen if the two of them ever met, and was quietly grateful that he would never have to find out.

Gustaf returned his attention to the board, then guffawed loudly, slamming his hands down on the table.

"Sorensen, you old dog! You thought you had me..." He wagged a fat digit at his opponent. "But you didn't see..." And with a flourish, he moved his piece. "Bishop takes Rook. Check." He paused, one hand to his fat face in mock astonishment. "No no! Wait, what's this...? Check... mate."

Sorensen looked at the board. It was over. A gamble on his skill as a chess player, for the highest of stakes. "You win. My generals will lay down their arms. My 'band of brigands' are yours, to do with as you will."

Both knew that the generals would be lined up and shot at dawn, and the soldiers offered the same fate if they refused to switch allegiances. However, it wasn't just the soldiers who had something at stake. The game was one which they played regularly, here at a neutral location in the centre of the town. It was Sorensen who had suggested 'a small wager'. Winner take all, in every sense. The war outside had been going on for too long; it was time to call an end to it. Gustaf had been suspicious, but his greed had taken the better of him, as Sorensen knew that it would. He knew that Gustaf craved power above all else, and would stop at nothing to control the city.

Godfrey returned with a tray which he put down on a small side-table, then removed a folded parchment from an inside pocket. He opened it, uncapped a pen and laid the document in front of Sorensen.

"Mister Sorensen. My condolences on your loss. If you would be so kind as to sign here?" Godfrey indicated a space near the bottom of the page.

Sorensen picked up the pen, his hand trembling. He signed, then threw the pen down onto the table. "Get it over with." He rolled up one sleeve and turned his head.

Godfrey picked up the remaining item on the tray, a compact silver case. He opened it and withdrew a syringe full of a milky substance.

Gustaf chortled and clapped, bouncing in his seat. "I've waited for this, *Sorensen.*" The name spat out with venom. "I've waited these long, long years." He cackled, spittle flying.

Godfrey leaned over, and pressed the syringe home.

Sorensen closed his eyes, his breathing slowed. He heard Gustaf giggle again and a champagne cork popping, a glass being filled.

"A toast, Godders! A toast to me!" said Gustaf.

"Indeed, sir. Shall I remove Mister Sorensen?"

"No, no. Leave him there. I want to gloat some more. I want to..." Gustaf stumbled over his words. He giggled. "Too much bubbly, Godders. Too much..."

Gustaf fell forward onto the board, pieces scattering as his bulk hit. He slid sideways, eyes frantic, scrabbling fingers trying to grasp the table. A guttural groan escaped his throat and he twitched his last.

Sorensen opened one eye. "Ah, splendid. Well done, Godfrey."

Godfrey nodded his head. "Quite so, sir."

"Poison in the champagne, I take it?" He straightened his tie, and smoothed down his sleeve.

"The sweetbreads, sir. He was so fond of them." Godfrey had taken Sorensen's call late the previous evening, and had taken little persuasion to agree to the poisoning plot. It appeared that he'd always despised Gustaf and his habit of referring to the manservant as 'Godders'. It had taken a short trip to a local supplier to procure the necessary ingredients, and the rest was left to Gustaf's prodigious appetite. Sorensen had promised Godfrey a handsome sum as a reward, plus a position as head of his personal staff.

"Splendid. I shall see that you receive your just rewards, Godfrey." Sorensen made a mental note to have Godfrey shot. What was the point of having an elaborate plan if there was someone who could tell tales? "A drink! Shame to leave all that champagne to waste. I'd be grateful if I could have a clean glass, though."

"Of course, sir."

Sorensen walked around the table and prodded Gustaf with his foot. "Greasy, despicable little man. Our country is better off without you. I will lead us into a better future, one where the people have hope, eh Godfrey?"

"Indeed, sir." Godfrey placed two champagne flutes on the table and filled them both, before passing one to Sorensen. The manservant raised his glass.

"A toast, if I may?" Sorensen nodded, raising his own glass. "To the future."

Sorensen drained his glass in one. "The future!" He grinned.

The grin faded. "You're not drinking, Godfrey."

"Indeed not, sir."

Godfrey turned and walked towards the door. It had seemed a shame to waste the rest of the poison, he had mused. Two birds with one stone, and with Fredrickson out of the picture too, it seemed that his city might have a chance at peace. He smiled as Sorensen's lifeless body slumped to the floor.

"Indeed not."

Cover by Ruby for Issue 8

Casamundi

Douglas Thompson

Summer evening at last. The centre of life. In our house that we have rebuilt together here, over many months and seasons. We stand at the summer window in the room that looks out over the trees and gardens of suburbia, the shadows of leaves falling and playing over our faces at the glass, as the evening breeze sighs.

The hour glass, the looking glass, at the vantage point where all the paths of the world have led us home to. And the clocks tick somewhere, echoing, in another room, echoing with the sound of polished wood and summer evenings, every evening of every remembered clock in each remembered house that told the time to here.

The evening and the town are full of summer, it pours out with the birdsong and distant sound of children's voices, and the sighs of cars, the faint buzzing of bees and motorbikes. We see and hear everything through this screen, this looking-glass, perched above the town, captains of our house tonight above the drifting sea of leaves.

Your face is beautiful, your eyes are blue glass, spinning the world around inside them as you smile, and your smile is the gap in the leaves, the opening in the clouds that lets the sun through: it breaks the world open like a cracking egg, pouring out the warm gold from within it. Your mouth opens slowly, with the inevitable motion of a breaking wave, and your words wash over my face like cool water, shocking, refreshing, impossibly slowly and deeply, shaking the walls:

This is the singularity, we are at the centre point now, at the pivot. The numbered years and moments from your birth can be spun around this point, and they will lead forward to your death, our death, in a car crash, in 18 years, nine months and 2 days…

But what are you saying…? – I start to recoil, but you place your hand on my lips, and your smile is a sun that obliterates the room, removing all shadows. The flowing strands of your brown hair are falling over your eyes like leaves and branches and filtering the light. And your eyelashes sweep across my brow like a witch's broom made of tiny insects. We kiss. And from this still point you suck time backwards and turn the room upside down.

I open my eyes, and you step backwards in the summer room and, stretching a leg behind you, rotate effortlessly with two steps until you are standing on the opposite wall. Now you are reaching out to me, looking upwards to meet my gaze, and when I take your hand, it is as if some invisible sea swell – an eddy in the river of time – is catching me from below, and I am gently swung up and around to join you on the wall.

Now what was a wall is a floor, and the view from the window is of our village before it was a suburb. I see a scarified landscape of open mines, from which they are building the great city to the south that will one day envelop us. Everywhere there is black smoke and ramshackle railway lines, spoil heaps, and the sound of metal tools on stone, chipping and chiselling.

What's happening? –I ask.

It is 1854 and we are moving through dimensions. You see, it's so easy really when you grasp what time actually is. Events form a landscape over which you can walk while standing still, just open your heart and the world will turn under you. We are falling through space and rotating around ourselves and the sun, and thus every moment is a unique place. We are the maps of this journey. You are a temporary conflagration of atoms, a quantum constellation, a fantastical spatter of paint by a celestial Jackson Pollock. When you say that you cannot alter the past, you are describing your own immortality. Your pattern through time cannot be altered, it is eternal, and you can revisit it endlessly, forwards, backwards, sideways.

Am I dead then? – I ask in horror, as you lead me onto the ceiling and the world rotates again.

Ha! – you laugh – *wrong question! You are always dead and always alive, if you truly understand what I have just told you.*

Now the inside of our house has changed, and as we stroll upside down along the ceiling, it is as if we peer through a subtle fog at former and future inhabitants of the house below. Wallpapers change, strange children run about, old ladies die in bed, dogs bark, somebody slits their wrists in the bath. We look upwards at these scenes, and the changing light from the world beyond reaches us in some diffuse underwater ambience, rotating in circular patterns, tunnelling us out. I feel as if I were Dante with his Virgil, traversing the underworld.

Then out of the cold mud of the Somme, like figures of grey clay, the bodies of young men regain life and stand up, and then march backwards by roads and by boats: to return home to here, and to the nail that has been here for a century – half-hammered into a skirting-board inside our hall cupboard. One of them lifts a hammer and sucks the nail out magnetically and retreats with his fellows, taking the gable of our home with him. We watch it disassemble, stone by stone, revealing the sky, as the scaffold deconstructs behind it. Drawn by the expanding light, we float down the staircase to the doorway, as each step disappears in turn.

Out to the garden: towards the yew tree, which seems slightly younger now. You look the same, but your eyes cloud with horror as a pair of boots sway into my chin. We step backwards and look up to see that a man wearing these boots is hanging from the tree with a rope about his neck. A crowd has gathered around about, but is unable to see us: a priest, a magistrate, an unwashed crowd, hecklers shouting abuse, policemen in antiquated uniforms and shining boots, relatives snivelling, women's mournful singing somewhere, Irish accents. This is Dennis Doolan, the railway labourer who allegedly killed his foreman and was executed for the crime, taking twenty minutes to die. A poor immigrant scapegoat for the indignant protestant crowd.

You lead me running, as if we are children, around the outskirts of the onlookers under a grey, bleak sky laden with rain, until the dull clouds fade and the yew tree, alone now in its meadow, grows magically younger in new sunlight as we advance upon it, enchanted. Daisies, buttercups, bluebells spin and flash around its base in the alternating patterns of seasons and years.

Turning around the trunk once more, this time we chance upon a well-dressed young man; Thomas Muir of Huntershill, home from his law studies in Edinburgh, his head hot under his new white wig or perhaps enflamed by the book he is reading; *The Rights of Man* by *Thomas Paine*, news of the French Revolution. Shaded by the yew tree, as he sits on the grass in this corner of his wealthy father's estate, what dangerous seeds take root in his mind? In less than two years, this living pillar of the landed establishment will find himself suddenly proclaimed a hero of the working man and an enemy of the state and deported to Australia. Just now he unexpectedly reaches up and catches a bee in his hand, its drowsily angry rumblings starting to echo within the cathedral of his fingers. He holds it gently, amazed by his own absent-minded daring, suddenly afraid as to whether to release it suddenly or to dare to crush it.

We run on, getting younger as our tree does, for another circuit of its branches. Now, the town around us is disappearing into farmland. Changing patchwork quilts of fields, flickering of forests encroaching. Farmhouses, barns, horse and carts, dirt track roads heavily creased by hooves and rain. Our tree is nearly a sapling, wagging up and down between seasons, as if wavering over the business of life, and how to negotiate the shading canopies of its competitors; all of whom will die before it.

Until the huge hand of William Wallace brushes it, the same hand that held at Stirling Bridge; held a broadsword to dazzle the effeminate generations of the future. Now, in a moment of absent-minded reflection, he is talking to a friend who he wonders if he can still trust, his other hand under his cloak just touching the hilt of his dagger, the familiar texture of it rubbing his skin; a thousand dizzying rotations of twine. He wanders incognito, outlaw in his own country, and begins the climb up the long hill and over to the pastures beyond: where soon he will pause at the fated well and the farm where he will be betrayed to the English soldiers.

Later, butchered alive, eyes closed in indescribable pain: he will focus his dying thoughts on the last pure thing he remembers: his strange memory of a sapling tree; its bark smooth as a woman's skin, its little leaves flickering like her hair in a breeze in the sunlight. His own body, breaking like branches, he feels growing outwards, reaching beyond himself. He thinks of the Yew that will outlive everything around it, patiently unnoticed, growing ever stronger. He imagines what a mighty longbow its wood will one day make, and where its last arrow might fall, far into the future.

But as the arrow strikes the earth, the tree of knowledge unmakes itself finally, and we wake up from our daydream.

Back in the house, we climb down the wall onto the floor again, in another room with another window and a different view of the same suburb that was once a town. And now it's later, and the sky is beginning to redden like blood over the trees and all the drowsy little roofs in rows. The bird song is quieter and slower, and strange light and reflections play on our walls like turning oceans and emerald armies, the quiet machinations of leaves and shadows. The bees and the mysterious distant motorcyclists have all gone home, their droning fading away to nothing.

Now your face is beautiful, and your eyes like dark pools where evening will grow until all the night overflows and pours out from them to fill and soothe the world with silence, as we walk the late streets together. Walking aimlessly, endlessly searching for something we've forgotten, sighing, debating, ruminating.

And nobody in any of the houses will know us, and none of them venture out, not daring to leave their televisions without the protection of their cars, their metallic insect-armour. Pale, frightened molluscs, retreated to the last chamber of their spiral shells, the sound of television static washing their ears like the memories of lost oceans. We will walk by, and it will be as if we are the only people left in the whole town, and the passing cars just empty machines running on rails. As if we are dead or in a dream. Adrift in our own constellation, marvelling at the night sky, the painted stars.

But our thoughts are suddenly interrupted. Here, in the last room, the ceiling collapses and the Apollo Moon Lander crashes through and lands on the floor on the carpet between us, shaking the whole building. Grey dust of plaster or moon rock swirls in slow motion through the room, and we are choking but unable to move. Our hands freeze to the armchairs, mouths forming words we cannot hear, as if in a vacuum. Then as the dust swirls, a metal hatch is thrown open, a ladder let down, and one after the other, two astronauts lumber down backwards, awkwardly, bouncing off the floor as if it is rubber.

And the last thing I see is the American flag being planted in the sofa in the background, the television filled with grey flickering static behind it, and a huge white helmet looming up closer to examine my immobilised face, the dark glass orb of the visor filled with blue water; swishing with fishes.

Author's Note

This story was written in a house I lived in for four years, in Springfield Square, in the Glasgow suburb of Bishopbriggs, in what was once the grounds of Huntershill House, where the godfather of modern democracy, Thomas Muir, was raised; a posh lawyer who got deported for dreaming up the idea of socialism. Everything else in the story, also really happened within a mile or two, right down to William Wallace's betrayal. My point in writing this was not that Springfield Square was a particularly interesting place, but the opposite: that every corner of our ancient nation is probably criss-crossed with many layers of stories if only we could reach them. There was indeed a nail on a door-facing that the original builders had neglected to hammer in: I hammered it in myself one night, thus completing a simple task begun and left unfinished eighty years beforehand, an act of solidarity and sympathy with the dead. But I've left the worst to last: the house was haunted by the ghost of the lover of my wife's old art teacher. He had beaten her and abandoned her with two kids and she had eventually lost her mind and killed herself in the bath, although we only found all this out quite a while after we'd moved in. There was a bad atmosphere in the bathroom and one night as I stripped the wallpaper I became aware (out of the corner of my eye) of her lying in the bath filled with blood. It wasn't a scary experience, just sad and matter-of-fact, I could feel her despair. A few months later a local woman in a curtain shop inadvertently broke the story to us when we gave her our address: "Oh, you live in THAT house, don't you know the story?" But before she could finish I said, "Was her hair black and did it happen in the bath?", and she looked at me amazed: "But I thought you never knew her?" I didn't, but I do now, I might have added. Poor old Rita; she used to make the electrics trip in the middle of the night, but I felt she was a good soul really, meant us no harm at all...

The Lady of the Fog

J.H. Fleming

It was common knowledge in Swallow's Bend that when the fog came into town, you shut your doors and stayed inside. Everyone there knew all about the fog. It was not just that people were afraid of getting lost. In our neck of the woods, the fog was more than just an inconvenience.

When I was a little girl, my mother would let my sisters and me play in the fields surrounding our house. We knew we had to be home well before dark, and we also knew that if the fog came we were to get home immediately, even though the last time the fog had come was before I was born. Everyone took the fog seriously. Little children would gather and listen to their grandmother or grandfather tell stories of children who had wandered into the fog. I remember listening to those stories with my sisters when I was a little girl. They were meant to warn us about the fog, and to keep us from wandering into it if it came. But more often than not they simply gave us nightmares.

I remember stories of little girls – only little girls, never boys – wandering into the fog who were never seen again. And then there were the stories where the little girl would go into the fog, and then be found the next day, dead, frozen to death, or worse. I know what you're thinking. What could be worse than death? But believe me, such things exist.

I remember one story in particular, to me the scariest of all that my grandmother told me and my sisters, about a little girl who, like my sisters and me, played in the fields around her house. One day the fog came, and instead of going home like a good girl, she went into it. Her mother noticed that she didn't come home and became worried, but her father wouldn't let anyone go look for her until the fog had cleared. The next day a search party had scaled the fields, hoping to at least find a body (that was seemingly the best anyone hoped for). To everyone's surprise, they found the little girl nestled against a tree in the woods, but she wasn't dead. They carried her home, and of course she was sick for having been out all night in the cold. But when she finally awoke, she told of meeting children in the fog who wanted to play with her, and a kind woman who looked after all of them. She said all the children had urged her to join them, and the woman had told her about all the fun they would have. But she had run from them and found the big tree where she'd spent the night. Her parents asked her if the children or the woman had followed her, and she told them that they had, but she had been clever and ran all around the trees until she found the great tree, and there she had hidden from them.

It scared me as a child, thinking that there were children in the fog. I believed they were all the children who had gone missing before, and that they were trapped in the fog with the woman. I thought the woman was some evil witch, or fairy, who had tricked the children into staying with her. Sometimes I would dream that she was coming for me, and I'd imagine her standing outside my window at night, calling me to her. My sisters all had similar ideas and fears. We were lucky that the fog never came during our childhood. We were scared enough by the stories; who knew what we would do if the fog actually came one day while we were playing in the fields?

When I made a family of my own, my mother terrified my children with the stories as soon as they were old enough to listen to them. My youngest daughter, Abriel, took them to heart the most. She believed anything you told her, no matter how outrageous because, being only five, she had a big imagination.

One day, when my mother, my sisters, and their families came over for holy day dinner, all the children played outside, while my sisters and I settled in the kitchen to talk. I tried to listen attentively, but I could hear my mother on the porch, telling fog stories to our daughters.

Later, I pulled my favourite sister Mica into the hallway.

"I wanted to talk to you about the fog stories," I said. "Do you remember how badly those stories frightened us as children?"

"Oh, they weren't that bad," she said.

"But Mica, the fog hasn't come in years. There's no point to those stories anymore, except to scare children. I don't want my daughters to have to listen to those."

"The girls are fine. They know the stories aren't true."

"What if we could get Mother to stop telling the stories? Kisha has such nightmares sometimes."

"All kids have nightmares, Alina. It's a part of growing up."

"Please, Mica."

"You're just overreacting," she said and went back to the kitchen.

A few days later, I invited my mother to dinner. After eating, she played games with the children and then of course began her fog stories. I went outside for a breath of fresh air. The night sky covered us like a blanket and the stars shone so clearly. When I went back inside, I sent my children to bed and then sat down to talk with my mother.

"I need to talk to you about the fog stories," I said. "I don't think you should be telling them to the children."

She laughed at me. "Your grandmother told them to you and your sisters, and her grandmother told them to her. What's wrong with stories?"

"But mother, all of us had nightmares. I don't want my children to be terrified."

"The fog is real, Alina," my mother said, sticking out her chin. "The children need to be warned."

"I can warn them myself," I snapped. "I don't need you scaring them to death."

My mother scowled at me, but I didn't budge. I wasn't going to change my mind.

"Well, I guess you've said all you need to say," she said. She rearranged her shawl around her shoulders and patted her hair. "I won't trouble you anymore."

With that she left in a huff, slamming the door behind her. I didn't let myself care. As long as the fog stories stopped, I was satisfied.

The next few months passed slowly. The winter season was always hard on us, and the children were forced to stay inside while it snowed heavily outside, which they did not enjoy at all. We spent our time telling stories (happy ones) and playing games that we made up in our boredom. But even though we all enjoyed these, we were relieved when the snow began to melt, and warmth, minimal though it was, returned to the air.

The children were in raptures when I finally agreed it was warm enough for them to play outdoors. They squealed in delight as they ran out, shouting and yelling to one another about how great it was that it was spring again.

As I got the children ready for bed that night, Abriel began to tell me of all the fun she had enjoyed that afternoon. She talked incessantly of playing hide and seek with her brothers and sisters, and tagging each other in the field.

"I had so much fun, Mama, and I tagged Bali six times! He's usually too fast for me, but I got him today!"

"Really, darling? That's wonderful." Bali was my eldest son, only twelve. I suspected he had probably let her tag him, and I silently praised him for giving his baby sister that satisfaction.

"I know, Mama, and then the lady by the creek said we should come by again tomorrow and she would give us some treats and teach us new games."

"What lady was that, darling?" I pulled her gown over her head and smoothed her hair.

"I told you, Mama, the lady by the creek. She has long blonde hair and a big white gown. She looks like an angel. Can we play with her tomorrow Mama, please?"

"Perhaps darling, we'll see tomorrow." I tucked her into bed and kissed her forehead. She smiled at me and then turned her head. I blew out the bedroom candle and closed the door.

As I got ready to sleep, I told Colin about Abriel's chattering. Something struck me then concerning the lady she mentioned. Who was she? Why had she not come to the house, as was proper? I told

Colin, but he didn't see anything strange about it. After all, there were other villages nearby, and plenty of younger, unmarried women who loved children. So I let it go and climbed into bed beside him.

Every day for the rest of that week, Abriel came home with stories about Veronica, the lady with the blonde hair. I asked Bali if he had seen this Veronica, but he said that Abriel always played by herself. Sometimes she would talk to herself, and laugh as if someone had told her a joke. But he didn't see anything unusual with it. She was only five, after all. So what if she wanted an imaginary friend? I put Veronica out of my mind.

The next week proved to be the same as the first. "Veronica this" and "Veronica that" was all I could get out of my little Abriel. I must say, I actually felt a touch of jealousy. She was my baby, and imaginary or not, I didn't want her to love anyone more than me.

So the next day I decided to go out with the children and play with her. We ran, laughing across the fields, and danced in a big circle. I grabbed Abriel up in my arms and held her close to me, kissing her cheeks and head.

"Mama, there's Veronica!" she said. She struggled to get out of my arms and ran over to a line of trees. Of course, I didn't see anyone there.

"Abriel, come back, honey. Come play with your brothers and sisters." But she didn't hear me. She didn't even acknowledge that I'd spoken. So I took off toward the line of trees after her.

When I got closer I found her sitting on the other side of a tree, laughing aloud.

"Mama, this is Veronica!" she said.

"Sweetheart, I don't see anyone," I told her, reaching my hand out to her. "Why don't you come with me, we'll go play tag with your brothers and sisters."

"But Mama, I want to stay here with Veronica. She said you can't see her because she doesn't want you to, because you'll make her go away, but you wouldn't do that, would you, Mama?"

"Of course not baby," I told her. "Just tell her you'll see her later and come with me."

"Okay," she grumbled. She hugged Veronica, or the air, since that was all I could see, then she took my hand.

"Ooh, sweetie your hands are freezing," I told her.

"I'm sorry, Mama. Veronica said she's always cold, because she can't come out in the sunlight. She said it would hurt her too bad."

"Well, maybe next time you shouldn't hug her, if she's always cold. You could get sick." She didn't say anything, and I led her away from the trees and back into the open field.

The next day I woke early. I'd had bad dreams about a tall blonde woman in a white gown, and my little Abriel going off into the woods with her. So I got out of bed and made myself something to drink. I usually slept the night through with no dreams that I could remember, but something niggled at my mind, preventing me from sleeping. I finished my drink and then went through my children's rooms to check on them.

Bali and Jeri, my two boys, were sound asleep, and I kissed each on the cheek and left them to their slumber. The next room was the girls' room where Mara, Kisha, and Abriel slept. Mara and Kisha, the elder two, my twins, were each asleep in their bed. I smiled and turned my attention to Abriel's bed. But she wasn't in it.

An electric shock ran through my body when I realised Abriel was gone. I already knew she wasn't in the kitchen, so I ran to my bedroom and woke my husband.

"Colin, wake up, Abriel's gone!" I said. He woke and, as soon as what I said sunk in, he jumped out of bed and began to get dressed. Of course, I was already halfway done with that by the time he began.

I ran to the front door, which stood open wide. My body stood frozen in terror when I looked out into the night. A blanket of fog covered everything outside, all the way to my doorstep, and I couldn't see a thing.

I ran blindly through the fog, searching for anything that I could grab onto to let me know which way I was going.

"Abriel! Where are you?!"

I called her name again and again, but I heard no answer. I walked with my hands out in front of me, hoping to run into anything that could help me. Finally I felt bark under my palms. A tree.

As I clung to it I reached out across the fog, searching for others. I found them and I knew I was either at the small line of trees, or in the forest. I reached out again and ran into something else.

But it wasn't bark. It was soft and slightly spongy. A woman.

She turned to look at me and I knew it was Veronica. She had on a long white gown, and she had blonde hair. Plus, I could faintly see that she was holding something in her arms. A child.

My daughter.

"Give her back to me!" I screamed.

She smiled. "You have four other children," she replied. Her voice was low and husky, causing a shiver up my spine. "Let me keep this one. I lost all of my children. Let me have one of yours and I will bother you no more."

"No! You cannot take my baby!" I cried. I tried to take Abriel out of her arms, but Veronica held her tight and ripped her from my grasp.

"I went into the fog, like you, searching for my lost young one," she told me. "The lady wouldn't give her to me, so I made a deal. She let my young one go home and I became the Lady of the Fog, so that she would be free. My young ones forgot about me. I vowed I would never take another woman's child, and I have kept my promise for over forty years. But I cannot be alone any longer! Let me keep this one child. I will take good care of her."

"I cannot let you take her," I said, reaching for my daughter again, but again she jerked her out of reach.

"When the fog clears I will be gone, and your daughter with me," she said. "So do not try to look for her, because you won't find her. Do not waste your time and bring yourself to grief."

I could see a little better, and I could tell that she had backed away from me, that she was trying to escape with the receding fog.

"Please! I'll do anything! Just do not take her!" I cried in panic. I couldn't leave Abriel with her in the fog, in that miserable world of grey and white.

Veronica eyed me through the blanket of white. "You say you would do anything?" she asked me.

I nodded my head. "Yes."

Veronica smirked and then laughed. She set Abriel down on the ground and rose to her full height to face me. "Take my place," she said. "Become the Lady of the Fog and set me free."

I shuddered, but I saw my little darling lying unconscious on the ground and I couldn't turn back. "I'll do it," I said.

Veronica raised her arms and laughed again. The fog intensified and surrounded me, pressing in on me, smothering me.

I gave myself to it.

The child looked at me blankly.

"Did that really happen, Alina?"

"Yes," I told her, making my voice as soft and smooth as I could, so as to keep her attention. "It really happened, and like Veronica, I have vowed never to take another woman's child. That was sixty years ago."

"Well, what if I kept you company?" she asked me, all innocence, just like my Abriel.

"Oh, that would be wonderful!" I exclaimed. "But we must keep it a secret. Don't tell your family that you've seen me, or that you're talking to me. It must stay just between us."

She nodded. "Okay. I promise."

"Good girl," I said. "Now go on back to your house. I hear your mother calling for you."

She gave me a hug and ran home. I smiled where I sat. For sixty years, I had not taken a child, had not seen my own family. But I was so very lonely.

And I was so tired of being alone.

Mother Mary

A. N. Calaway

I had a cat before I found God.

Truthfully, she was a stray that only returned to me for the promise of milk and a few leftover fish-heads that I stole from the kitchen. I didn't mind. Her pelt was like milk, somehow unsoiled by the filth of my family's decrepit ancestral manor. It was incomprehensible to me then, how my cat, my stray, navigated the filth of the dying gardens and dust of the deserted hallways without the least trace of a blemish upon her innocence. I remember staring into her swirling, faceted orbs of golden yellow and thinking that her eyes must have been a sort of portal into heaven. I often wondered why no one else seemed to notice her beauty, or even her presence. She would hiss and snarl at my father most violently when he entered my room, on the darkest and quietest of nights. I often imagined her little claws tearing into the flesh of his exposed back as he towered over me and bade me be silent. Now, as I wait for a fellow sister to find and escort me to the greatest trial of my faith, I think fondly of my cat. However, I cannot help but fear those feline eyes of celestial allure might be the only glimpse of heaven I will ever see.

The convent in Killone was a difficult life for me, though the abbess could not possibly be found at fault. Abbess Catherine was a kind woman. She never once mentioned the large donation that my mother made to the abbey shortly before my arrival. Despite her compassion, I became her trial. I was young, stubborn, callous and had already given birth to a bastard. My mother had never spoken to me of my son. Abbess Catherine told me that I was not to dwell on my past sins.

My child, my infant boy, was a sin, and no one would even tell me if he was alive when the doctor ripped him from my womb. I highly suspect he was dead at birth. Something in my soul died during that procedure and I think that must have been where his soul would have resided, if he had been born properly.

My first years at the abbey were fraught with disobedience and discontent. I stole bread for a hungry street urchin. I was unmoved during the sermon of the Christ's suffering. I wailed uncontrollably at night for my most grievous sin, the child that would forever be a stranger to my conscious mind, though not to my heart.

Still, Abbess Catherine was ever patient and kind. My bitterness eventually gave way to her gentleness. She gave me a new name. She told me that Mary Magdalene had been tormented by demons because of her immorality and Christ had freed her from perpetual misery. I wished greatly to be freed and so from then on, I became Sister Magdalene. Abbess Catherine beseeched me to take a vow of one year's silence and to keep my vow while serving amongst the unfortunate orphans. It would be the hardest trial she ever asked of me.

But I must remain resolute that only God receive my love and no worldly thing. For only God, my sisters have taught me, is worthy of such a sacred thing.

It is nearly half past nine when the shuffling steps of my fellow sister alert me to her presence. Her habit melts out of the blackness which engulfs the chapel of Portrush. I have stood on these deserted, crumbling steps since my ride by carriage, earlier in the afternoon. She states my name and gives me her own. Sister Esther does not say anything more and I am thankful. She must know of my vows. I am not surprised when she motions for me to mount a buggy drawn by a single chestnut mare. The orphanage depends on the charity of the people of Portrush, but these citizens are no different from the citizens of any other city. They are filled with greed and gluttony, with no room for grace. This is why the orphanage is isolated, to keep the blessed children from the corruption that is so widespread in society.

The ride is long and uncomfortable. I am jarred forwards and back, the stiff-backed seat bruising the flesh of my lower back with each little rut in the winding road. It is nearly unbearable but I do not utter a single cry. My sister notices the unnatural purse of my lips, and the corners of her own lips curve upwards into a sort of sad, sympathetic smile. She is an older woman, silver strings of hair peeking from underneath her veil, with beautiful, dark eyes the colour of flint but not as hard.

"We have almost arrived, Sister Magdalene. Rough as it may be, this is the only safe path through these moors and remember, we are called to suffer in the name of our beloved Christ," she tells me.

I nod and attempt to smile, but I find my teeth are gritted. A white spot emerges from the shadowed horizon and distracts me from my anguish. I lean forward, straining my vision in desperate hope of a reprieve. This singular spot of brightness is joined by many others, though only one white spire towers above the buildings.

My sister notices my interest and answers the questions that have formed in my mind but must not form on my lips. "Yes, the large building is our church. We hold our daily devotional there and it also serves as a schoolhouse for the children. That building to the far right," she says, motioning with her hand, "Yes, that one there. That is our dwelling. We have a kitchen, a room for meals and of course, our own private rooms. They're very small but you'll grow to appreciate the simplicity. The building to the left is the priests' dwelling and in between, yes, those two small buildings are the boys' and girls' dormitories."

Sister Esther tugs on the reins and with a snort, the mare halts. It is a relief for my bruised body to feel the earth under my thin-soled shoes. As I wait for the horse to be unharnessed, a great moaning is carried out the windows from one of the white buildings. Children scream and bawl, and I am almost in hysterics after only a few minutes.

"Don't worry. It's only the children frightened by the dark again. They go through stages every now and then. One of them frightens the others by recounting a bad dream or memory. They'll be fine in a few minutes," my sister tries to assure me.

I want to wrench myself from the comforting hand on my shoulder but I know I cannot. I cannot go and console the children as a mother. I am not a mother. I am a nun. My heart belongs to God.

I am led to the adjacent building but Sister Esther stops, alarmed that the door, splintered and scratched at its base by some sort of animal, is already ajar. She rushes in, her kerosene lamp held aloft. The light flickers for a few moments, but reveals a disastrous scene. Flour, eggs, milk and other assorted supplies are tossed all around the shelves and floor. She bustles about, checking the shelves and pantries and muttering to herself.

"God be merciful! Who would do such a thing? Spoil food and not take a morsel of it? I told Abbess Sara we needed to – Oh, never mind. Come along, Sister Magdalene. No, no, I'll clean it up myself. You need your rest. Come on, this is where you'll stay," she insists.

My cell is not far from the kitchen. As I was told, it is very small, having only a little cot and a single nightstand that is barely large enough to set my Bible upon. I make a sort of awkward bow to express my gratitude to my fellow sister, but she scurries away, seemingly intent on cleaning. I close my door and lie down.

As I open the Holy Scriptures, another chorus of screaming begins. I close the heavy tome and try to sleep.

Time passes and I grow accustomed to St. Andrew's Orphanage for the Misfortuned. I have a strict schedule, but I am grateful for it. I wake early, help prepare breakfast, supervise the children while they eat, and then I attend to the garden while the children go to their lessons. This is my cherished time. There are few nuns here and workloads are heavy. Although I spend hours pulling weeds, watering the soil and gathering the harvest of the day, the garden is quiet. I am under no one's scrutiny. I do not have to turn my eyes downward to respect a sister of higher rank, or grip my rosaries in prayer, or pretend to enjoy the stinging of a thorn in my hand because I suffer with Christ. Here, I pretend that I am not Sister Magdalene. Here, it is safe to be Mary and know that it is enough. I even found a tiny rock that is flat and square. I set it underneath the green canopy of the potato plants. It is a secret headstone for my son, but since I have placed it there, I feel even more ashamed that I have never wept openly for him. I have never expressed the pain of his loss to the world, as a mother should, and I wonder if demons or angels or both will punish me for it.

I must confess, outside my secret paradise, I find the orphanage to be strange. The children, both boys and girls, number hardly a dozen. I have seen the throngs of abandoned children on the streets of Dublin, but these children, here at St. Andrews, possess a different sort of mood. They are the calmest children I've ever encountered. Surely, this serenity would seem an admirable characteristic but it is an eerie calm, as though they are silenced by some fear they cannot speak of. But what horror, I cannot imagine.

This horror is not so dormant during the hours of night. It creeps into the boys' quarters and torments them till they scream and wail and cry. I wake to their hellish moans every night but no one is permitted to enter. Sister Esther continues to assure me it will pass. But I also overhear her mention the fits have never lasted so long before.

Worried, I inspect the exterior of the boys' dormitory. The door and window seem secure. However, on the white paint near the window, there are scratch marks made by what looks like a small animal desperate to break in.

I silently bring my discovery to the attention of a priest, but he is callous in his remarks. Boys must learn not to fear the dark. They must learn not to fear such small creatures. They must mature. They must learn to become adults.

I think it is an abominable practice, but there is nothing I can do. I have vowed silence. I have vowed that only God, the Creator of All, may stir my heart to love.

"They are not simply orphans, Sister Magdalene," Abbess Sara tells me. She has noticed me observing our charges, instead of praying like I ought during evening devotional. She takes me aside and I keep myself at a distance from her. The Abbess smells of dust and that sort of heaviness that hangs about a room with no windows. I do not wish to disturb her by my own smell, which is mixed with the dirt and breath of the moors.

"These children witnessed atrocities before they were brought here. They survived fires, while the rest of their families perished. They are children of prostitutes, who rotted from the inside out, leaving them with nothing but a corpse. They are all of delicate minds, Sister. I think your Abbess was trying to protect you when she suggested you take your vow of silence. It's best if you don't speak with them," she says.

I think she is trying to be kind to me, but I feel a cold chill, as though I've reached down into a bucket of ice and the tingling, stinging sensation has filled my entire body. I imagine myself striking her chubby, red-splotched face, running to the nearest child and falling upon them to coddle and weep and kiss them. This frightens me, this terrible urge to sin. I nod my head obediently and she continues her pacing of the aisles, making sure the children are saying their prayers properly.

I step outside while she is not looking, because my chest is tight and my vision spotted with flecks of black fluff. I do not know where I am going, until I am in the garden and begin to feel safe again. I can breathe here. I sit down underneath an apple tree and close my eyes. The snapping of a twig startles me. I look up and standing before me is an angel. He is a small boy, probably only eight years old. He gazes at me silently and I can tell he is afraid. Like me, he is meant to be in the chapel, clutching rosaries and praying the psalms he was taught. I remember seeing him at meals. He always sits alone, and I never see him speak to anyone. I wonder if, like me, he holds a deep sin in his heart that others shy away from in fear of their own damnation. I smile at him, and the muscles of his pale, smooth face seem to relax. I stare at his halo, the curly, wild locks of golden honey, and I am transfixed.

"Are you sad?" he asks me. His accent is thick. He must have spent his formative years on the streets. I am surprised that he has spoken to me and I long to reply. I must remember my vow; I remind myself. I shake my head but he frowns at me. "You look sad. I'm sad too. My name's Abel," he says.

I pick up an apple that has fallen from the tree and toss it to him. He catches it, a smile finally brightening his features, and he sits next to me. He chomps away at the apple greedily, and I find myself laughing softly to myself. I wish to reach out, caress the golden locks, but I remain still. Such a show of affection would never be allowed. When he finishes, he throws the apple core away and stands up. He stares out of the garden, towards the distant horizon that is already greying with twilight. "My father... he was a bad man too," he says.

I choke, catching the question that was already on my tongue and strangling it until only a whimper of surprise breaks my silence.

The boy looks down at me. His eyes are the same deep, moss green of my father's and I feel cold again. "It's all right. I won't tell them what he did to you. She made me promise not to," he says.

Suddenly, I am standing and although he is tall for his age, I am taller still. He stares up at me with my father's eyes and I can keep my silence no longer.

"Who did?" I whisper. My voice is strange. It sounds hollow, more like the hiss of a deceitful serpent than the voice I remember as being my own.

The boy does not seem to notice. but puts his hands in his trousers, turning his gaze back towards the moors. "My sister. She says you and her were friends, but it was a long time ago. She misses you; I can tell," he answers confidently.

My brow furrows, the muscles of my forehead tensing. I feel my veil tugging painfully at my hair but I ignore it. "Who is your sister? What is her name?" I ask. Again, my voice is more earnest than I intend it to be, desperate.

The boy does not look at me. "You know once someone has your name, they got power over you?" he asks me. He is looking at me again and there is something unbearable about his gaze.

I cannot look at him. I stare at the apple tree, the plump fruit, shiny and red and glistening. "Where is she? Your sister?" I ask.

He nods his head towards the moors.

Shaking my head, I put a hand on his shoulder and turn him towards me. "Your sister can't live out there. It's impossible. The moors are too dangerous. What would she do for food?" I am trying very hard to convince him of what I know to be the truth. This is why the Abbess does not wish for me to talk to these children. They are consumed with delusions and fantasies and nightmares.

The angel's lips stretch back until his teeth are bared at me like a stray animal's might and he does not look so angelic. I let him go, suddenly afraid he might bite at my flesh.

"She's smart; she is! She steals food from the kitchen!" he snarls.

I take a few deep breaths. It does not surprise me that he has heard of the kitchen being broken into. It would be a logical thing to weave into one's fantasy, though he doesn't know that food hasn't been stolen, only spoiled. I sigh, and feel weary, as though speaking with the child has somehow drained me of energy.

"And how then, child, does she navigate the moors at night?" I ask quietly.

To my surprise, the grin graces his features and he is an angel again. He looks as though he carries a wonderful secret and I am the first he trusts enough to bequeath the treasured words to. "She can see in the dark, just like a cat! She's special, my sister." He laughs.

I shake my head. The boy's mind is not ready to accept reality. I understand the safety of his created world and I decide to leave him to it. Perhaps that is best for him, for now.

It is a strange coincidence that he would perceive the nature of my father. I take a certain comfort in this. Perhaps souls wounded in the same manner can somehow recognise one another at that certain level of unconsciousness that children are ever so in tune with, if only for the purpose of gaining comfort and companionship. I smile with him but as my mind hovers over other unanswered questions, the smile fades from my face. I lean down to his level and, as every child does, he knows now that we must speak of a serious, grave subject.

"Do you cry at night with the other boys? What frightens you all so?" I ask. I recognise my voice now. It is soft and tender, a purring sound of affection and gentleness. The boy turns away from me again.

"It ain't me... it's my sister. She's angry, 'cause we can't be together. She says nobody got the right to keep us apart, so she comes up to the windows at night and scratches at them and makes scary sounds. I think it's kinda funny but the other boys are frightened, 'cause she's got silvery hair and yellow eyes. They call her the white lady," he says softly.

I do not know what to say now. His delusion is too broad, too complex and I cannot reason him out of it. I withhold the disappointed sigh. His mind keeps him from the truth of the matter and myself as well. I reach out to pat his back softly, but he flinches as we hear footsteps. Before I can speak, he rushes in the other direction, disappearing in only a second behind the shrubs.

Sister Esther appears as my little angel disappears. Her face is white, the wrinkles of her old face stretched in anger or disgust. I cannot tell. My cheeks prickle with shame.

"I heard voices," she accuses.

I shake my head, but she grasps my hand, dragging me away from my garden and back to the confines of the dusty chapel.

I have been locked in my room for three days and three nights. I have spent much of my time pacing, peeking out of my little window and when there is nothing else to do, I sleep. I am told that I should be praying and meditating, asking for forgiveness, because I forsook my vow of silence. I know Abbess Catherine will be disappointed in me. More so because the child I spoke with was a thief, instead of an angel. He stole away my heart that I kept locked away so carefully for God. He is all I can think of.

Sister Esther checks on me regularly. I muster my courage, knowing that this is the last night I will spend at the orphanage. Tomorrow, I am to be sent back to my abbey in Killone. Then, I do not know what will be decided. I ask her about the child, but I am vague. I do not tell her I spoke with him. I simply ask her of a boy named Abel. She tells me she knows of no such boy and that I should not think of it any longer.

I do not believe her. I spoke with him, didn't I? Do they think they can convince me that I am mad? Their heartlessness is the true madness!

Sister Esther leaves me, nervous and agitated, and so she forgets to lock my door. I lie down on my bed and weep into my pillow until sleep takes me.

A great crash awakens me. Without taking time to think, I light my kerosene lamp and hurry out of my room towards the kitchens. As I round the corner, I can hear scuffling and sniffing, but my light finds nothing but an open door, newly scratched, and a pound of flour that is still drifting in clouds about the room. The children begin to wail and I pause, gazing out into the night.

I have failed as a nun. There is nothing left in life that I have to be anxious of losing. I wonder if even God could strip me of anything that I cared for. I will find Abel, and I will comfort him, as a boy should be comforted by his mother. Striding out into the cold air, I cross the little quadrant and hurry up the steps to the boys' quarters.

As I open the door, the wailing increases greatly. My kerosene lamp flutters and I see the familiar faces of seven boys. Abel is not among them.

"Where is Abel? Tell me where Abel is!" I say. I am frightened that he might be out on the moors, and I cannot tolerate their weeping. They are all piled in a corner, holding each other and gazing at me with fearful, tearstained eyes. They are cringing away from me.

"We already told you! We don't know where he is!" one of the boys screams.

I advance upon them and they scream louder. Their nonsense is wearying. My patience is spent and I am more and more frightened for Abel's sake.

"Tell me where Abel is!" I demand.

"Please don't hurt us, White Lady!" another boy yelps. I pause, gazing down at my habit. It is covered in flour. I am beginning to lose hope that I will ever find my angel. I cross the room, ignoring the crescendo of wailing and look outside. I see a glimpse of golden hair flash below it.

"Abel!" I call.

The boys continue to wail, as if the name itself frightens them. I no longer care about their misery. I know that my little angel is outside, in danger of the moors' treacherous cliffs and I must be his salvation. If not I, then who?

The moon is full. I leave my lamp, knowing that the cold winds will soon extinguish it and it is too cumbersome for me to carry in pursuit. I can see the golden-haired child running ahead of me. He is led by another child who I have not seen before. This child is taller, cloaked in white and with hair that is as milk, which streams out behind her as she bounds gracefully over the moors. I call for them to stop. A ravine could be hidden over the next hill and our pace is too quick to correct our direction in time to keep us all from tumbling to our deaths.

Finally, when I feel my lungs will collapse, I see the children slow and stop. Abel stares ahead and does not heed my breathless requests. He acts as though he cannot hear me any longer. But the girl turns and looks at me. The remainder of what little oxygen was left to me is stolen away. Unearthly orbs of celestial yellow glow brightly and I think I see heaven in them. Before I can speak, the young girl with milky, white hair and glittering yellow eyes takes a knife from her white robe and draws the blade across Abel's throat. I cannot scream, and Abel is motionless, silent before the slaughter. I am frozen, and I watch as she drops the knife, pushing Abel forward into the blackness. The night swallows him, as if the gates of hell have opened to steal the last bit of purity from the world.

I crawl forwards, weeping and wailing, and tearing my habit and veil until they are shreds. My hair, once resembling Abel's golden curls, is now stained dark with the moss and peat of the moors. As I reach the precipice, I look down to see his crumpled corpse, broken and crushed by the cruel rocks of the ravine's pit.

Pain shoots like needles driven into my hands as I steady myself on my knees, to bend further over the pit. There seem to be little flecks of white underneath my bloodied fingernails but any thought for myself is swept away by the moor's merciless winds and the crushing despair at my beautiful, fallen angel. The apparition that murdered my little angel, who sacrificed Abel to a God that I can no longer believe in – she is gone.

I gaze down again, leaning forwards but Abel's body is gone. I peer into the blackness with a vision strained by shadows and tears. He must be down in the pit! I know I cannot leave him here, before a heartless God who did not care about me or him. I look back towards the orphanage. The buildings look like nothing more than whitewashed tombs, full of despair and hopelessness and decay.

I look back into the pit. A white glow has risen and I know, somewhere behind this ethereal light, Abel is waiting for me. The white blaze surrounds me and fills me with warmth. I feel strength for the first time, and the yellow and gold in my eyes reflect the light before me. I refuse to abide by the law of false love any longer. I will go down to my Abel, my sweet angel. Together, we will exist in our loving blasphemy, until God himself crumbles into faded memory. I

A.N. Calaway

begin to climb carefully towards his final resting place, but I have
forgotten my stained hands are freshly wet with our blood.

Appendix 1
Lex Visionaria

Jamie Spracklen

I am a bad general; in that I lose more battles than I win. But it is in our defeats, as well as our small gains against the mediocrity of life, that the divine map of our existence is inscribed for what passes as eternity. And it is in this stark fact, that the very genesis of *Visionary Tongue* Magazine can be found.

Let me, dear reader, try to explain.

For me, writing can, and indeed *should*, be the great *confession* of our hopes, desires, successes and lamentations of that terrible drug we must explore. But the act of writing, of creating, has within its very bones a powerful and eternal sin, the sin of our pride. For we attempt to goad our words into performing slights of hand for us – we force our imagination into the bodies of murderers, poets, the sacred and the reviled. And we do all this for our own amusement and yours, and because, as writers, we can. Or at least we think we can.

So, once you set yourself to write, to draw, to compose, there is no turning from the fold. From the first time we dared trust in ourselves that *we could, we will*, set *our* seal to this virgin paper or a blinking screen, with only our *will* and *courage* to sustain us, we embark on a lonely voyage, and one from which we may not make landfall.

But, we are *not* alone. There are others groping in the dark for those delightful symbols of success, be that publication, or that life-long moment when you get a paragraph just right. And that is where VT struck a bright match, and cast the shadows into deeper corners, lighting those seafarers to shore, safely.

As you would have read in the pages of this anthology, VT sprang, kicking into the world in the mid-1990s from the beatifically simple idea of writers *helping* other writers. Storm had gathered a like-minded collection of altruistic writers and authors together with the view of supporting neonate creative types who were also interested in dark fantasy fiction.

And that is where, gentle reader, I appeared on that plutonian shore – a naïve writer with a small store of adolescent verse and the beginnings of an idea for a short story. I had followed Storm's work closely, and we shared connections with our interests in the Gothic subculture. Early fan publications, which were run by helpful and supportive people, had cheerfully provided access to what was for me, the first *professional author* (insert hushed reverential whisper here, reader) I had known.

For just because you write, you have no idea if your literary squibs are *any good*, and it's not always easy to receive free, impartial advice. Mum doesn't count, I'm afraid!

So when Storm put out the call for interested, beginning writers to contribute to her own small press magazine, I was naturally both excited and full of trepidation to chance sending an ink-stained missive. At the time, I was studying, somewhat riotously, Archaeology in darkest West Wales, but had a small body of grim work, which would later form the core of my first poetry collection, one of which was the poem, *Penetration*.

And so, from this dark crossing of literary waters, far from being shipwrecked, I had found a home. You can imagine my delight when my poem was selected to appear in the second issue of VT. For a brief time, the mediocrity of life had been challenged, and defeated. And what great reads those early issues were – slim volumes as they were of around 45 pages, A5, with card-stock coloured covers, but brimming with delightfully sensuous artwork by Ruby, and established writers as editorial consultants such as Graham Joyce, Brian Stableford and Freda Warrington, and of course, Storm. And there was little old me, in the same publication!

And so, VT flourished part of, but divinely *apart* from that wonderful heterogeneous mix of small press magazines that existed in those days, which struggling writers such as myself threw ourselves into, and became part of.

For VT was special in many ways – here was a publication that wanted to help, and provided, essentially for free, access to successful writers. All you needed to do was read, digest, listen and learn – call it the *Lex*

Visionaria if you will, the Law of *Visionary Tongue*. And I was privileged to go through this process when the magazine provided my first literary 'break', the publication of my first short story, *Harry's Tape* in Issue 6 (which, should you wish to test your patience my dear reader, you can read in this anthology under the revised title of *Ptolemy's Recording*).

I kept tabs on VT from then on, and although the cruel machinations of study and later work allowed me little time to send submissions, the magazine grew, developed and continued to inspire me with the wealth of talent it contained. VT was also forward thinking, going completely online for several issues, during a time when most small press magazines were print only.

And so, patient reader, this is where I enter again as one of the *dramatis personae*, if you will, in this delightfully dark fairytale of literary success. Storm's writing commitments had continued to grow, so she kindly asked if I would become the editor of VT, which I was honoured to accept from issue seventeen.

Shortly afterwards, while attending a convention organised by Storm, I met for the first time my dear friend Donna Bond. Donna, being a truly gifted writer and editor, was very quickly persuaded by me to serve as co-editor of VT, and the rest, as they say, is our little piece of VT history.

Drink deep of the stories and poems from the latter years of the magazine, and you too will savour just some of dark blooms we saw grow amongst the pages of this venerable magazine, which we hawked at conventions and poetry events when time and life allowed. A small addition to the format was the creation of the very modest VT Press, which provided an outlet for new writers to produce their first collection of stories/poetry/artwork by being sponsored and promoted by VT.

I would ask that if you would look for the heart of VT, then read the words it helped to nurture, and in that small silence that follows a truly good read, smile. For we owe it to ourselves to keep faith in literature, to look into the dark and *refuse* to be told that somebody new to writing cannot spark fire with their very first match, and in doing so, light their way, safely to shore.

Appendix 2
The Female Fool

Donna Scott

Many years ago, I wrote an editorial for *Visionary Tongue* on daring to read my writing out before a crowd of strangers. It was still quite new to me then, all my performing malarkey, but as the magazine was a sort stepping stone for fledgling writers, I thought it might be useful to recount my own experiences of taking the plunge into these dark, unfathomable waters. After all, it's a brave thing to share your writing with the world in any context, and I knew there might be readers thinking, *could I? Should I?* – just about submitting their story to a magazine, never mind speaking their words before a crowd of people they don't know.

Anyway, this is how it was for me. First I would read pieces of flash fiction before friends and strangers at Wolverhampton's City Voices at The Clarendon Hotel. Before long, it was poetry, shouted to disinterested shoppers at a spoken word event in The Mander Centre, a toughening experience that prepared me for the soar and swoop of adrenalin that you encounter at a poetry slam.

However, comedy was the challenge I had skirted round. I'd avoided it, resigned myself to just being a 'fan', ever since my student days when I had dared mention my hopes of being a stand-up one day to friends on the top deck of a Potteries Meridien Transport bus, looping its way back from Hanley to Keele University campus. "Don't do it," my friends urged, eyes wide with horror. "They'll eat you alive!"

They will?

"You're too, erm… nice."

Curses! Just too *nice* for comedy! In truth, it was what I wanted to hear. I mean the same friends would find house sharing with me an absolute nightmare, when I moaned at them for doing normal student things, like pissing in the kitchen sink, or walking round bottomless, but them telling me I was "too nice" was an affirmation of character – and I needed that after some other people at uni had told me that they thought I had a really screechy voice, only exacerbated by my Black Country accent, and would avoid being in the same place as me because of it. In fact, I decided to wait another sixteen years to make sure I was a miserable nearly middle-aged bat, who could never be accused of being too nice by anyone, before I even attempted doing a stand-up routine, which I did for the first time in Kettering eight years ago, shaking with nerves. The tiny audience was softly blurred by the couple of pints of cider I had most unwisely downed before going on stage. I ended up doing fourteen minutes instead of ten, but the audience didn't eat me alive at all. In fact, they rather liked me. I celebrated with more cider and, on the way home, I ate some cheesy chips. *Alive?* Well, *I* was.

I knew I was hardly a pioneer in my field. I'd been to gigs before to see Victoria Wood, Jo Enright and Josie Long, so I knew there were loads of female comedians out there – a lot fewer than there were male comedians, it seemed, at least when it came to line-ups. I knew how French and Saunders had been among the select few chosen acts at the inception of the Comedy Store, and how Jo Brand had battled her first hecklers in the late 80s. Jenny Eclair had been the first woman to win the coveted Edinburgh Comedy Award in 1995 – and I was still a student then. These women were the vanguard, or so I thought. Behind them we can all proceed to victory!

I do, on occasion, encounter the odd audience member who is utterly incredulous that a woman is allowed to appear before them and speak in any situation whatsoever, let alone on a stage for the purpose of performing a comedy routine. (I don't say telling jokes. I know quite a few joke-based comics, but there are dozens of ways of finding your route through this craft, and mine is the sort rarely to be found in a cracker.) Thankfully, this is a rare occurrence. However, most people assume that women never tried being comedians before the 1980s. And most people would be wrong. Look a little more deeply at history and you will find it is full of women who are sharp-tongued, silly, childish, witty… proper funny women, who have in some form or other used humour to make a living. And yet, so often they are brushed over, or re-touched, to make their historical worth about something else entirely. Here I hope to shed a little spotlight on some of those funny women who inspire me.

Jane the Fool and Lucretia the Tumbler (1540s)

Given that Jane was one of the most celebrated jesters of the Tudor age, the details of her origins and her act remain fairly obscure, where fuller records seem to be kept of other jesters. She went by many stage epithets: Jane Foole, The Queen's Fool and possibly Beden the Jester, which was likely her original surname. Having been around in Catherine Parr's time in King Henry VIII's court, she was a definite favourite of Queen Mary I, who lavished dresses, caps and shoes on her.

Queen Mary I loved Jane so much, that the most famous jester of her father's reign, Will Somers, was reduced to being Jane's sidekick in her court. There are many who think that Jane and Will married, but there is no clear evidence of this. It is also believed that Jane may have had a learning disability. Nonetheless, it is clear she had a definite talent for humour to have maintained her place for so long.

Lucretia, or Lucrece the Tumbler, was a trained professional jester who was also employed by Queen Mary I for her court. She was given many identical outfits to Jane, and it is also thought that she may have been her carer, as well as a fellow amuser of Her Majesty. They were good friends nonetheless.

Both these women, despite the luxurious clothes they were gifted, would have been made to look the part of the fool by having their heads completely shaved, just as male jesters would. Now much as I admire these pioneers of British comedy, and love a bit of dress-up, my tonsurephobia would always prevent me from emulating this aspect of their act. Nobody's fool, me – especially not a bald one.

Nell Gwyn (1660s)

Pretty, witty Nell is the mostly kindly way in which historians tend to remember Eleanor Gwyn. Nell, selling oranges in the theatre, catching the eye of the King. Nell, the actress. Nell the harlot, who nicknamed her regal lover "Charles the Third", because she had been the lover of another two men named Charles before. Was this all there was to this infamous mistress?

The popular image of Naughty Nell, proffering an orange to the King, is, however, anachronistic. Orange-selling was her first job in the theatre at the age of fourteen, shortly before she tried her hand at acting. Sadly, it is more than likely that her boss, Orange Moll, also pimped out Nell and her sister Rose at this time, but they were poor, desperate children, and their own mother was an alcoholic brothel-keeper, so even this horror may not have been a new experience to them. Restoration theatre was a tough environment to make one's way in, and competitive in more ways than one, but here Gwyn spotted an opportunity to raise herself in the world, and she had the brains and ambition to go for it.

Gwyn studied at a school for young actors set up by Thomas Killigrew, but she may not have been the most literate of readers and, struggling with the high turnover of scripts, she fared better in humorous parts than serious roles, where her sharp wit could happily fill in where her recall failed. She initially gained popularity with a character act on the stage called William Nell, for which she dressed as a bearded man and told funny stories on stage. But it was in Restoration comedy plays that she truly made her name.

During the Great Plague, Nell joined the company as an official servant of the King to play a series of private comedy productions away from London. Following one performance, the diarist Samuel Pepys said, "[…] so great performance of a comical part was never, I believe, in the world before". She had more than proved her funny bones.

Were there lingering looks from the stage to where the King was watching? Alas, no such romance for Nell. It was a managed arrangement between George Villiers, 2nd Duke of Buckingham and herself, just because there was an available vacancy for a new royal mistress. But at least there was some comedy, it is rumoured, when she got her mate Aphra Behn to lace a rival's food with laxatives shortly before she was due in the king's bedchamber. Apparently, she was also quite the prankster.

Dame Ellen Terry (1850s, and onwards)

Alice Terry, better known by her middle name of Ellen, was one of those actresses you might never had heard of, but she seems to turn up everywhere in literature. She's mentioned in Bram Stoker's *Dracula*. She's there in the poetry of Oscar Wilde. She's the passionate correspondent of Sir George Bernard Shaw (who underlines every other word). She's the pretty ginger-haired girl sniffing scentless camellias in George

Frederick Watts' portrait *Choosing*. She ghosts the characters of Mina Harker, Sybil Vane and, to some extent, Alice in Wonderland. Virginia Woolf wrote a play about her... and she was the greatest Shakespearian actress of her age (making her *one* Nell who could play the serious parts). Plus, she was a brilliant burlesque performer.

Now, get your minds out of the gutter. "Burlesque" simply means a performance that is light-hearted or humorous in design, often in parody of more serious pieces, and may include sketches, dancing, singing, or a bit of everything. It's the heart-root of the variety show, the cabaret, musical comedy, and yes – those naughty nude-y ladies who jiggle their bits behind giant ostrich-feather fans, the addition of whom to American playbills at the end of the 19th Century became the focus of burlesque shows over there, and on both sides of the pond in the revival of the genre a hundred years later, (not forgetting the thirty-or-so-year-reign of the Windmill Theatre in London in between, with its infamous *tableaux vivants*).

I get annoyed when I hear of burlesque shows that don't have this aspect of fun and variety at their centre, featuring stripper after morose stripper, introduced by a leery male comedian. The best shows I have seen have included music, magic, comedy, poetry, magic and drama, as well as dances of all sorts, with diversity a consideration among all the performers. My favourite stripping act, Khandie Kisses, is also a great MC, foregrounded in stand-up, and her dances are full of humour, her "Gorilla" routine being her most well-known. If baring flesh is at all empowering for women, then let us own the humour of that flesh, male gazers!

If versatility is the mark of a great performer, then Dame Ellen Terry was surely that. As she became renowned for her portrayals of the fearsome Lady Macbeth, or sweet Margaret in *Faust*, or quick-witted Portia in *The Merchant of Venice*, she never forgot her childlike delight at her earlier forays into comedy. After the performance of many a serious play at the Lyceum, her stage partner, Henry Irving, would entertain VIPs in what they called "The Beefsteak Club" after the male-only dining society that had once been housed at the theatre. You will scarce find a writer do anything but namecheck the various worthy men whom Irving invited to dine, (but I know Ellen ate there, and Sarah Bernhardt too). Ellen, however, wrote a lot of things down herself, including the little burlesque skits and jokes she performed alongside her good friend, Lillie

Langtry there. If it were not for the persistence of Terry's fans, this would remain a male-only space in history. So many people in her life tried to tell her off for wearing funny clothes, or sliding down the bannisters on the way to meetings she knew would be wearisome. She wasn't all serious and gothic. Not all the time, anyway.

Dolly Allen (1960s -1980s)

At last in my brief list, a proper stand-up! A professional circuit comedian. Dolly was a contemporary of the likes of Bernard Manning, who may not have achieved anything like his level of fame despite her local popularity, but you can still laugh at her immensely funny routines, if you can understand the accent. His jokes? Not so much...

With her trademark straw hat with a turkey feather stuck in it, this little old woman from Wordsley in the Black Country would come on stage saying, "Hello my luvvers!" And then would come monologue-type stories, with joke after joke loaded with her deadpan wit.

Dolly actually started her time as a comedian even later in life than I did, at the age of forty, when she began performing in church halls. She'd been making her work colleagues laugh for years before then, though.

In 1975, she was invited to join the regular touring show A Black Country Night Out, featuring other regular guests like Aynuk & Ayli, Tommy Mundon, and Harry Harrison. They not only entertained the local crowds, but travelled as far as Canada and visited ex-pats in Spain. Dolly was so sought after, she even got to make guest appearances in the soap *Crossroads* in the Eighties.

She carried on performing until her death in 1990 at the age of 84. If you are interested in finding out what her act was like, there are audio recordings out there, and occasionally tribute acts in the Black Country put on live shows in the style of Dolly.

As I am about to take part in the Old Comedian competition for the third time (you have to be thirty-five to qualify, but good news – you *stay* qualified!), I remain inspired by the likes of Dolly Allen, who never let age be a deterrent. Funny's funny and that's all that matters. And Mistress Nell may have been a right cow, with a rude reputation; Lucretia and Jane, mainly remembered for what they looked like; Ellen Terry, somewhat written out of the history of the burlesque nights she helped to organise. But I certainly don't worry these days about being too nice, too old, too absurd or too anything. It's my stage, and I'm going through it however I like.

And I think, too, about some of the people whose work I first encountered in these pages – some of their earliest published fiction in some cases – and how they are now inspiring other writers in their turn. This includes people who are now among the best known speculative writers in the UK, such as Justina Robson and Jaine Fenn. I am blessed that I got to work with, and will always, *always* remain inspired by, my awesome friends: the inimitable poet, Jamie Spracklen, and Powder Monki Sarah. And forever grateful to Storm, who started all this, and who found me those two. May we all keep on dreaming and doing.

About the Contributors

Storm Constantine is the creator of the *Wraeththu Mythos*, the first trilogy of which was published in the 1980s. Her other novels include *Burying the Shadow* and *Hermetech*. Storm is the founder of Immanion Press, created initially in 2003 to publish her out-of-print back catalogue, but which evolved into the thriving venture it is today. She has written over thirty books, including full length genre-crossing novels, novellas, short story collections and non-fiction titles. She is currently working on two non-fiction titles, several collections of stories, and a new novel. She can be found at stormconstantine.co.uk and immanion-press.com

Chris Amies was born in South London. He is a Languages graduate and taught English as a Foreign Language in Greece before working for the British Civil Service, which he left in 2010. His novel *Dead Ground* was reissued in 2013 by Clarion and his non-fiction *Images of England: Hammersmith and Fulham Pubs* appeared in 2004. A novel in progress *Walking on the Bones* deals with weird happenings in the inner London district of Hammersmith. In recent years he has taken up painting, mostly pictures of significant places near his home. chrisamies.com

Tanya Brown has been reading, writing and thinking about fiction since she was at primary school. Her short stories have appeared in *Visionary Tongue*, *Strange Attractor*, *Inception* and *Matrix*. She's served as a judge for the Arthur C Clarke Award, and was a Reviews editor for Vector, the critical journal of the BSFA. Find her book reviews at tamaranth.blogspot.co.uk. She lives in Greenwich, London, with a cat, some books and a well-stocked Kindle. Some day she intends to polish and publish at least one of the novels languishing in her virtual desk drawer.

Alexandra N. Calaway was born somewhere in the Deep South, the only day it snowed that winter in 1989. She graduated from the University of Central Arkansas with a Bachelor's Degree in Creative Writing. She lives in Austin, Texas, where she works very happily in a library. She gratefully cares for and considers herself property of two exceptional cats; one of whom is very affectionate. The other is a calico. Alexandra can be found hiking in the early dawn hours reserved mostly for insomniacs, turning in overdue library books at her own library, reading copious amounts of fantasy, drinking writerly amounts of coffee and stopping at street corners to bid hello to a passing cat. Blog:calawaycat.tumblr.com

Louise Coquio is a sometime writer, free-lance editor and world-class procrastinator. She is currently a post-graduate studying Creative Writing and specialises in Gothic fiction. Having worked in assorted jobs, she returned to education full-time in her late thirties, after which she qualified as a teacher and taught Creative Writing at Stafford college. Now working in student support while she completes her studies, she has at last achieved her long-cherished dream of being paid to attend lectures. When not working on a Gothic novel with a mind of its own, and two ghost-filled children's books, she can be found attending to the every whim of her cats, watching deeply uncool teen movies and cooking obsessively. She can be found on Twitter at @Louisecoquio

William Eve was one of the original contributors to *Visionary Tongue*. While we've been unable to trace him to update his biography, the information we have on file for him tells us he lived in Wales, with his wife and a feline companion. He was a graduate in Classical Studies and Ancient History and completed an MA in Mythology and Ancient Philosophy. He contributed to various pagan magazines in addition to his fiction for *Visionary Tongue*.

Jaine Fenn's short fiction has appeared in various publications over the last fifteen years, including *On Spec* and *Alfred Hitchcock's Mystery Magazine*. A recent short story published by Newcon Press, *Liberty Bird*, was shortlisted for the 2016 BSFA Short Story Award. Her *Hidden Empire* series of far future space opera novels is published by Gollancz. *What You Came For* is a rare foray into darker realms, and was inspired by a derelict house on the other side of the world, though not by real events. At least, not as far as anyone knows.... www.jainefenn.com

J.H. Fleming started her first novel in the 9th grade. It sparked something that has resulted in numerous short stories and 8 novels so far. She received a Bachelor's Degree in Creative Writing from the University of Central Arkansas, and hopes to try for a Master's at some point. She owns roughly 1,200 books and spends her free time befriending dragons, fighting goblins, and learning the craft of the bards. J.H. lives in Northwest Arkansas with three companions: a giant teddy bear, a miniature Cerberus, and a water dragon. www.someplacetobeflying.com

Ray Girvan was born in Portsmouth, but relocated to the Midlands in the 80s. Although he graduated from Selwyn College, Cambridge with an MA in Natural Sciences, his chief interest was in writing and computers, and he happily combined the two (as well as writing erotic fiction as Thomas Gomez, for Olympia press). His stories include *Mad Love* and *Lord of the Files*, and several Sherlock Holmes parodies. In 2012, he wrote a biography of Maxwell Gray, a little-known Edwardian author from the Isle of Wight, published by Wren Publications. Ray had a remarkable sense of humour and produced many fun pieces. He was diagnosed with cancer in 2012 and died in June 2015 at the age of fifty-six.

Jason Gould was born in Hull in 1971. He is the author of numerous short stories, which have appeared in a variety of anthologies and magazines. His short crime story, *Not the '60s Anymore*, won joint first prize in the *Dead Pretty City* crime writing competition in 2017. Other stories have been published in magazines and anthologies including *Terror Tales of Yorkshire* (Gray Friar Press), *Structo*, *Beneath the Ground* (Alchemy Press), *Neon Lit: The Time Out Book of New Writing Vol 1*, *Crimewave*, *The Third Alternative* and *Black Static*. He lives in Hull, where he is in the final year of a degree in Creative Writing. www.facebook.com/jasongoulduk

Dave Graham is an occasional writer, photographer, coffee-lover, cyclist, and stationery geek. Brought up on a diet of Pratchett, Gaiman and Banks, he's been writing stories for a dozen years or more. 'Chess' was his first published story. http://espressococo.com

Chris Green attended Storm's creative writing workshops at Stafford College in the 1990s, producing both poetry and short stories. After the workshop folded, we learned some time later that Chris had died, when still very young but, unfortunately, we've been unable to trace his relatives and are unable to provide any more information about him.

Suzanne Gyseman works as an artist and illustrator, creating images inspired by myth, folklore and dreams. Graduating with a BSc in Botany she has worked in a variety of jobs including nature conservation, botanist, mother, and church warden. She writes stories and articles in her free time. Her paintings are included in private collections worldwide and her work has been published as book covers, illustrations, calendars, designs for cross stitch and needlepoint, greetings cards and prints. Her writing has appeared in *West Coast Magazine*, *Visionary Tongue* and *Faerie Magazine*. She lives on the outskirts of a tiny seaside village in Wales with her elderly black cat. www.suzannegyseman.co.uk

Lauren Halkon contributed a few stories to *Visionary Tongue*. She published several novels, including *Night Seekers*, and a short story collection, *Chrysalis*. The information we have on file for her says that her main love was fantasy, inspired by her pagan beliefs. There is no information on the internet about her later than around 2005, but at that time it seems she was mostly working as an artist and photographer.

Colin James is another of our enigmas. He contributed poems to the magazine when Jamie was editing it, but no contact details remain. There are a couple of poets with this name mentioned online, but no email addresses or web sites. Get in touch if you read this, Colin!

Lachesis January, another of our mysterious, untraceable writers, contributed several stories to *Visionary Tongue* over its various incarnations. The only information we have on file for this author is that she lived in London with a company of Gothic-types! The last we heard of her she was about to collaborate on a cyber-novel.

Janine Jones contributed the story *Féa* to one of the issues of *Visionary Tongue* that only appeared online. As the pages were all lost for this site, and we've been unable to trace Janine via the internet, we regret we can't offer any information about this author, other than her strange and bewitching story in this collection.

Sian Kingston attended Storm's writing workshops at Stafford College for a number of years, which helped her find her writer's 'voice'. She learned that what really drives a story is the choices people make, and the consequences of those choices. In the late 1990s she had a few short stories published by White Wolf in America. She now uses her storytelling skills in photography. Her images have been published in a number of magazines, and exhibited internationally. As a portrait photographer, she considers she is a privileged narrator of someone's life, or the tableau they create together. She is captivated by each chapter she glimpses through her lens. And wherever she goes, there is always someone to meet who she just knows has a special tale to tell.

Dylan Kinnett is a writer, critic, and publisher. He has written a non-linear, web-based novella, a stage play about a street preacher and another about astronauts. He is the Founding Editor of *Infinity's Kitchen*, a literary journal. He is also a member of the Second Land audio-visual collective, where he performs improvisational spoken word to experimental musical accompaniment. He has work published with or performed by Industry Night, Otoliths, the Annex Theater, the University of Baltimore, and others. Dylan works as a web developer for the Walters Art Museum in Baltimore, Maryland and holds a BA in Writing from Maryville College in Tennessee. http://nocategories.net

Tim Lebbon is a New York Times-bestselling writer from South Wales. He's had over thirty novels published to date, as well as hundreds of novellas and short stories. His latest novel is the supernatural thriller *Relics*, and other recent releases include *The Silence*, *The Family Man*, and *The Rage War* trilogy. He has won four British Fantasy Awards, a Bram Stoker Award, and a Scribe Award, and has been a finalist for World Fantasy, International Horror Guild and Shirley Jackson Awards. The movie of his story 'Pay the Ghost', starring Nicolas Cage, was released Hallowe'en 2015, and several other novels and screenplays are in development. www.timlebbon.net

Austin McCarron is another missing poet. His work is online, but we couldn't find any contact details. Austin contributed poems to the magazine when Jamie was the editor. If you read this, Austin, get in touch!

Fiona McGavin is the author of *The Dream and a Lie* trilogy published by Immanion Press and had several short stories published in *Visionary Tongue* magazine. She is originally from the Scottish Highlands but now lives in Buckinghamshire. She has been making up stories and writing from a very young age, and has always been interested in all things strange and spooky. She is currently working on several half-written novels and hopes one day to actually complete one of them.

Brian Maycock was a regular contributor to *Visionary Tongue* throughout its history, but again we are rather short of information about him since then and have been unable to trace him. He began writing in 1993 and was published in several small press magazines, including *Bats and Red Velvet*. The last we heard of him he was working on a novel.

Lisa Pallin never provided us with a great deal of biographical information, other than she lived in Staffordshire with her tree surgeon husband, Andy, and several cats. We've been unable to trace her to find out what she's writing now. She contributed several stories and poems to *Visionary Tongue*.

Katherine Roberts won the Banford Boase Award for her debut novel *Song Quest*, which led to a decade of writing fantasy and historical fiction with a focus on legend and myth for young readers. More recently, she has indie-published some of her historical fantasy with a touch of romance for older readers under the name Katherine A. Roberts. Before becoming self-employed as an author, she trained as a mathematician at Bath University, had a short-lived career as a computer programmer, and then worked with racehorses for many years, while writing short stories for magazines such as *Visionary Tongue*. She lives in the west country with a pink-eared white cat, which is obviously a witch's cat in disguise. www.katherineroberts.co.uk

Justina Robson was born in Leeds, and studied philosophy and linguistics at the University of York. She worked in a variety of jobs – including secretary, technical writer, and fitness instructor – until becoming a full-time writer. She was first published in 1994 in the British small press magazine *The Third Alternative*. Her debut novel *Silver Screen* was shortlisted for both the Arthur C Clarke Award and the BSFA Award in 2000. Justina has written twelve novels and one short story collection. Her work has been noted for its sharply-drawn characters, and an intelligent and deeply thought-out approach to the tropes of the genre. She has been described as 'one of the very best of the new British hard SF writers'.

Donna Scott is Chair of the British Science Fiction Association, a member of Northampton Science Fiction Writers Group and Northampton Arts Lab, which has produced various events, publications and media productions. As an editor, she has previously worked for Immanion Press, Angry Robot, Games Workshop and most recently worked on Alan Moore's Jerusalem. Her current project is the Best of British Science Fiction 2016 anthology for Newcon Press. She was the first ever official Bard of Northampton and has performed comedy and poetry all over the UK. She recently performed her first solo show *The Pleasant Revolt* about the history of social justice in Leicester's beautiful Tudor Guildhall.

Jamie Spracklen, born in 1973, began to write poetry and dark fantasy fiction in the early 1990s and has since been published in many anthologies and magazines worldwide. In addition to his regular writing, Jamie has been editor of two small press magazines, *Monas Hieroglyphica* and *Visionary Tongue Magazine* and his first collection of verse *Burying October* was introduced by Storm Constantine. Jamie's association with *Visionary Tongue* goes back to the earliest issues, with an early poem appearing in the second issue. *Ptolemy's Recording* (originally entitled Harry's Tape) was Jamie's first published short story. Currently working on his next collection of verse, *Embracing Medusa*, outside of his writing and editorial work, Jamie is a Teacher of Archaeology.

Isabel Taylor was a young student, who had dreams of starting a writing career, when she was originally published in *Visionary Tongue*. However, she says that was not to be and the two stories she had published by VT (the other story published was 'Mirage' in Issue 7) were the pinnacle of that career. Any writing she does now is of the non-fiction work-related kind. She now works in Higher Education. When not working, she still likes creative pursuits, though nowadays this tends to be mostly sewing dresses and learning to knit. She lives in Newcastle with no husband/wife, kids or cats and that's how she likes it.

Douglas Thompson's short stories and poems have appeared in a wide range of magazines and anthologies, including *Ambit*. His first book, *Ultrameta*, was published by Eibonvale Press in August 2009, and included the story 'Casamundi', originally published in *Visionary Tongue*. He has produced 8 novels and short story collections: including *Sylvow* (Eibonvale Press, 2010); *Apoidea* (The Exaggerated Press, 2011); *Mechagnosis* (Dog Horn Publishing, 2012); *Entanglement* (Elsewhen Press, 2012); and *The Sleep Corporation* (The Exaggerated Press, 2015). His first poetry collection will be published by Red Squirrel in early 2018. https://douglasthompson.wordpress.com/

Ian Whates is a British speculative fiction author and editor. In 2006, he launched the independent publisher NewCon Press by accident. Some seventy of his short stories have appeared in a variety of venues, resulting in three collections in English: *The Gift of Joy* (2009), *Growing Pains* (2013) and *Dark Travellings* (2016) and one in Spanish: *Torres de Babel* (2017). His work has twice been shortlisted for a British Science Fiction Award and once for a Bram Stoker Award. He has written seven novels, most recently the space opera romps *Pelquin's Comet* (2015) and its sequel *The Ion Raider* (2017) and co-written two more. He lives with his partner Helen in Cambridgeshire.

Paul Whyte is another poet who contributed to the magazine while Jamie was editor. Again, we've been unable to trace him, so please get in touch, Paul, if you read this.

Liz Williams is a science fiction and fantasy writer living in Glastonbury, England. She has been published by Bantam Spectra (US) and Tor Macmillan (UK), also Night Shade Press and appears regularly in Asimov's and other magazines. She is involved in the Milford SF Writers' Workshop, and also teaches creative writing. Her novels include *The Ghost Sister*, (Bantam Spectra), *Winterstrike* (Tor Macmillan) and *The Iron Khan* (Morrigan Press). She has also had three short story collections published through Night Shade Press and NewCon Press. Her novel *Banner of Souls* been nominated for the Philip K Dick Memorial Award.

Simon Williams is the author of the *Aona* dark fantasy series, of which five books have been published so far – *Oblivion's Forge*, *Secret Roads*, *The Endless Shore*, *The Spiral Heart* and *Salvation's Door*. He has also written a science fiction/fantasy/supernatural book, *Summer's Dark Waters* aimed at younger readers. He cites his influences as Alan Garner, Clive Barker, Cecilia Dart-Thornton, Tad Williams, C.J Cherryh and Ian Irvine. He is currently working on a new standalone novel separate to the *Aona* series. www.simonwilliamsauthor.com

Tanith By Choice

Tanith Lee

Tanith Lee is one of the finest writers to ever grace the field of speculative fiction. The author of around 100 novels and several hundred short stories, she wrote two episodes of the iconic TV series *Blake's 7*, was the first woman to win the British Fantasy Award – which she followed with two World Fantasy Awards, shortlistings for all manner of accolades including Nebula and BSFA Awards – and in 2013 she received a 'Lifetime Achievement Award' from the organisers of World Fantasycon…

Tanith has left one heck of a legacy. I would never dream of attempting to compile a 'Best of' collection, so instead I've let others do so for me.

TANITH BY CHOICE

features many of her finest stories, as chosen by those who knew her.

With contributions from **Storm Constantine, Craig Gidney, Mavis Haut, Stephen Jones, John Kaiine** (Tanith's widower), **Vera Nazarian, Sarah Singleton, Kari Sperring, Sam Stone, Cecilia Dart-Thornton, Freda Warrington**, and **Ian Whates**, each story is accompanied by a note from the person responsible for selecting it explaining why this tale means so much to them.

Released September 2017. Available as a paperback and a numbered limited edition hardback.

www.newconpress.co.uk

Splinters of Truth
Storm Constantine

Cover art by Danielle Lainton

Storm Constantine is one of our finest writers of genre fiction. This new collection, **Splinters of Truth**, features fifteen stories, four of them original to this volume, that transport the reader to richly imagined realms one moment and shine a light on our own world's darkest corners the next. A writer of rare passion, Storm delivers here some of her most accomplished work to date.

"Constantine's talent for twisting the mundane and making it dark and delicious shines out on each page"

– Starburst

"Storm Constantine is a myth-making Gothic queen. Her stories are poetic, involving, delightful and depraved. I wouldn't swap her for a dozen Anne Rices." *– Neil Gaiman*

"Storm Constantine... is a daring romantic sensualist, as well as a fine storyteller." *– Poppy Z Brite*

"Storm Constantine is a literary fantasist of outstanding power and originality. Her work is rich, idiosyncratic and completely engaging. Her themes have much in common with Philip K Dick – the nature of identify, the nature of reality, the creative power of the human imagination – while her sensibility reminds me of Angela Carter at her most inventive." *– Michael Moorcock*

Available now from NewCon Press
www.newconpress.co.uk

IMMANION PRESS
Purveyors of Speculative Fiction

The Weird Tales of Tanith Lee

This anthology of twenty-eight tales comprises all the short stories by Tanith Lee that were published in the seminal magazine *Weird Tales*. Some of them are previously uncollected, so will be new to many of Tanith's fans. Tanith Lee's highly-respected and influential work spanned every genre, and this sumptuous collection demonstrates the range of her versatility. From the dark high fantasy of 'The Sombrus Tower', through the achingly beautiful 'Stars Above, Stars Below', the sinister retelling of a fairy tale in 'When the Clock Strikes', to the almost whimsical steampunk of 'The Persecution Machine', *The Weird Tales of Tanith Lee* showcases the myriad styles of the writer rightly known as the High Priestess of Fantasy. ISBN: 978-1-907737-79-4 £13.99 $18.99

A Raven Bound with Lilies by Storm Constantine

Androgynous, and stronger in mind and body than humans, naturally magical, sometimes deadly, and often possessing unearthly beauty, the Wraeththu have captivated readers since Storm Constantine's first novel, *The Enchantments of Flesh and Spirit*, was published in 1988, regarded as ground-breaking in its treatment of gender and sexuality. This anthology of 15 tales collects all her published Wraeththu short stories into one volume, and also includes extra material, including the author's first explorations of the androgynous race. The tales range from the 'creation story' *Paragenesis*, through the bloody, brutal rise of the earliest tribes, and on into a future, where strange mutations are starting to emerge from hidden corners of the earth. With sumptuous illustrations by official Wraeththu artist Ruby, as well as pictures from Danielle Lainton and the author herself, *A Raven Bound with Lilies* is a must for any Wraeththu enthusiast, and is also a comprehensive introduction to the mythos for those who are new to it. ISBN: 978-1-907737-80-0 £11.99, $15.50

Immanion Press
http://www.immanion-press.com
info@immanion-press.com

www.ingramcontent.com/pod-product-compliance
Lightning Source LLC
Chambersburg PA
CBHW030107260626
47156CB00008B/2560